Praise for the novels of Alex Kava

"Criminally readable, murderously enjoyable."
—*Closer* (U.K.)

"Kava uses a strong supporting cast to provide
Scarpetta-like authenticity and the psychological
insights of Alex Delaware…. Add to that a clever surprise
ending, and this one is sure to be spotted all over the
beach by summer's end."
—*Publishers Weekly*

"Alex Kava has crafted a suspenseful novel and created
a winning character in Agent O'Dell."
—*Washington Post Book World*

"A tight, tension-building tale much enjoyed…"
—*The Bookseller* (U.K.)

"A suspense thriller with enough twists and turns to keep
the reader guessing until the last page."
—*Mystery Scene*

"Alex Kava's thriller is a roller-coaster read.
Although your heart is in your throat the entire time,
you enjoy every scary minute."
—*Woman's Own*

"This debut thriller pumps the suspense out….
Maggie is gutsy and appealing as an FBI agent
facing constant danger."
—*Library Journal*

"A well-crafted page-turner."
—*Publishers Weekly*

"Ms. Kava's…novel is a formidable one, filled with
characters comfortable with themselves and acting out
their roles intelligently and believably."
—*Dallas Morning News*

ALEX KAVA

AT THE STROKE OF MADNESS

MIRA®

ISBN 0-7783-2055-3

AT THE STROKE OF MADNESS

Copyright © 2003 by S. M. Kava.

All rights reserved. Except for use in any review, the reproduction or utilization of this work in whole or in part in any form by any electronic, mechanical or other means, now known or hereafter invented, including xerography, photocopying and recording, or in any information storage or retrieval system, is forbidden without the written permission of the publisher, MIRA Books, 225 Duncan Mill Road, Don Mills, Ontario, Canada M3B 3K9.

All characters in this book have no existence outside the imagination of the author and have no relation whatsoever to anyone bearing the same name or names. They are not even distantly inspired by any individual known or unknown to the author, and all incidents are pure invention.

MIRA and the Star Colophon are trademarks used under license and registered in Australia, New Zealand, Philippines, United States Patent and Trademark Office and in other countries.

www.MIRABooks.com

Printed in U.S.A.

This book is dedicated to
Amy Moore-Benson,
who believed and coached and encouraged
and never gave up on me.

And to
Deborah Groh Carlin,
who listened and inspired and cared
and never allowed me to give up on me.

ACKNOWLEDGMENTS

My sincerest appreciation goes to all the professionals whose expertise has, once again, proven invaluable. And to my family and friends who put up with my long absences while I'm in writing marathon mode. Special thanks to:

Patricia Sierra for the occasional swift kick in the pants, the numerous pats on the back and always, always being there.

Leigh Ann Retelsdorf, Deputy County Attorney, who over lunch one afternoon helped me create an intriguing M.O. for a killer.

Laura Van Wormer, fellow author and friend, for taking time out of your crazy schedule to show me around Connecticut and for sharing your enthusiasm for your adopted hometown of Meriden.

Leonardo Suzio of York Hill Trap Rock Quarry Company for an interesting tour despite it being in the middle of a blizzard.

Lori O'Brien for being my go-to person whenever I had a question about the area.

Dianne Moggy and the rest of the team at MIRA Books, including Tania Charzewski, Craig Swinwood, Krystyna de Duleba, Stacy Widdrington, Kate Monk, Maureen Stead and Alex Osuszek.

Megan Underwood and the crew at Goldberg McDuffie Communications, Inc.

Mary Means for a friendship that includes loving and caring for my kids while I'm on the road.

Tammy Hall for filling in the gaps and always being available at a moment's notice.

Sharon Car, fellow writer and friend, for once again helping me weather the good and the bad.

Marlene Haney, Sandy Rockwood and Patti El-Kachouti for unconditional friendship that withstands absences, that knows no guilt and that celebrates strengths while allowing and unmasking vulnerabilities.

Kenny and Connie Kava for listening and encouraging.

And to the rest of my family and friends whose continued support is greatly appreciated: Jeanie Shoemaker Mezger and John Mezger, Patricia Kava, Nicole and Tony Friend, LaDonna Tworek, Mac Payne, Gene and Mary Egnoski, Rich Kava, Annie Belatti, Natalie and Rich Cummings, Jo Ellen Shoemaker, and Lyn and David Belitz.

Also a sincere and humble thank-you to:

The many book buyers, booksellers and librarians for recommending my books.

The readers, who are truly the ones responsible for keeping Maggie O'Dell alive.

The residents of Meriden and Wallingford, Connecticut, for welcoming me into your community. Please forgive me for any liberties I may have taken with the geography and for dumping dead bodies in your backyard.

Last, to Mike Vallier. MIRA Books lost one of its brightest stars October 26, 2002. I always thought it was appropriate that Mike was the very first person I met from MIRA, because he genuinely exemplified its generosity, enthusiasm and dedication. We're going to miss you, Mike, but your spirit will always be a part of this team.

CHAPTER 1

Saturday, September 13
Meriden, Connecticut

It was almost midnight, and yet Joan Begley continued to wait.

She tapped her fingernails on the steering wheel and watched for headlights in her rearview mirror. She tried to ignore the streaks of lightning in the distance, telling herself the approaching storm was headed in the other direction. Occasionally, her eyes darted across the front windshield. She barely noticed the spectacular view of city lights below, more interested in getting a glimpse in the side mirrors, as if she could catch something the rearview mirror may have missed.

"Objects may be closer than they appear."

The print on the passenger-side mirror made her smile. Smile and shiver at the same time. Not like she could see anything in this blasted darkness. Probably not until it was right on top of her car.

"Oh, that's good, Joan," she admonished herself. "Freak yourself out." She needed to think positively. She needed to keep a positive attitude. What good were all her sessions with Dr. Patterson if she threw out everything she had learned so easily?

What was taking him so long? Maybe he had gotten here earlier and had given up on her. After all, she was ten minutes late. Not intentionally. He'd forgotten to mention the fork in the road, right before the final climb to the top. It had taken her on an unexpected detour. It was bad enough that it was pitch dark up here, a canopy of tree branches overhead so thick even the moonlight couldn't penetrate it. What moonlight was left. The thunderheads would soon block out, or rather they would replace, the moonlight with what promised to be a hell of a lightning show.

God, she hated thunderstorms. She could feel the electricity in the air. Could almost taste it, metallic and annoying, like leaving the dentist with a fresh filling. And it only added to her anxiety. It pricked at her nerves like a reminder that she shouldn't be here. That maybe she shouldn't be doing this…that she shouldn't be doing this, again.

Those stupid, distracting thunderclouds had even caused her to lose her sense of direction. Or at least that's what she was blaming, though she knew full well all it took was getting into a rent-a-car. As soon as she closed the car door her ability to tell direction flew right out the window. It didn't help matters that all these Connecticut cities were made up of streets that ran every which way except at right angles or in straight lines. She had gotten lost plenty of times in the last several days. Then tonight, on the entire trip up here, she kept taking wrong turns, despite telling herself over and over that she would not, could not, get lost again. Yet, if it hadn't been for the old man and his dog, she would have been driving around in circles, looking for the West Peak.

"Walnut hunting," he had told her, and she hadn't thought anything of it at the time, because she was too anxious, too preoccupied. Now, as she waited, she remembered that he wasn't carrying a bag or bucket or sack. Just a flashlight. Who went walnut hunting in the middle of the night? Odd. Yes, there had been something quite odd about the man. A lost, faraway look in his eyes, and yet he didn't hesitate in giving her animated directions to the top of this wind-howling, branch-creaking, shadowy ridge.

Why in the world had she come?

She grabbed her cell phone and punched in the number from memory, crossing her fingers, only to be disappointed when the voice-messaging service picked up after the second ring. "You've reached Dr. Gwen Patterson. Please leave your name and phone number and I'll get back to you as soon as possible."

"As soon as possible might be too late," Joan said in place of a greeting, then laughed, regretting the words because Dr. P. would try to read between the lines. But then wasn't that what she was paying her the big bucks for? "Hey, Dr. P., yes, it's me again. Sorry to be such a pain in the ass. But you were right. I'm doing it again. So no, I guess I haven't learned my lesson, because here I am in the middle of the night, sitting in my dark car and waiting for…yeah, you guessed it, a man. Actually Sonny is different. Remember I told you about him in my e-mail? We've been getting together to talk, just talk. At least so far. He really does seem like a nice guy. Definitely not my type, right? Not like I'm a good judge of character when it comes to men. For all I know he could be an ax murderer, huh?" Another forced laugh. "Look, I was just hoping. I don't know. Maybe I was hoping you would talk me out of this. Save me from…oh, you know… Save me from myself, like you always do. Who knows, maybe he won't even show up. Anyway, I'll see you Monday morning for our usual rendezvous. You can yell at me then. Okay?"

She hung up before the string of prerecorded options, one of which would have allowed her to review her message, revise it or even delete it. She didn't want to be faced with any more choices, not tonight. She was sick and tired of making decisions. That's all she had done the last few days: The Serenity Package or the Deluxe-in-case-you're-feeling-guilty Premium Package? White roses or white lilies? The walnut casket with brass trim or the mahogany with silk lining?

Good heavens! Who would have thought there were so many stupid decisions involved in burying someone?

Joan tossed the phone into her bag. She drew her fingers through her thick blond hair, batted impatiently at damp strands to push them off her forehead. She glanced in the rearview mirror, turning on the overhead light to get a look at her dark roots. She needed to take care of those soon. Being a blonde sure took a lot of work.

"You've become high maintenance, girlfriend," she told the eyes in the mirror. Eyes she hardly recognized some days with new ravens cutting into what were once cute little laugh lines. Would that be her next project? A part of the new image she was creating for herself? God! She had even visited a plastic surgeon. What was she thinking? That she could re-create herself like one of her sculptures? Mold a new Joan Begley out of clay, dip it in brass, then solder on a couple of new attitudes while she was at it?

Maybe it was hopeless. Yet she did seem to be gaining control over the yo-yo dieting. Okay, *control* might not be the right word, because she wasn't totally convinced she did have control, but she had to admit that her new body felt good. Really good. It allowed her to do things she could never do before. She had more energy. Without the extra weight she could get back to maneuvering around her metal sculptures and didn't get winded every five minutes, waiting like her blow torch for more fuel to pump through before she could get going again.

Yes, this new slender self had an impact on her work, too. It made her feel like she had a whole new lease on work, on life. So why in the back of her mind was she unable to stifle that damn annoying little voice, that constant nag that kept asking, "How long will it last this time?"

The truth was, no matter how wonderful things were, she didn't trust this new person she was becoming. She didn't trust it like she didn't trust sugarless chocolate or fat-free potato chips. There had to be a catch, like a bad aftertaste or chronic diarrhea. No, what it came down to was that she didn't trust herself. That was it. That was the real problem. She didn't trust herself and that was what got her into trouble. That was what had brought her to the top of this ridge in the middle of the fricking night, waiting for some guy to make her feel good, to make her feel—Jesus, she hated to admit it—waiting for some guy to make her feel complete.

Dr. P. said it was because she didn't think she deserved to be happy. That she didn't feel worthy, or some psychobabble crap. She had told Joan over and over again that it didn't matter that there was a new improved exterior as long as the old interior didn't change.

God! She hated when her shrink was right.

She wondered if she should try calling her again. No, that was ridiculous. She glanced at the rearview mirror. He probably wouldn't show up, anyway.

Suddenly Joan realized she was disappointed. How silly was that? Maybe she really did think this guy was different. He was different from her regular fare—quiet and shy and interested. Yes, actually interested in listening to her. She hadn't imagined that part. Sonny did seem interested, maybe even concerned about her. Especially when she gave him that load of bull about her weight problem being caused by a hormone deficiency, like it was something out of her control that made her overeat. But instead of treating it like the gutless excuse it was, Sonny believed her. He *believed* her.

Why kid herself. That's why she was up here in the middle of nowhere, waiting in the dark. When was the last time a man had taken an interest in her? A real interest in her and not just in her new slender exterior with the artificial blond hair?

She shut off the overhead light and stared out at the city lights below. It was quite beautiful. And if she would relax, she might be able to see that it was quite romantic, despite that annoying rumble of thunder. Was that a raindrop on the windshield? Great! Wonderful! Just what she needed.

She tapped her fingernails on the steering wheel again and went back to her vigil, checking the side mirrors, then the rearview mirror.

Why was he so late? Had he changed his mind? Why would he change his mind?

She grabbed her handbag and searched inside, digging to the bottom until she heard the crinkle. She pulled out and ripped open the bag of M&M's, poured a handful and began popping them, one after another, into her mouth, as if they were Zoloft tablets, expecting the chocolate to calm her. It usually worked.

"Yes, of course, he'll come," she finally announced out loud with a mouthful, as if the sound of her voice was necessary for confirmation. "Something came up. Something he had to take care of. He's a very busy guy."

After all he had done for her in the last week…. Well, surely she could wait for him. She had been kidding herself to think that losing Granny hadn't had a tremendous impact on her. Granny had been the only person who truly understood and supported her. She was the only one who had stood up for her and defended her, insisting Joan's predicament of still being single and alone at forty was due to her independent nature instead of just being pathetic.

And now Granny, her protector, her confidant, her advocate, was gone. She had lived a long and wonderful life, but none of that could fill the void Joan was feeling. Sonny had been able to see that loss in her, that void. He had gotten her through the last week, allowing and encouraging her to grieve, even encouraging her to "rant and rave" a little.

She smiled at the memory of him, that serious look creasing his forehead. He always looked so serious, so in control. It was strength and a sense of authority that she needed in her life right now.

Just then a pair of headlights magically appeared as if they were her reward. She watched the car weave through the trees. It rounded the twists and curves with a smooth, steady ease, finding its way to this hideaway far above the city as if the driver knew the dark road. As if the driver came here often.

She felt an unexpected flutter in her stomach. Excitement. Anxiety. Nervous energy. Whatever it was, she chastised herself. Such emotions befitted an immature schoolgirl and not a woman her age.

She watched his car drive up behind her, feeling on the back of her neck the startling, powerful glare of his headlights as though they were his strong hands, hands that sometimes had just the slightest scent of vanilla. He said the vanilla removed the other pungent odors he worked with on a regular basis. He had said it as if embarrassed by it. She didn't mind. She had come to like that scent. There was something comforting about it.

The thunder rumbled overhead now and the droplets grew in number and size, splatting on the car's windows and blurring her vision. She watched his shadow, a hat-brimmed, black silhouette, get out of the vehicle. He had cut the engine but left on the headlights, making it dif-

ficult for her to see him against the glare and through
the wet splotches.

He was getting something out of the trunk. A bag. A
change of clothes? Perhaps he had brought her a going-
away gift? The thought made her smile again. But as he
approached, she noticed the object was long and narrow.
Something he could carry by a handle...a duffel bag,
perhaps?

He was almost at her car door. In a flash of lightning
she caught a glimpse of metal. She recognized the
chainlike mechanism around a blade. She saw the dan-
gling pull cord. She had to be wrong. Maybe it was a
joke. Yes, a joke. Why else would he bring a chain saw?

Then she saw his face.

Through the flickering lightning and now a steady
rain, his features looked dark and brooding. He stared
at her from under the hat's brim. He wore an angry
scowl, piercing eyes she didn't recognize, eyes that held
hers despite the rain-streaked glass between them. There
was something wrong, horribly wrong. He looked as
though he were possessed.

Joan's mind scattered into fragments as panic took
hold of her. He stood at her car door, staring in at her. A
clap of thunder startled her, making her jump and sending her body—like electric shock treatment—into action. Instinctively, her hand flew to the locks. Her fingers
fumbled in the dark, searching, feeling, racing. Her heart
throbbed in her ears. Or was that more thunder? Her fin-

gers pushed, punched, clawed at buttons. A wheeze as the glass lowered. The wrong button—damn rent-a-car—and she punched again.

Oh, Jesus! Too late.

He was pulling the car door open. The car's dinging sound joined the tap-tap-tapping of the rain. That annoying dinging sound, warning her that the keys were still in the ignition, warning her that it was too late.

"Good evening, Joan," he said in his gentle tone, but now combined with the scowl on his face, it only seemed to telegraph his complete madness. That was when Joan Begley realized no one would hear her rant and rave this time. No one would hear her final scream.

CHAPTER 2

Monday, September 15
Wallingford, Connecticut

Luc Racine pretended it was a game. That was how it had started a couple of months ago. A silly guessing game that he played with himself. Except now, standing in his stocking feet at the end of his driveway, he stared at the plastic-encased newspaper on the ground as if it were a pipe bomb left just to trick him. What if today was the day? What if he got it wrong today? What the hell would it mean?

He turned around, full circle, to see if his neighbors were watching. Not an easy task for any of them. From atop his lane, Luc could barely see their houses, let alone their windows, well hidden by thick foliage. The sun, which had just broken free over the mountain ridge, couldn't penetrate the thick canopies created by huge oak and walnut trees along Whippoorwill Drive. And it was impossible to see anything up or down the lane, even cars, which were there one second and gone the next.

The road twisted and curved—surrounded by trees and vines on both sides and sometimes twisting together overhead—showing only the next fifty feet, if that. It took anyone who drove it on a winding roller-coaster ride, climbing and climbing, only to send drivers plunging down and around ninety-degree corners. Like some ancient NASCAR track, it could be three to four seconds of exhilaration, shoving your stomach up into your throat while your foot hovered over the brake pedal. The beautiful surroundings, as well as the dramatic plunge, literally took your breath away. It was one of the things Luc Racine loved about this area, and he told anyone who would listen. Yes, they had it all, right here in the middle of Connecticut: mountains, water, forest and the ocean minutes away.

His daughter often ribbed him, saying that he could be "a fucking ad for the tourism department." To which he gave his usual answer, "I didn't raise you to swear like a sailor. You're not too big I can't still wash your mouth out with soap."

He smiled, thinking about his little girl. She did have a mouth on her, more so now that she was a big-shot detective in…blast it! Why couldn't he remember the city? It was easy. It was where all the politicians were, the

White House, the president. It was on the tip of his tongue.

Just then he realized he was almost all the way to his front door and both his hands were empty.

"Shoot!" He looked back down the lane. The newspaper lay exactly where the carrier had tossed it. How in the world could he guess what day it was if he couldn't remember to pick up the stupid newspaper? That couldn't be a good sign. He dug a small notepad and pen out of his shirt pocket, jotted down the date—or at least, the date he believed it to be—and wrote, "Walked to end of lane and forgot newspaper."

As he put the notepad back he noticed he had buttoned his shirt wrong—two buttons off this time. He loved his cotton oxford-cloth shirts—short sleeves for the summer, long for the winter—but unfortunately, they would need to go. And as he padded out to the end of the lane he tried to envision himself in a T-shirt or polo shirt, untucked over his trousers. Would it look silly with his black beret? And if it did, did he care?

He scooped up the *Hartford Courant,* pulled it out of its plastic bag and unfolded it, swinging it open like a magician. "And the date today is…yes, Monday, September 15." Pleased, he folded it without glancing at a single headline and tucked it under his arm.

"Hey, Scrapple," he yelled to the Jack Russell terrier coming out of the woods. "I got it right again." But the dog paid no attention, focusing instead on the huge bone he had in his mouth, losing what looked to be a balancing act as he half carried, half dragged his prize.

"One of these days, Scrap ole boy, those coyotes are going to catch up with you for stealing their kill." Just as Luc said it, a loud noise came from the other side of the woods, sounding like metal slamming against rock. Startled, the dog dropped the bone and raced to Luc's feet, tail between his legs as though the coyotes *were* coming.

"It's okay, Scrapple," Luc reassured the dog as another slam shook the earth. "What the hell?"

Luc headed down the footpath that led into the woods. There was about a quarter of a mile of trees and brush that separated his property from what had once been a working rock quarry. The owner had gone out of business years ago, deserting the place, leaving behind equipment and piles of rock waiting to be crushed and hauled away. Who'd have guessed that the precious brownstone would someday not be able to withstand all the gas emissions of New York City?

Someone had started using the secluded quarry as a free dumping ground. Luc had heard that Calvin Vargus and Wally Hobbs had been hired to remove the garbage and clean up the area. So far, Luc had only seen additional huge yellow equipment parked alongside the old rusted stuff. He remembered thinking that perhaps Vargus and Hobbs—or Calvin and Hobbs as many of the townspeople called them—had taken advantage of using the quarry for safe, private and cheap equipment storage.

Now on the other side of the trees, Luc could see the earthmover with its heavy bucket shoving rocks the size of Rhode Island from side to side. He had forgotten how secluded the area was and could barely see the one dirt road through the woods that acted as the only opening. Otherwise, this overgrown pasture was completely boxed in by a stripped mountain, bled of its precious brownstone on one side and thick with woods on the other three sides.

He recognized Calvin Vargus at the monster machine's controls inside the open-air cab. He could see Calvin's bloated forearms shove and grab and pull at the levers, making the machine's bucket scoop up rock like a giant mouth. Another lever shoved forward and the huge yellow body twisted to one side and spit out the rock with a slam and thump.

Calvin's head bobbed, the orange baseball cap shielding his eyes from the morning sun, but he still caught a glimpse of Luc and waved. Luc waved back and took it as an invitation for a closer inspection. The machine drummed in his ears. He could feel its vibration all the way from his toes to his teeth. It fascinated Luc. It scared the dickens out of Scrapple. What a wuss. Stealing bones from coyotes and yet here he was scared by a little noise, following close behind Luc, bumping his nose into the back of Luc's leg

The machine's giant yellow mouth took another bite

of rock and debris—debris that looked to be part crushed rock, part brush and garbage. This time a discarded rusted barrel broke free and came rolling down the pile of boulders. It crashed against the sharp rock edges, splitting open and sending the lid flying like a Frisbee.

Luc watched the lid, amazed by its speed and distance, so that he only saw the spilled contents out of the corner of his eye. At first he thought it was old clothes, a bunch of rags. Then he saw an arm and thought maybe a mannequin. It was a garbage dump, after all.

Then he noticed the smell.

It wasn't what ordinary garbage smelled like. No, it smelled different. It smelled like…it smelled like something dead. It didn't really scare him until Scrapple began to howl, an uncontrollable, high-pitched howl that broke through the noise of the equipment and sent a chill up Luc's spine.

Calvin stopped the bucket in midair. He cut the engine. And suddenly, Scrapple's howl came to an abrupt stop, too, leaving an unsettling silence. Luc could see Calvin push back his cap. He glanced up at the big man who now sat paralyzed in the cab. Luc stood still.

The vibrations from earlier seemed to be replaced by throbbing in his ears. Only now did Luc realize the throbbing wasn't the aftereffects of the equipment. The throbbing was his own heart pounding, hammering so hard he could barely hear the geese overhead. There were dozens of them, a flood of squawking as they made their daily pilgrimage to or from the McKenzie Reservoir. In the distance he could hear the hum of rush-hour traffic on I-91. All the routine sounds of an ordinary day.

An ordinary day, Luc thought as he watched the morning sun peek through the trees and highlight the bluish-white flesh that had spilled from the fifty-five-gallon barrel. Luc caught Calvin's eyes. He expected to see his own panic mirrored on Calvin's face. And there may have been a little panic, maybe even a little disgust at the sight. But what struck Luc Racine as odd was what he didn't see. What Luc didn't see on Calvin Vargus's face was surprise.

CHAPTER 3

The FBI Academy
Quantico, Virginia

Maggie O'Dell reached for the last doughnut, a choco-late-frosted number with bright pink and white sprin-kles, and already she heard a "tsk-tsk" sound scolding her. She glanced over her shoulder at her partner, Spe-cial Agent R. J. Tully.

"That's what you're having for lunch?" he asked.

"Dessert." She added a cellophane-wrapped platter of one of the cafeteria's daily specials. Something listed on the chalkboard as a "tacorito" supreme. Maggie couldn't help thinking even the FBI couldn't screw up something as good as Mexican food.

"Doughnuts are not dessert," Tully insisted.

"You're just jealous because it's the last one."

"I beg to differ. Doughnuts are breakfast. Not dessert," he told her as he held up the line, waiting for Arlene's attention behind the counter, waiting for her to put down the steaming hot-out-of-the-oven pot of creamed corn, before he pointed to the roast beef. "Let's ask the expert. Doughnuts are breakfast. Wouldn't you agree, Arlene?"

"Sweetie, if I had Agent O'Dell's figure you'd see me eating doughnuts at every meal."

"Thank you, Arlene." Maggie added a Diet Pepsi, then indicated to the cashier, a little mole-faced woman she didn't recognize, that she'd pay for the tray coming behind her, too.

"Wow!" Tully said when he noticed her generosity. "What's the special occasion?"

"Are you saying I never buy unless there's a special occasion?"

"Well, there's that…that and the doughnut."

"Couldn't it be that I'm having a great day?" she said while leading him to a table next to the window. Outside on one of Quantico's many running trails, a half-dozen recruits were finishing their daily run, weaving through the pine trees single file. "Classes just ended for this session. I have no nightmare cases keeping me awake nights. I'm taking a few days off for the first time in…oh, about a hundred years. I'm actually looking forward to working in my garden. I even bought three dozen daffodil bulbs to add to the southwest corner. Just Harvey and me, enjoying this amazing fall weather, digging in the dirt and playing fetch. Why wouldn't that put me in a good mood?"

Tully was watching her. Sometime around the daffodil bulbs she realized he wasn't convinced. He shook his head and said, "You never get this excited about time off, O'Dell. I've seen you before a three-day federally approved weekend, and you're chomping at the bit for everyone to get the hell back in their offices first thing Tuesday morning so they don't hold you up on whatever case you're working. I wouldn't be surprised if your briefcase is stuffed and ready for the backyard breaks. So really, what gives, O'Dell? What has you grinning like the cat that swallowed the parakeet?"

She rolled her eyes at him. Her partner, ever the profiler, always "on" and solving puzzles. Hard to argue with him for something she did herself. Perhaps it was simply an occupational hazard. "Okay, if you must know, my lawyer finally got the last—the very, very last—of the divorce papers back from Greg's lawyer. This time everything was signed."

"Ah. So it's all over. And you're okay with that?"

"Of course, I'm okay with that. Why wouldn't I be okay with it?"

"I don't know." Tully shrugged as he tucked his tie—already stained with morning coffee—into his shirt, then scooped up mashed potatoes, gravy and all, and dumped them on top of his roast beef.

Maggie watched as he dipped his shirt cuff into the gravy, completely unaware while he concentrated on building a dam out of his mashed potatoes. Maggie only shook her head and restrained herself from reaching across the table to wipe at his newest stain.

Tully continued, fork and now knife working at his lunch creation, "I just remember having lots of mixed feelings when mine was final." He looked up, checked her eyes and paused with fork in midair, as if waiting for a confession that might be prompted by his own admission.

"Yours didn't drag on for almost two years. I've had plenty of time to get okay with this." He was still looking at her. "I'm fine. Really. It's understandable that you had mixed feelings. You and Caroline still have to raise Emma together. At least Greg and I didn't have kids. That's probably the only thing we did right in our marriage."

Maggie started unwrapping the tacorito, wondering at Arlene's overuse of cellophane. She stopped. She couldn't help herself. She took her napkin from her lap, reached across the table and dabbed at the gravy on Tully's cuff. He no longer got embarrassed when she did these things, and this time he even held up the errant wrist for her.

"How is Emma, by the way?" she asked, going back to her lunch.

"Good. Busy. I hardly ever get to see her anymore. Too many after-school activities. And boys...too many boys."

Maggie's cell phone interrupted them.

"Maggie O'Dell."

"Maggie, it's Gwen. Is this a good a time to talk?"

"Tully and I are just having an early lunch. What's wrong?" Maggie knew Gwen Patterson well enough to recognize the urgency in her friend's voice, despite Gwen's attempt to disguise it with a clipped professional tone. She and Gwen had known each other for almost ten years, having first met when Maggie was in Quantico's forensic program and Gwen was a consulting psychologist frequently called in by Maggie's boss, Assistant Director Kyle Cunningham. The two women, despite their age difference—Gwen was thirteen years Maggie's senior—had become instant friends.

"I was wondering if you might be able to check on something for me."

"Sure. What do you need?"

"I'm concerned about a patient. I'm afraid she might be in some kind of trouble."

"Okay." Maggie was a bit surprised. Gwen rarely talked about her patients, let alone asked for help with one. "What kind of trouble?"

"I'm not sure. It may be nothing, but I'd feel better if someone checked on her. She left a disturbing voice message late Saturday night. I haven't been able to reach

her. Then this morning she missed our weekly session.
She never misses a session."

"Have you tried contacting her employer or any of
her family?"

"She's an artist, self-employed. No family that I know
of other than her grandmother. Actually she was out of
town for her grandmother's funeral. Another concern.
You know how funerals can be emotional triggers."

Yes, Maggie did know. Over a decade later and she
still wasn't able to go to one without visions of her
heroic, firefighting father lying in that huge mahogany
box, his hair combed to the wrong side, his burnt hands
wrapped in plastic and tucked at his sides.

"Maggie?"

"Could she simply have decided to stay an extra day
or two?"

"I doubt she would do that. She didn't even want to
be there for the funeral."

"Maybe her car broke down on the trip back?" Maggie couldn't help wondering if Gwen was overreacting.
It made sense that the woman may have wanted to be
away from everyone and everything for a day or two
without running back here for a session with her shrink
to dissect how she was feeling. But then Maggie knew
not everyone reacted to stress and tragedy like she did.

"No, she rented a car up there. See, that's another
thing. The car hasn't been turned in yet. The hotel told
me she was scheduled for departure yesterday but she

hasn't checked out, nor has she contacted anyone about staying longer. And she missed her flight yesterday. She's not like this. She has problems, but organization and reliability are not on the list."

"You said yourself that funerals can be emotionally draining. Maybe she just wanted a few more days before coming back to the everyday routine. By the way, how were you able to find out that she missed her flight?" Airlines didn't just hand out their passenger manifest. After years of Gwen lecturing her about playing by the rules, Maggie waited for an admission of guilt. Now that she thought about it, Gwen had managed to get a lot of information that wasn't usually handed out freely.

"Maggie, there's more to it." The urgency returned to Gwen's voice, dismissing any confession to rule breaking. "She said she was meeting someone…a man. That was the message and she was calling me to talk her out of it. She has this…this tendency…" She paused. "Look, Maggie, I can't share the intimacies of her case. Let's just say that in the past she's made some bad choices when it comes to men."

Maggie glanced across the table to find Tully watching her, listening. He looked away quickly as if caught. She had noticed recently—although he tried to disguise it—that he seemed interested in anything related to Gwen Patterson. Or was it simply her imagination?

"What are you saying, Gwen? That you think this man may have done something to her?"

Silence again. Maggie waited. Was Gwen finally realizing that perhaps she was overreacting? And why was she being so overprotective with this particular woman? Maggie had never known Gwen to baby-sit her patients. Her friends, yes, but not her patients.

"Maggie, is there some way you could check on her? Someone you might be able to call?"

Maggie looked at Tully again. He had finished his lunch and now pretended to be watching out the window, another group of recruits down below in sweaty T-shirts and jogging shorts snaking through the woods.

Maggie picked at her own lunch. Why had Gwen suddenly decided to become this patient's caretaker? It seemed like a simple case of a grieving woman shutting herself away from her world for a while, perhaps even finding solace in a friendly stranger. Why didn't Gwen see that?

"Maggie?"

"I'll do what I can. Where was she staying?"

"The funeral was in Wallingford, Connecticut, but she was staying at the Ramada Plaza Hotel next door in Meriden. I have the phone numbers and addresses right here. I can fax over some other information later. All I know about the man she was meeting was that she called him Sonny."

Maggie's stomach gave a sudden flip while she took down the information. All the while she kept thinking, "Not Connecticut."

CHAPTER 4

Sheriff Henry Watermeier shoved his hat back and swiped at the sweat on his forehead.

"Fuck!" he muttered, wanting to walk, to pace off his frustration, but reminding himself to stand in one place. And so he did, hands on his belt buckle, waiting and watching and trying to think, trying to ignore the stench of death and the buzzing of flies. Jesus! The flies were a pain in the ass, miniature vultures, impatient and persistent despite the plastic tarp.

It wasn't the first body Henry had seen stuffed into a strange and unusual place. He had seen more than his share during his thirty years with the NYPD. But not here. Crimes like this weren't supposed to happen in Connecticut. This was exactly the kind of stuff he had hoped to escape when his wife talked him into moving to the middle of nowhere. Yeah, sure, Fairfield County and the shore got its share of this kind of thing all the time. There were always plenty of high-profile cases—big fucking cases—like that stupid publicist driving her SUV over sixteen people, or even the Martha Moxley murder that took decades to solve, or Alex Cross, Connecticut's very own preppy rapist. Yeah, there were plenty of crimes on the shore and closer to New York, but in the middle of Connecticut things were quieter. Crap like this wasn't supposed to happen here.

He had instructed his deputies to set up a wide perimeter, having them string up yellow crime-scene tape. It was going to take a hell of a lot of tape. He watched two of his men stretching it from tree to tree, Arliss with a fucking Marlboro hanging from his lips and that kid, Truman, screeching like a banshee at any of the outsiders who dared come within ten feet.

"Arliss, make sure your butts don't end up on the ground." The deputy looked up, startled, as if he had no idea what his boss was talking about. "I mean the damned cigarette. Get it out of your mouth. Now."

Finally, a look of recognition crossed Arliss's face as he grabbed at the cigarette, stubbed it out on a tree, started to fling it but stopped with his hand in midair.

Henry could see the red start at his deputy's neck as he tucked the rest of the cigarette under his hat and over his ear. It almost made Henry as mad as if Arliss had flung it. First major crime scene as New Haven County sheriff, maybe his last major crime scene of his career, and these goddamn screwups were going to make him look like a fucking idiot.

Henry glanced over his shoulder, pretending to assess the scene when all he really wanted to know was if Channel 8 still had their camera on him. Should have known, the fucking lens was still pointed at his back. He could feel it like a laser beam slicing him in two. And that's exactly what it could do if he wasn't careful.

Why the hell had Calvin Vargus called the goddamn media? Of course, he knew why, and he didn't know Vargus except by reputation. The son of a bitch was living up to that reputation in spades, flapping his yap to that pretty little reporter from Hartford even after Henry told him to shut the fuck up. But he couldn't make Vargus shut up. Not without locking him up. Although that wasn't entirely out of the question.

He needed to concentrate. Vargus was the least of his worries. He lifted the tarp and forced himself to look at the body again, or at least at the part sticking out of the barrel. From what he could see the blouse looked like silk with French cuffs. The fingernails were once professionally manicured. The hair may have been dyed— the roots were a bit darker. It was hard to tell since it was now matted and caked with blood. A shitload of blood. Definite death blow. Didn't have to be a forensic scientist to know that.

He dropped the tarp and wondered again if this poor woman was a local. Was she some bastard's mistress? Before he left the station he had run the list of missing persons, highlighting those in New Haven County, but none of them fit the preliminary description. The list included a male college student who had skipped out on classes last spring, a teenage drug addict who had probably run away from home, and an elderly woman who supposedly went out for milk one morning and hadn't been seen since. Nowhere on the list had Henry found a fortysomething-year-old female with long hair, an expensive silk blouse and manicured fingernails.

Henry took a deep breath to clear his mind, to help him think. He looked up into the cloudless blue and watched another flock of geese. Lucky bastards. Maybe he was getting old and tired. Maybe he was simply ready for that fantasy retirement of endless days fishing off the banks of the Connecticut River with a cooler full of Budweiser and a couple of smoked turkey sandwiches with salami and provolone. Yeah, a sandwich, but not just any sandwich. One with the works from Vinny's Deli, wrapped all neat and tight in that white paper that Vinny used. He could go for one now.

He glanced at the barrel again. The flies were sneaking under the tarp, their buzzing amplified instead of muffled. Goddamn vultures. They'd be swarming the moist areas and taking up residence before the M.E. arrived. Nothing worse than flies and their fucking offspring maggots. He'd seen the damage they could do in a matter of hours. Disgusting. And here he was thinking about Vinny's sandwiches. Well, hell, it took a lot for him to lose his appetite.

His wife, Rosie, would say it was because he had become "jaded." Jesus! She actually talked like that, using words like *jaded.* Henry claimed instead that he was simply pissed dry, burned out. This short stint as New Haven County's sheriff was supposed to help him make some sort of transition. It was supposed to help him ease his way from the head-banging stress of New York to the laid-back routine of Connecticut to finally the peace and quiet of retirement.

But this… No, he hadn't signed up for this. He didn't want or need a messy unsolved murder to screw up his reputation. How the hell were he and Rosie going to retire here if he had to listen to the stories, the second-guessing, the snickers behind his back?

He glanced at Arliss again. The goddamn idiot had some crime-scene tape stuck to the bottom of his shoe, a stream of it following him like toilet paper and fucking Arliss completely unaware.

No, this was definitely not the way he wanted to end his career.

CHAPTER 5

R. J. Tully watched O'Dell sort through some file folders stacked on her desk.

"So much for vacation," she said, her good mood put on hold.

He thought her mood had changed because of the phone call from Dr. Patterson, but O'Dell seemed to be ignoring the fax machine behind her as it spit out page after page of details about Patterson's missing patient. Instead of retrieving and examining those pages, O'Dell was searching for something already lost in her stacks.

Perhaps a case she had planned on taking home with her to peruse during those backyard digging breaks. What was one more if she added Dr. Patterson's?

Tully sank into the overstuffed chair O'Dell had managed to cram into her small but orderly office. It always amazed him. Their offices down in BSU—Behavioral Science Unit—were Cracker Jack boxes, yet hers included neatly stacked bookcases—not one errant hardcover squashed on top. Now that he had a closer look, he could see they were categorized. And alphabetized.

His office, on the other hand, looked like a storage closet with stacks of files and books and magazines— not necessarily each in separate piles—on his shelves, on his desk and guest chair and even on the floor. Some days he was lucky to find a path to his desk. And underneath his desk was a whole other matter. That's where he kept a duffel bag of running shoes, shorts and socks, some of which—especially the dirty ones—never managed to stay put in the bag. Now that he thought about it, maybe that was the mysterious smell that had recently begun to take over the room. He missed having a window in his office. In Cleveland he had left behind a corner office on the third floor in exchange for a Cracker Jack box three floors underground. He missed the fresh air, especially this time of year. Fall used to be his favorite season. Used to be. Back before the divorce.

Funny, but that was how he kept track of time these days—before the divorce and after the divorce. Before the divorce he had been much more organized. Or at least he hadn't been such a mess. Since his transfer to Quantico he hadn't been able to get back on track. No, that wasn't true. It had little to do with the move. Ever since his divorce from Caroline his life had been a mess. Yes, it was the divorce that had caused this nosedive, this spiral into disorganization. Maybe that's what bothered him right now about O'Dell's attitude. She really seemed to be taking this finalization of her divorce as a form of liberation. Maybe he envied her just a little.

He waited while O'Dell continued her search, still ignoring the wheeze of the fax machine. He wanted to say something to retrieve her good mood, something like, "What? No color-coded filing system?" But before he could say it he noticed the files she had pulled out of the stack all had red tabs. He rubbed at the beginning of a smile. For as predictable as his partner was, why couldn't he figure out what the hell she was up to most of the time? Like, for instance, how long did she intend to taunt him with that last doughnut? She had brought it down from the cafeteria with her, still wrapped in cellophane, untouched and now sitting on the corner of her desk— yes, sitting on the edge of her desk, tempting him.

Finally she slipped the file folders into her briefcase and turned to collect the faxed pages. "Her name is Joan Begley," O'Dell said, looking over the information as she put the pages in order. "She's been a patient of Gwen's for more than ten years."

Gwen. Tully still hadn't allowed himself to call her by

her first name. To him she was Dr. Gwen Patterson, D.C. psychologist, best friend to his partner and sometimes consultant to the FBI and their boss, Assistant Director Cunningham. Usually the woman drove Tully a little nuts with her arrogant, know-it-all psychobabble. It didn't help matters that she had strawberry-blond hair and nice legs.

He and Dr. Patterson had gotten carried away on a case last November. Exchanged a kiss. No, it was more than that. It was…it didn't matter. They had decided it was a mistake. They had agreed to forget about it. O'Dell was looking at him as if expecting an answer, and only then did Tully realize he must have missed a question. Patterson's fault.

"I'm sorry, what did you say?"

"She was up in Connecticut for her grandmother's funeral and no one's seen or heard from her since late Saturday."

"Seems odd that Dr. Patterson would be so concerned about a patient. Is there a personal connection?"

"Now, Agent Tully, it would be highly unprofessional of me to ask Dr. Patterson that question." She looked up at him and smiled, which didn't prevent him from rolling his eyes at her. O'Dell might be organized, but when it came to protocol and procedure or sometimes even common courtesy, she conveniently forgot to look at whose toes she might be stepping on.

"Actually, just between the two of us, I think it's a bit odd, too."

"So what are you going to do?"

"I told her I'd check it out, so I guess I'll check it out." But O'Dell sounded nonchalant about it. "Do you know any law enforcement officers in Connecticut I could call?" she asked him, her attention already on another red-tabbed file folder she had missed on her desk. She picked it up, opened it for a quick glance, then added it to her briefcase.

"Where in Connecticut?"

"Let's see. I know she told me." O'Dell had to flip through the faxed pages, and Tully wondered why she didn't remember the basic details from the phone call. Or was her mind simply already focused on her back-yard retreat? Somehow he doubted that. His bet was that she was focused on the contents of those red-tabbed file folders, stuffed safely in her briefcase. "Here it is," she finally said. "She was staying in Meriden, but the funeral was in Wallingford."

"Wallingford?"

O'Dell double-checked. "Yes. Do you know anyone?"

"No, but I've been through that area. It's beautiful. You know who might be able to tell you who to call? Our buddy Detective Racine is from there."

"Our buddy? I think if you know where she's from, she's your buddy."

"Come on, O'Dell, I thought you two made nice...or

at least called a truce." The D.C. detective and O'Dell clashed like night and day, but on a case almost a year ago, Julia Racine ended up saving O'Dell's mother. Whatever their differences, the two women now seemed to have what he'd call a healthy tolerance of each other.

"You know my mother has lunch with Racine once a month?"

"Really? That's nice."

"*I* don't even have lunch with my mother once a month."

"Maybe you should."

O'Dell frowned at him and went back to the faxed pages. "I suppose I could just call the field office."

Tully shook his head. For a smart woman his partner could be annoyingly stubborn.

"So what was this Begley woman seeing Dr. Patterson for?"

O'Dell looked at him over the faxed pages. "You know Gwen can't tell me that. Patient confidentiality."

"It might help to know how kooky she is."

"Kooky?" Another frown. He hated when she did that, especially when it made him feel like he was being unprofessional, even when she was right.

"You know what I mean. It could help to know what she's capable of doing. Like, for instance, is she suicidal?"

"Gwen seemed concerned that she may have gotten involved with a man. Someone she met up there. And that she might actually be in some danger."

"She was there for how long?"

O'Dell shuffled through the pages. "She left the District last Monday, so it's been a week."

"How did she get involved with a man in less than a week? And you said she was there for a funeral? Who meets someone at a funeral? I can't even pick up a woman at the Laundromat."

She smiled at him, quite an accomplishment. O'Dell hardly ever smiled at his attempts at humor. Which meant the good mood lurked close to the surface.

"Let me know if you need any help, okay?" he offered, and now she looked at him with suspicion and he wondered, not for the first time, if Dr. Patterson had confided in O'Dell about their Boston tryst. Geez, tryst wasn't right. That made it sound…tawdry. Tawdry wasn't right, either. That made it sound…O'Dell was smiling at him again. "What?"

"Nothing."

He got up to leave. Wanting her to believe his offer had been genuine, he added, "I'm serious, O'Dell. Let me know if you need any help. I mean with any of your cases, not with the backyard digging. Bad knee, remember?"

"Thanks," she said, but there was still a bit of a smile.

Oh, yeah, she knew. She knew something.

CHAPTER 6

Wallingford, Connecticut

Lillian Hobbs loved her Mondays. It was the one time she left Rosie alone during the busy rush hours, steaming milk for lattes, collecting sticky quarters for cheese Danishes and the *New York Times*. Not a problem. According to Rosie, the busier, the better. After all, it had been Rosie's idea to add a coffee bar to their little bookstore.

"It'll bring in business," Rosie had promised. "Foot traffic we might not get otherwise."

Foot traffic was just the thing Lillian had dreaded. And so at first she had revolted. Well, maybe *revolted* was too strong a word. Lillian Hobbs had never really revolted against anything in her forty-six years of life. She simply hadn't seen the wisdom in Rosie's side enterprise. In fact, she worried that the coffee bar would be a distraction. That it would bring in the gossipmongers who would rather make up their own stories than purchase one off their shelves.

But Rosie had been right. Again. The coffee crowd had been good for business. It wasn't just that they cleaned them out of the daily *New York Times* and *USA TODAY.* There were the magazine sales, and the occasional paperbacks that got picked up on impulse. Soon the regular coffee drinkers—even the mocha lattes with extra whipped cream and the espresso addicts—were browsing the shelves and wandering back into the store after work and on the weekends. Sometimes bringing their families or their friends. Okay, so foot traffic hadn't been such a bad thing, after all.

Yes, Rosie had been right.

Actually, Lillian didn't mind admitting that. She knew Rosie was the one with a head for business. Business was Rosie's forte and books were Lillian's. That's why they made such excellent partners. She didn't even mind Rosie rubbing her nose in it every once in a while. How could she mind when she was allowed to revel in her own passion every single day of the week? But Mondays were the best, like having Christmas once a week. Christmas sitting in a crammed, dark storage room, soothed by her cup of hazelnut coffee and armed with a box cutter.

Opening each box was like ripping into a precious gift. At least that's what it felt like for Lillian, opening each new shipment of books, pushing back the cardboard flaps and taking in that aroma of ink and paper and binding that could so easily transport her to a whole different world. Whether it was a shipment of eighteenth-century history books or a boxful of Harlequin romances or the latest *New York Times* bestseller, it didn't matter. She simply loved the feel, the smell, the sight of a box of books. What could be more heavenly?

Except that this Monday the stacks of ready and waiting cartons couldn't keep Lillian's mind from wandering. Roy Morgan, who owned the antique store next door, had raced in about an hour ago, breathless, ranting and raving and talking crazy. With his face flushed red—Lillian had noticed even his earlobes had been blazing—and his eyes wild, Roy looked as though he would have a stroke. Either that, or he was having a mental breakdown. Only Roy was probably the sanest person Lillian knew.

He kept stumbling over his words, too. Talking too fast and too choppy. Like a man panicked or in a frenzy. Yes, like a man who was losing his mind. And what he was saying certainly sounded like he had gone mad.

"A woman in a barrel," he said more than once. "They found her stuffed in a barrel. A fifty-five-gallon drum. Just east of McKenzie Reservoir. Buried under a pile of brownstone in the old McCarty rock quarry."

It sounded like something out of a suspense thriller.

Something only Patricia Cornwell or Jeffery Deaver would create.

"Lillian," Rosie called from the door of the storage room, making Lillian jump. "They have something on the news. Come see."

She came out to find them all crowded around a thirteen-inch TV set that she had never seen before. Someone had slid it in between the display of pastries and the napkin dispenser. Even Rosie's coveted antique jar that she used for the pink packages of Sweet'n Low had been shoved aside. As soon as Lillian saw the TV, she knew. First a coffee bar, now a TV. She knew that whatever was happening would change everything. Not for the better. She could feel it, like a storm brewing. Could feel it coming on like when she was a child, and she had been able to predict her mother's temper tantrums before they started.

On the small TV screen she saw Calvin Vargus, her brother's business partner, standing in front of the petite news reporter. Calvin looked like a plaid railroad tie, solid and stiff and bulky but with a silly boyish grin as if he had discovered some hidden treasure.

Lillian listened to Calvin Vargus describe—although they were getting his bleeped version—how his machine had dug up the barrel out of the rocks.

"I dropped it. Bam! Just like that. And its *(bleep)* lid sort of popped off when it hit the ground. And *(bleep)* if it wasn't a *(bleep bleep)* dead body."

Lillian checked the huddled crowd—about a dozen of their regulars—and looked for her brother. Had he come in yet for his daily bear claw and glass of milk? And his opportunity to complain about today's aches and pains. Sometimes it was his back, other times it was the bursitis in his shoulder or his ultrasensitive stomach. She wondered what he would think about his partner's discovery.

Finally, she saw Walter Hobbs sipping his milk as he sat at the end of the counter, three empty stools away from the frenzy. Lillian took the long way around and sat on the stool next to him. He glanced at her and went back to his copy of *Newsweek* opened in front of him, more interested in the headlines about dead Al Qaeda members found a world away than the dead body in their own back yard.

Without looking up at her and without waiting for her question, Walter Hobbs shook his head and mumbled, "Why the hell couldn't he have stayed away and left that fucking quarry alone?"

CHAPTER 7

Luc Racine felt sick to his stomach. And embarrassed—because the dead body hadn't made him as nauseated as the TV camera did. He had been fine before they turned the camera on him, before the girl reporter had simply asked him questions. He had been more fascinated by the way her eyes bulged behind the thick glasses. Huge and blue, they reminded him of some exotic fish eyes stuck behind a glass tank. But then the glasses came off and the camera went on and it was pointed right at him, right at him like a high-powered rifle sight.

The girl reporter's questions came faster now. Already he couldn't remember her name, though she had just introduced herself to the camera lens. Maybe it was Jennifer...or Jessica...no, it was Jennifer. Maybe. He needed to pay closer attention. He couldn't think and answer as fast as she could ask. And if he didn't answer quick enough, would she turn her attention to Calvin again?

"I live right over there," Luc told her, his arm waving high over his shoulder. "And no, I didn't smell anything unusual," he added, almost spitting on her. "Not a thing." She stared at him instead of asking another question. Oh, crap! He had *spit* on her. He could see it—a little glistening spot on her forehead. "The trees sorta block this area off." He waved again in the other direction. Maybe she hadn't noticed the spit. Why did his arm go up so high? "All this area is very secluded."

"Very remote," Calvin said, and Luc glanced at him in time to catch the scowl meant especially for Luc, though hidden from the camera by the girl reporter's back.

But Calvin's comment caught her attention and now she was turning in his direction again, reaching the microphone up to him. It was a stretch. Calvin Vargus stood well over six feet. Earlier inside the big earth-moving machine, Luc thought Calvin looked like part of the machine—thick, heavy, strong and durable like a giant chunk of steel. Yeah, a chunk of metal with few defining marks, like a neck or waist.

She looked like a dwarf next to Calvin, practically standing on tiptoes to reach the microphone up to his fleshy lips, but content to give Calvin her full attention now, despite his earlier colorful description of the morning's discovery. Of course she preferred Calvin's version, especially since he would only say it and not spray it. Who wouldn't prefer a giant no-neck to an arm-waving spitter?

Luc watched. What else could he do? He'd had his chance and he blew it. And this wasn't even his first time. He had been on TV before. Once during the anthrax scare. A woman on his route had gotten sick, and Luc had delivered the letter. For a week they closed down the postal station in Wallingford, tested all facilities and grilled the carriers about precautions they should take. Luc had been interviewed on TV, though he hadn't been allowed to say much. That woman died. What was her name? How long ago was that? Last year? The year before? Certainly it hadn't been long enough ago that he couldn't remember her name.

Now he would be on TV again because some other woman was dead. And he didn't know her name, either. He looked back. They were a safe distance from the crime-scene tape and the deputy who screamed at them anytime they ventured an inch or two closer. Yet Luc could still see the barrel toppled over, its side dented in. One big chunk of brownstone kept it from rolling down the pile of rocks. A blue plastic tarp now covered her, but he could still see the image of that gray-blue arm flung out of the barrel, protruding halfway, as if the body were trying to crawl out. That was all he had been able to see—all he needed to see—that arm and a hunk of matted hair.

Luc felt a nudge at the back of his leg and, without looking, he reached down for the dog to lick his hand. Only there was no lick. He glanced at Scrapple, who immediately went into his defensive stance, gripping harder on the prize he had brought to show his owner. Another bone. Luc ignored him, and his attention went back to the excitement beyond the trees.

Suddenly, it hit Luc. Why hadn't he thought of it before? He looked back at the dog working his paws to hold his large treat as he chewed on the fleshy end and tried to get his teeth around the perimeter. Luc's knees went weak.

"Holy crap, Scrapple. Where in the world did you get that?" he said to the Jack Russell, but now everyone around him went silent as they twisted and turned to see.

Luc glanced at the girl reporter and asked, "You think that's what it looks like?"

Instead of answering—or as if confirming it—she began vomiting on Calvin Vargus's size-thirteen boots. Her hand went up to block the camera and in between gags she yelled, "Shut it off. For God's sake, shut off the camera."

CHAPTER 8

Sheriff Henry Watermeier didn't need a forensic expert to tell him what he was looking at. The larger bone Luc Racine held out to him had enough tissue to keep the smaller bones attached. And although some of the smaller bones were missing and the flesh was now black and deteriorated, there was no question as to what the Jack Russell terrier had dug up. What Luc Racine held out in shaking hands—his palms faceup as if making an offering—was definitely a human foot.

"Where the hell did he find it?"

"Don't know," Luc said, stepping closer, his eyes never leaving Henry's as if willing himself not to look at the dog's discovery any more than necessary. "He brought it to me. But I don't know where he found it."

Henry waved over one of the mobile-crime guys, a tall, skinny Asian man with a name tag reading "Carl" on his blue uniform. He reminded himself that it wasn't a bad thing he didn't know all the mobile-crime guys by name, even if they were from up the road at Meriden's Police Crime Lab. Just meant the really sick bastards were committing their crimes somewhere outside the boundaries of New Haven County. For the second time today, Henry found himself hoping this sick bastard didn't seriously fuck up his own retirement plans. He had come this far with a perfect record—no unsolved mysteries during his reign—and he'd sure as hell like to keep it that way.

"That didn't fall out of the barrel, did it?" Carl asked as he shook open a paper evidence bag, then held it under Luc's outstretched hands, positioning it for Luc to drop the bones into the bag.

But Luc, who had seemed anxious to get rid of the thing, now only stared at Henry. He nodded at Luc to put it into the bag, and like a sleepwalker waking suddenly, Luc jerked—almost as if snapping back to reality—and he dropped the bone.

Henry kept an eye on him, studying him. Luc Racine had been one of the first people Henry had met when he and Rosie moved here. Hell, everyone knew Luc. He was the best, friendliest postal carrier in the area, making it a habit to remember his customers by name. Henry remembered a package that Luc had delivered when

Henry wasn't home, wrapping it in plastic and leaving it on Henry's front portico with a note explaining that it had looked like rain. That wasn't so long ago, and now Luc Racine had taken early retirement. Word was he had early-onset Alzheimer's disease.

How was that possible? The man looked younger than Henry. Though his hair was silver-gray, he had a full head of it, not like Henry's, which seemed to get thinner and thinner and receded away from his forehead more each day. Racine looked fit and trim, too, arms tanned and twisted with muscles from lifting and carrying years' worth of junk mail. Although Henry had a bit of a paunch around the middle, he prided himself on the fact that he could still fit into his NYPD police uniform that he had worn…God, had it been thirty-some years ago?

As Henry assessed the man standing in front of him, he couldn't help thinking that Luc Racine appeared the picture of health for a man in his sixties. Except for that blank stare, the one that came out of nowhere. The one staring back at him right now that looked lost, gone, miles away.

"I think there are others," Luc said, reaching under his trademark black beret and scratching his head, his fingers digging into the shaggy hair as if penetrating his scalp would help him remember.

"Others?" Henry checked Luc's eyes. Was this part of the disease? What was he talking about? Did he forget where he was? Did he forget what had just happened? "Other what?"

"Bones," Luc said. "I think ole Scrap maybe brought me some others. He's always bringing me stuff, scraps, bones, old shoes. But the bones…I just thought he found leftovers from the coyotes' kill. You know, from down by the pond."

"Do you still have any of them?"

"I don't."

"Damn."

"But Scrapple probably does. I'm sure he's got some of them buried around our place somewhere."

"We'll need to look. You don't mind us doing that, do you, Luc?"

"No, no. Not at all. Do you think the bones belong to that lady in the barrel?"

Before Henry could answer, one of his deputies, Charlie Newhouse, yelled for everyone's attention. Charlie and two of the crime lab guys had been trying to carefully lift the barrel with the woman still inside down off the rocks. All the photos had been taken, the evidence gathered, and the assistant M.E. had made his initial examination. It was time for the transport, but Charlie seemed all excited about something. Charlie Newhouse, the one guy Henry remembered never getting excited except after a few beers and then only when the Yankees managed to make a triple play.

"Okay, you got our attention." Henry joined the others and looked up at Charlie, putting his hand to his forehead to block out the sun. "What the hell is it, Charlie?"

"Might not mean a thing, Sheriff," Charlie said, securing his balance as he paced from rock to rock, looking down into the pile as if trying to locate lost change. He then squatted to get a better look. "Might not mean a thing at all, but there're more barrels under here. And something sure smells to high heaven."

CHAPTER 9

Adam Bonzado shoved aside Tom Clancy with one hand while he maneuvered the winding road with the other, twisting and pulling at the stubborn and cracked vinyl steering wheel. At each incline the old El Camino pickup groaned as if there were another gear it needed to be shifted into. Adam stirred up the pile of cassettes strewn across the passenger seat, the pile that some-where included the other three cassettes for Tom Clancy's *Red Rabbit*. He searched with stray glances for something else, something that fit his mood. All he knew was that Clancy wasn't going to cut it. Not today.

Sheriff Henry Watermeier had sounded strained,

maybe even a bit panicked. Not that Adam knew Henry all that well. They had worked a case last winter. A skull found under an old building that was being demolished in downtown Meriden. All Adam could determine was that it was a small Caucasian man older than forty-two but younger than seventy-seven who had died about twenty-five to thirty years ago. It was difficult to tell with only the skull. The body must have been buried somewhere else. With all their digging, they had found nothing more, and so, the time of death had been a major guess, based more on architectural facts than archeological ones. Despite the lack of evidence, Watermeier seemed convinced it had been a mob hit.

Adam smiled at the idea. He couldn't imagine the mob operating in the middle of Connecticut, although Watermeier had quickly filled him in with a couple of tall tales. Or at least that's what they sounded like to Adam, who had grown up in Brooklyn and figured he knew a little something about mob hits. But he also knew Henry Watermeier had begun his career as a New York City beat cop, so maybe ole Henry knew a thing about mob hits, too.

Adam Bonzado couldn't help wondering if that was what they had on their hands this time. Dead bodies stuffed in rusted fifty-five-gallon drums and then buried under several tons of brownstone in a deserted rock quarry sounded like something the mob might come up with. But if there were bones scattered around the area, as Henry reported, somebody didn't do a very good job of disposing of the victims. The mob wasn't usually that careless.

Adam reached for the cassette caught between the door and the seat. He read the spine. Perfect. His fingers fumbled with the plastic container. He slowed down to wind around another S in the road as he pried open and freed the Dixie Chicks from their confinement. Then he gave them a gentle shove into the cassette drive and cranked up the volume.

Yes, this was exactly what he was in the mood for. Something upbeat to get the feet tapping and the blood flowing. He couldn't help it. Digging up bones got him excited. Pumped up his adrenaline. There was no better puzzle. Sure, he enjoyed teaching, but that was only to make a living. This—dead bodies in barrels and scattered bones—this was what he lived for.

Unfortunately, after ten years, his parents still didn't get it. He had a Ph.D. in forensic anthropology, was a professor and department head at the University of New Haven, and his mother still introduced him as her youngest son who was single and could play the concertina, as if those two things were his most admirable characteristics. He shook his head. When would it no longer matter? He was a grown man. He shouldn't care what his parents thought. The fact that he cared—no, not cared but worried about what they thought—he could even track back to their influence. For Adam Bonzado knew he had inherited his quiet, rebellious spirit from his Spanish father and his stubborn pride from his mother's ancestral Polish blood.

After creeping up the S in the road, it was time to come back down, and the old pickup flew. Adam didn't brake. Instead, he sat back and enjoyed the roller-coaster ride, working the rigid steering wheel, twisting, turning and pulling to the sexy rhythm of the Dixie Chicks. The intersection appeared suddenly. Adam slammed on the brakes. The pickup came skidding to a halt inches in front of the stop sign and seconds before a UPS truck rolled through.

"Crap! That was close."

His hands were fisted, his fingers red and still gripping the steering wheel. But the UPS driver simply waved, full hand, no choice fingers extended, no lips moving to the tune of "fuck you." Maybe the guy simply hadn't realized how close Adam had come to plowing into him. He reached over as an afterthought and turned down the volume on the Dixie Chicks. As he did so, he noticed the metal pry bar that had slid out from under the passenger seat.

Adam checked his rearview mirror to make sure he wasn't holding up traffic, then he leaned down, grabbed the pry bar, slid open the rear window and tossed the tool into the enclosed pickup bed. It clanked against the lining and he cringed, hoping he hadn't cracked the makeshift shell he'd just installed. It was a tough, waffle-weave polyurethane that was supposed to be easy to clean and would protect the bed from rust and corrosion, no matter how much mud and bones and blood he stuffed back there. It was just another measure he took to keep his pickup from becoming a smelly mobile morgue.

He checked the floor for more tools. He needed to remind his students to put their tools back whenever they borrowed his pickup. Maybe he shouldn't complain. At the least the pry bar was clean. That was a start.

CHAPTER 10

Maggie juggled her briefcase in one hand, a pile of mail under her arm and a can of Diet Pepsi and a rawhide chew bone in the other hand as she followed Harvey out onto their patio. Harvey had convinced her as soon as she walked in the front door that they should spend their first afternoon of vacation in the backyard.

She had only planned on making a brief visit to her office at Quantico to finish up some paperwork. She'd had no intentions of bringing work home with her. Now, as she unloaded the files from her briefcase onto the wrought-iron patio table, she wished she had left these back on her desk, hidden under the stacks where they had been for the last several months.

She watched Harvey, nose to the ground, doing his routine patrol of the fence line. Her huge two-story, brick Tudor house sat on almost two acres, protected by the best electronic security system money could buy, as well as by a natural barrier of pine trees that made it difficult to see even her neighbors' roofs. Yet the white Labrador went into guard duty every time they stepped out of the house, not able to relax or play until he checked out every inch.

He had been this way ever since Maggie adopted him. Okay, *adopted* wasn't quite right. She had rescued him after his owner had been kidnapped and murdered by serial killer Albert Stucky, targeted only because she happened to be Maggie's new neighbor. Of course, Maggie had rescued poor Harvey. How could she not? And yet, the ironic part was that Harvey had rescued her, too, giving her a reason to come home every evening, teaching her about unconditional love, forgiveness and loyalty. Lessons she had missed out on growing up with an alcoholic, suicidal mother. Important qualities that had also been missing from her marriage to Greg.

Harvey was at her side now, having performed his routine patrol and nudging her hand for his reward. She scratched behind his ears and his big head lolled to the side, leaning against her. She gave him the rawhide chew bone and he pranced off, flopping himself down into the grass, monster paws holding the bone as he chewed while he kept one ear perched, listening, and his eyes on Maggie. She shook her head and smiled. What more could a girl want? Loyalty, affection, admiration and constant protection. And Tully wondered why she was content to have her divorce settlement over with, behind her. In ten years of marriage she had never felt any of those things with Greg.

Maggie grabbed the file folders, hesitating and glancing at the can of Diet Pepsi. She hadn't gone through these before without a glass of Scotch in hand. There was a bottle in the cabinet, the seal unbroken. It was supposed to be there only as proof that she didn't need it. Proof that she wasn't like her mother. It was supposed to be proof, not temptation. She caught herself licking her lips, thinking one short drink wouldn't matter. She wouldn't have it neat. It could be on the rocks, watered down, hardly a drink at all. It would take the edge off, help her to relax.

Just then she realized she had bent the corner of the first file folder. Bent it, hell, she had mutilated it into an accordion fold. This was ridiculous. She grabbed the Diet Pepsi, took a long gulp and opened the folder.

It had been a while since she had sorted through these papers. She had added to them, piece by piece, but avoided sitting down to review all the information. She had treated this profile—she had treated *him*—like a project. No, she had treated him like one of her cases, even leaving the folders stacked on her desk alongside profiles of serial killers, rapists and terrorists. Maybe it was the only way she could deal with his existence. Maybe it was because she didn't want to believe he really did exist.

In the collection of documents, articles and downloaded records there wasn't a single photo. She probably could have found one, had she tried. All she would have had to do was send for a high school yearbook or request a copy of his driver's license. Certainly someone in the Wisconsin Department of Motor Vehicles would have accommodated her, especially with a simple mention of her FBI badge number. But she hadn't done any of those things. Maybe because seeing a photo would have made him too real.

Maggie found the envelope her mother had given her last December, the envelope that had started all this…this spiral…this…whatever this was. Last year, when she first learned that she had a brother, she immediately thought her mother had been lying, that it was another drunken ploy, another way to punish Maggie for loving and missing her father so much. And why wouldn't she believe her mother capable of such cruelty? Maggie had been raised with a double dose of Kathleen O'Dell's punishments. Even the woman's failed suicide attempts felt as if she had been lashing out at Maggie, punishing her. So when her mother, in a fit of anger, told Maggie that her father had been having an affair right up until the night he died, Maggie had refused to believe it. That was until she gave her this envelope.

She opened the envelope the way she had so many times before and carefully pulled out the single index card inside, handling it like fragile material, touching it only by the corner. She stared at her mother's handwriting, the cute curlicues and circles above the "i's." He had been named for Maggie's uncle, her father's only brother, Patrick, whom Maggie had never met, the legendary Patrick who had never come home from Vietnam. It seemed heroism ran in the O'Dell family. The same kind of heroism that had taken Maggie's father away from her when she was twelve. Heroism that she continued to curse.

She slipped the card back into the envelope. She didn't need to see it. She had the address memorized by now. And though her mother had given it to her almost a year ago, Maggie's current research indicated that it was still accurate. He was still in West Haven, Connecticut, only twenty-five miles away from where Gwen's patient had gone missing.

Her cellular phone started ringing, startling her and making Harvey leave his bone to come sit in front of her. Habit, she supposed. To Harvey, the phone ringing usually meant Maggie would need to be leaving him.

"Maggie O'Dell," she said, wishing she had shut the damn thing off. She was on vacation, after all.

"O'Dell, have you been listening or watching the news?" It was Tully.

"I just got home. I'm on vacation."

"You might want to check this out. AP is reporting a woman was found dead outside of Wallingford, Connecticut."

"A homicide?"

"Sounds like it. Early reports say she was found in a quarry, stuffed in a fifty-five-gallon drum and buried under rock."

"Oh, God. You think it's Gwen's patient?"

"I don't know," he admitted. "Just weird that it's the same town. Almost too much of a coincidence, don't you think?"

Maggie didn't believe in coincidences, either. But no, it couldn't be. Tully was jumping to conclusions and so was she. Maybe she was simply feeling guilty, and yet, she wanted to kick herself. She hadn't taken Gwen seriously this morning. In fact, she hadn't even called anyone to see if she could track down Joan Begley or file a missing persons report. "Why is it making the news down here?"

"Because it might not be the only body. There might be others. Maybe a dozen more."

She recognized that tone in Tully's voice. She could tell that his mind was already working, mulling over the possibilities, another occupational hazard. No, more than an occupational hazard. It was hard to describe, but she could already feel it taking hold of her. It was like an itch, a drive, an obsession. Like Tully, her mind sorted through the possibilities, raising questions and wanting answers. But one nagging question pushed to the forefront. What if one of the bodies was Joan Begley's?

In all the years Maggie had known Gwen, she had never asked anything of her. Not until now. And instead of doing everything she could, instead of doing anything, Maggie had shrugged off her friend's panicked request because it had reminded her of someone and someplace she didn't want to be reminded of.

"Hey, Tully."

"Yeah?"

She knew he wouldn't be surprised. Instead he would understand. Why else would he have called to tell her the news? "Do you think you and Emma might be able to take Harvey for a couple of days?"

CHAPTER 11

This was bad. Really bad. How could this have happened?

He rode the brakes. Watched the car in front. He needed to keep his distance. Needed to keep his eyes straight ahead, only allowing quick glances to check the rearview mirror. A monster SUV followed, right on his tail, with two idiots straining their necks to get a better look. But there was nothing to be seen. Too much distance. Too many trees. Nothing could be seen from the road. He knew that and yet he had to force himself to not look. *Don't look.*

There had to be a dozen patrol cars. And media vans. How could this have happened? And he hated hearing about it on the news. Hearing it from that anorexic bimbo reporter, sounding so cheerful as she broke the news that the sky was falling.

What the hell was Calvin Vargus thinking? Why did he need to clear that property now? It had been sitting vacant for more than five years. The owner didn't care about it. He wanted it only for a tax write-off. He didn't even live around here. Some hotshot attorney from Boston who probably hadn't seen the place. So why the hell did Vargus suddenly start moving stuff around? Or did he know? Had he suspected something? Had he seen something? Was Vargus trying to destroy him? Did he know? Know? How could he know? *Know, know, know—no!* Impossible. Not possible. Simply inconceivable. He didn't know. He couldn't know.

Breathe. He needed to breathe. He couldn't breathe. He felt a cold sweat breaking out, and it wasn't even midnight. The tingle began in his fingers. The chill slid down from his neck to the small of his back. He needed to stop it. *Stop, stop, stop it.* Stop the panic before it grabbed hold of his stomach.

He fumbled through the duffel bag on the passenger seat, fingers searching while his eyes stayed on the road. The car in front moved too slowly. Heads still turned. Stupid gawkers. What could they see? By now they should know they couldn't see anything beyond the trees. Assholes! Stupid assholes! *Move it, move it, move it!*

Already he could feel the nausea. The panic was

starting, a cramp deep in his bowel. Soon it would slice across his abdomen, a sharp knife piercing him from the inside out and slowly slitting its way along the same course. His muscles tightened, a stiff reflex to prepare for the pain, the dread, the agony. Sweat slid down his back as his fingers grew more desperate, shoving, clawing, searching.

Finally, his fingers found and grabbed on to the plastic bottle. He wrenched it free from the bottom of the stuffed bag. He fumbled, angry with the shaking in his hands, but still he managed to twist off the child-protective cap while steering. Like a man dying of thirst, he guzzled the white chalky liquid, not bothering to stop at the recommended dose. Once the pain had begun, it was a race to squelch it. He took another swallow just for good measure, wincing at the taste. The stuff made him want to gag, and he would if he thought about it.

Don't think. Stop thinking.

It was a taste he associated with childhood, with a dark stuffy bedroom, his mother's cold hand on his forehead and her soft voice cooing, "You'll feel better soon. I promise."

He put the cap back on the bottle and wiped his mouth with the sleeve of his shirt. He waited. Stared at the road ahead. Stared at the flaming-red taillights of the car in front. Demon red eyes blinking as the idiots inside continued to gawk. He wanted to tap his car horn, but he couldn't. Couldn't draw attention to himself. He would need to wait. Stay in line and wait. He needed to *stay, stay, stay* put.

Maybe it wasn't Vargus. His mind began racing again. What about the other guy—Racine. Luc Racine. Luc with a "c" was how they had spelled it at the bottom of the TV screen. That name sounded familiar. Had he seen him before? Yes, he was sure that he had. But where? *Where, where, where?* Where had he seen him before? Had the old man been following him? Was he the one who got Vargus interested? What could the two of them be up to? Had they gone to the quarry digging? Digging for something…or no, digging for someone?

But how? How could they have found out? Vargus was stupid, a brute, but that Racine guy. Maybe he wasn't. Maybe he knew something. Luc Racine knew something.

But how? He had been careful. Always very careful. *Careful, careful, careful.* Yes, he had been careful. Even when he used the equipment, he left everything as he found it. Nobody could know. Yes, he had been careful. Always very careful.

It didn't matter, though. Not now. He'd never be able to use that old quarry again. *Never, never, never.* The whole area was crawling with cops and reporters. And here he was, stuck in line, like one of the gawkers. This was worse than the idiots who jammed the roads every fall looking at the trees. And they would be starting up soon, within weeks. Long lines winding the byroads, gawking like they'd never seen leaves turn colors before. *Stupid, stupid, stupid idiots.* But he pretended to be one of them. Just this once. Just so he could see the commotion, scope things out, figure out what was going on.

Finally he could turn off, escaping onto a side road. No one followed. They couldn't. They wouldn't miss any of the excitement. He made his way up the winding road, and felt the tension in his back ease. But only a little. He still had things to worry about. Things to take care of. He needed to settle down, calm himself. He couldn't let the panic return. Couldn't handle the pain. Not now. Not when he needed to think. That panic, that pain could paralyze him if he let it. *Couldn't let it. Couldn't let it.* That pain, the same pain from when he was a kid, could still come out of nowhere, sharp and intense stabs as if he had swallowed a pack of shingling nails or maybe even a fillet knife.

He needed to stop thinking about it. He needed to get to work. How could he work, thinking about this? How could he function? What would he do? What could he do now that he no longer had a safe dumping ground?

CHAPTER 12

Adam Bonzado looked over the bits and pieces the crime-scene tech named Carl had spread out on a plastic tarp. He had already bagged and labeled some according to where they had been found and what he guessed they might be. From his preliminary once-over Adam could already tell the specimens were from at least two different corpses.

"The dog brought this one," Carl said, pointing to what looked to be a left foot.

Adam picked it up carefully in double-gloved hands and examined it from all angles. Most of the phalanges were gone. The metatarsals and some of the tarsals were held together by what little tissue remained. Even the calcaneus, the heel bone, appeared to be still attached.

"Have you found the rest of the body?"

"Nope. And I doubt if we will. A couple of the barrels look like they rusted through. Coyotes probably helped themselves. There might be pieces scattered all over this county."

"How much do you need to identify a person?" Sheriff Henry Watermeier asked, looking over the assortment.

"Depends on a lot of things. This has some tissue left," Adam said, handing the foot back to Carl, who placed it in a brown paper sack. "We probably have enough for DNA testing. But it won't matter if we don't have anything to match it to."

"So let me see if I can remember how this works," Watermeier said in a tone that Adam thought already sounded exhausted. "If a person is missing, we couldn't test for DNA to see if this is that missing person unless we already had something from that person, like hair samples, to match?"

"Exactly. You can do reverse DNA when you're looking for someone in particular. We did it to identify some of the World Trade Center victims."

"What do you mean, reverse DNA?"

"Say a person is missing, but we have nothing of his to match our DNA sample to. We could do a DNA test on one or both parents, and in some cases siblings, to see if there are enough hits. It can be a bit complicated, but it does work."

"So in other words," Watermeier said, "we may never know whose fucking foot that is."

"If we find more parts and identify them as belonging to the same person I might be able to piecemeal a profile. You know, narrow it down to male or female. Maybe give you a ballpark age. That way you have something to check against the missing persons lists."

"You know how many people go missing every year, Bonzado?"

Adam shrugged. "Yeah, okay, so you're right. We might not ever know whose fucking foot that is."

Carl brought several more pieces, some Adam could tell had been buried, absorbing the soil and turning the bone reddish black. He pointed to a small white one. "I don't think that one's a bone."

"No?" Carl picked it up for a closer look. "You sure? It looks like bone." He handed the piece to Adam.

"There's an easy way to tell," Adam told them, and took the piece, lifting it to his mouth and touching it with the tip of his tongue.

"Jesus Christ, Bonzado. What the hell are you doing?"

"Bone, unlike rock, is porous," Adam explained. "If it's bone it sticks to your tongue." He tossed the piece to the ground. "This one's just a rock."

"If it's okay with everyone else," Carl said, still wincing from Adam's demonstration, "I'll just pick up stuff and let you figure it out."

"Which reminds me—" Adam looked to Watermeier "—you mind if I bring a few of my students to help me sort through some of this stuff?"

"I can't have you teaching class out here, Bonzado."

"No, of course not. Come on, give me a break. Just two or three graduate students. Looks like you could use the help. I mean help, real physical help to dig up and bag what might be out here. We'll only touch what you tell us we can touch. Look, Henry, if Carl's already gathered up this much crap just from looking on the surface, think what might be buried in the rubble."

"You got that right." Watermeier reached under his hat and scratched at thin wisps of graying hair. Adam could see a slight slump of shoulders in the tall sheriff's normal rod-straight posture.

"How many barrels are there?" Adam asked.

"Don't know for sure. Could be almost a dozen. I'm having the crime-scene guys go over the area first, take their pictures and pick up stuff. 'Cause once we start digging out barrels, anything lying around here could get buried or trampled."

"Makes sense."

"We're gonna need one of those fucking earthmovers to get at some of the barrels. And we have to wait for Stolz. He's testifying up in Hartford, probably won't be able to get here until tomorrow morning. He had an assistant pick up the first barrel. That was before we realized there were more. Now he says he better be here himself for the rest. I don't blame him. I've asked the state patrol to bring in a few guys to stand guard tonight. That's all I need, one of these media mongrels sneak-

ing in here. I'm not taking any chances. We're likely to
have the governor up our asses on this one."

"That bad?"

Watermeier moved in closer to Adam and looked
around, making sure the others were out of earshot,
"There're a few barrels with the sides rusted open
enough to take a peek inside."

"And?"

"It doesn't look good, Bonzado," Watermeier said in
a low voice. "I've never seen anything like it, and I've
seen some pretty freaky shit over the years. This is one
fucking mess."

CHAPTER 13

Luc Racine stared at the TV. He really liked this show. It was on every night at the same time. Syndicated repeats, but each episode seemed new to him. He couldn't remember the characters' names, except the old guy, the father, reminded him of himself. Perhaps only because he had a Jack Russell terrier, too. Eddie—that was the dog's name. Figures he'd remember the dog's name.

He looked around the living room, thinking he needed to turn on a light, the TV screen the only illumination in the darkening room. When had it started to get dark? It seemed like he had just sat down for lunch. He hated the dark. Sometimes he worried that he might eventually forget how to turn on the lights. What if he honestly couldn't figure out how they worked? It had already happened with that box in the kitchen. That thing, that box…that food-warmer thing. Shoot! See, he couldn't even remember what the damned thing was called.

He reached over and switched on two lamps, glancing around, wishing he knew what had happened to the remote control. He was always misplacing it. Oh well, he liked this show. No need to change the channel. He sat back and watched, absently scratching Scrapple behind the ears. The dog was worn out from their day's adventure. It was still Monday, wasn't it?

The phone startled Luc. It always did, only because he received few phone calls. Still, for some reason it was close by, within reach.

"Hello?"

"Hey, Pops. The department sergeant told me he saw you on the evening news."

"How did I look?"

"Pop, what the fuck's going on?"

"Jules, you know I don't care for that language."

"He said you found a dead body in McCarty's old rock quarry. Is that true?"

"Calvin Vargus was moving some rocks and a woman fell out of a barrel."

"You're kidding. Who the hell is she?"

"Don't know. Sounds like something you'd have down there in D.C., huh?"

"Just be careful, Pop. I don't like the sound of this. And I don't like you being out in the middle of nowhere by yourself."

Luc stared at the TV screen. "*Frasier,*" he said, seeing the show's title on the screen.

"What's that, Pop?"

He felt it this time like a flipping of a switch. He blinked several times, but it didn't help. He looked around the room and the panic caught him off guard. Outside the windows it looked dark. He hated the dark. Inside there were shelves with books, a pile of newspapers in the corner, pictures on the walls, a jacket by the door. None of it looked familiar. Where the hell was he?

"Pop, are you okay?" Someone was yelling in his ear. "What the hell's going on?"

Yelling, but it sounded like it had come through a wind tunnel. There was a bit of an echo. An echo with words jumbled and then interrupted by a bark. A bark followed by another and another.

Sometimes it felt like jerking awake suddenly from a deep sleep. This time it was Scrapple sitting in front of him, looking up at him and barking as if in Morse Code.

"Pop, are you there?"

"I'm here, Jules."

"Are you okay?"

"Oh, sure."

Now there was silence on the other end. He didn't want to worry her. What was worse was that it was embarrassing. He didn't want her to know, to see what her father was becoming.

"Listen, Pop—" her voice was soft, reminding him of when she was a little girl, so sweet and shy "—I'm gonna try to get up there as soon as I can. Maybe in a couple of days, okay?"

"Jules, you don't have to do that. I'm fine."

"I'll let you know what my schedule is as soon as I check it."

"I don't want you changing your schedule for me."

"Damn! They're paging me, Pop. I gotta go. You stay out of trouble. I'll talk to you soon."

"You stay out of trouble, too. I love you, Jules." But she was already gone, a dial tone buzzing in his ear. Next time she called he'd convince her he was fine. He had to. As much as he loved seeing her, he couldn't risk her seeing him fumble and forget. He couldn't stand her being embarrassed of him, or worse, feeling sorry for him.

Luc glanced around the room again, comforted and calmed by the simple recognition of his things. He looked back at the TV, but as he did so he thought he saw someone move outside the window. He stopped. Had he imagined it? Had there been movement? A shadow walking right by the back window?

No, it was crazy. He hadn't heard a car door. No one would be out walking around in the dark. It was the stress of the day. He had to have imagined it. But as he crossed the room to pull the blinds shut and make sure the door was locked, he saw that Scrapple was still watching the window. The dog's ears were pitched, listening, and his tail was tucked between his legs. Luc had assumed the dog had barked to get him out of his daze. But had Scrapple seen someone, too?

CHAPTER 14

It was almost midnight.

He watched from the top of the ridge, crouched low and hidden in the trees. From here he could see down into the rock quarry, although most of the action was now limited to state patrol officers waving flashlights and setting up flares. Some of the media vans had left. Those that stayed had mounted glaring strobe lights atop the vans. What the hell did they think they would see?

His anger had given in to exhaustion for the time being. His stomach ached from all the retching. He hadn't thrown up that much since he was a boy. He hated when he lost control. *He hated, hated, hated it.*

Even now, as he watched his hiding place being invaded and desecrated, he couldn't control the cramps, the slicing sensation that ripped at his guts.

And to think it was all because of one man. One man who must want to destroy him. He could see the old man's house in the distance. Actually all he could see was the diffused yellow light through the blinds in the front room, what he knew from a closer inspection to be the living room. He had memorized where the sofa sat in the middle of the large space. How it faced the main window with a TV set on a cheap rolling cart right in front of the window, where he imagined the old man could watch the news and still catch anyone coming up the long driveway.

When he had seen Luc Racine earlier on TV he knew the old man looked familiar. He knew he had seen him around town, but still there was something that nagged at him all day. Then suddenly he remembered as if in a flash of lightning. Yes, lightning, the storm.

The old man had been there Saturday night. He had been in Hubbard Park, wandering around with that stupid little dog. Wandering around despite the dark and despite the storm. How could he have forgotten? Yes, he remembered seeing him with that strange little black hat on his silver head. He had even watched him give Joan directions to the West Peak. He had taken extra precautions so the old man wouldn't see him. He had waited until he was gone, making him late, and he hated to be late.

Yet, despite all the precautions, the old man knew. He knew something. Had he seen him that night? Had he

CHAPTER 15

Tuesday, September 16

Maggie picked up her keys, badge and cellular phone from the airport security conveyor belt while shoving the plastic basin aside and trying to grab her laptop off the oncoming tray all at the same time. She pushed several buttons on the cell phone and tucked it between her neck and shoulder while she slid her laptop back into its case. She should be an expert at this by now, but still she struggled with the Velcro straps that held the computer in place.

"Hello?" said a voice in her ear.

"Gwen, it's Maggie. I'm glad I caught you."

"Where in the world are you? It sounds like you're calling from the bottom of the Potomac River."

"No, no. Not the bottom of the Potomac. Worse. Airport security at National." She smiled when she saw one of the security officers scowl at her words. The woman wasn't amused. She waved Maggie to the side with her wand. "Oh, shoot, hold on a minute, Gwen."

"Arms at your sides and out," the woman barked at Maggie. She set her laptop case on a nearby chair, the cell phone on top, and followed the instructions she knew by heart. It never failed. She was always getting pulled aside. And as usual she immediately set the security wand chirping. She dug her keys and badge out of her pocket and tossed those on the case, too.

"Sit down and remove your shoes, please."

Maggie slipped off the leather flats and held up the soles of her feet for the wand. The entire time she still smiled at the woman, who refused to return the gesture. With only a nod of release, she left Maggie and went back to the trenches to capture the next potential terrorist or the next wiseass.

Maggie picked up the cell phone. "Gwen, are you still there?"

"You'll never learn, will you?" her friend started the lecture. "You're an FBI agent. You of all people know how important airport security is, and yet you insist on egging them on."

"I don't egg them on. I just don't understand why I

have to check my sense of humor with my luggage at the ticket counter."

"I thought you were taking some time off. Where's Cunningham sending you this time?"

"I'm going to Connecticut."

Silence. Such a long silence that Maggie thought she may have lost the connection.

"Gwen?"

"You found something out about Joan?"

"No, not yet." Maggie searched for Gate 11. Of course, it was the one with the line already boarding. "I thought I'd go check on her myself. Who knows, maybe I'll find her at the Ramada Plaza Hotel's pool, drinking piña coladas."

"Maggie, I didn't expect you to do that. I just thought you might be able to make a few phone calls. I didn't mean for you to go to Connecticut, especially on your vacation."

"Why not? You're always telling me I need to get away." Where had she put her boarding pass? Usually she slid it into her jacket pocket.

"Yes, get away and go on a real vacation. When was the last time you took a real vacation, Maggie?"

"I don't know. I was in Kansas City last year." She started to search her computer case's many pockets. Somewhere she knew she had a boarding pass. Maybe Tully's disorganization was rubbing off on her.

"Kansas City? That was two years ago and it was for

a law enforcement conference. That's not a vacation. Do you even know what a vacation is?"

"Of course, I know what it is. It's that thing where you sit around on a beach somewhere, getting drunk on piña coladas with those little pink umbrellas and ending up with a miserable sunburn and sand in places where I really don't like to have sand. That's just not something that interests me."

"And looking for a missing person on your vacation does interest you? You know, if you're going to Connecticut, maybe you could finally look up a certain man in the vicinity?"

"Here it is," Maggie said, relieved to find that the boarding ticket must have slipped behind her laptop when she was mastering the Velcro straps. She ignored Gwen's comment about "a certain man," knowing full well she meant a certain assistant D.A. in Boston. "Gwen, if there's anything you haven't told me about Joan Begley, now would be a good time."

Her friend was silent again.

"Gwen?"

"I've faxed you everything I could."

She noticed Gwen's careful choice of words.

"Look, Gwen, before you hear about it on the news, there's something you should know. Yesterday morning a woman's body was found outside of Wallingford in a rock quarry."

"Oh, my God! It's Joan, isn't it?"

She hated hearing the panic in her friend's voice. This was a woman Maggie always looked to for strength.

"No, I don't know that. I wouldn't have even told you, but it's made the national news already. They haven't identified her yet. I'm trying to get in touch with the sheriff who's heading the investigation. He's supposed to be calling me back, but I'm sure I'm on the bottom of a very long list." Maggie tucked the phone into her neck again as she prepared her ID and ticket for the attendant. "Look, my flight's boarding, Gwen. I'll give you a call as soon as I know something, okay?"

"Maggie, thanks for doing this. I hope it's not Joan, but I have to tell you, I just don't have a good feeling about this."

"Try not to worry until it's time to worry. I'll talk to you later."

She shoved the phone into her pocket just as the attendant reached for her ticket.

On board, Maggie unzipped pockets, searching—why was she suddenly so disorganized?—for the paperback she had bought in the airport bookstore: Lisa Scottoline's latest legal thriller. Past titles had succeeded in keeping her mind off being 38,000 feet above control. With the paperback came the envelope she had shoved into the side pocket at the last minute while deciding to leave the file folders behind.

She slid her case into the overhead compartment and

squeezed into the window seat. A small gray-haired woman fussed and fidgeted into the seat next to her, and Maggie opened the paperback to read but, instead, stared at the envelope.

Maggie knew Gwen had meant Nick Morrelli when she asked if she would attempt to see "a certain man in the vicinity." And why wouldn't she? Nick was in Boston, probably only an hour's drive from the middle of Connecticut. Whatever had started between Nick and Maggie several years ago while they worked on a case together in Nebraska had fizzled out during Maggie's prolonged divorce. She had refused to start a relationship before her divorce was finalized, not so much out of legalities or principles, but perhaps because she couldn't risk the emotional drain. Quite honestly she had never trusted her feelings for Nick—too much heat and intensity. What they lacked in common interests, they made up for in chemistry. It was the exact opposite of her relationship with Greg. Maybe that's what had attracted her to Nick in the first place.

Then last year, sometime before Thanksgiving, she had called Nick's apartment, except a woman answered, telling Maggie Nick couldn't come to the phone because he was in the shower. Since then, Maggie had kept the distance between them, increasing it by increments with shorter phone conversations replaced by missed phone calls and then never-returned voice messages. She hadn't expected Nick to wait for her to be free. And, though she had been surprised—and yes, a bit hurt—to discover that he had moved on, in the days that followed, she felt an unexpected sense of relief that only galvanized her decision. It was better to be alone, she had decided. At least for a while.

The flight attendant interrupted her thoughts with preflight instructions, something Maggie politely ignored. The woman beside her seemed frantic to find the laminated guide in the seat pocket in front of her. Maggie took out her own and handed it to the woman, who thanked her quickly as she searched with an index finger to catch up.

Maggie opened her paperback again and began to read, using the envelope as a bookmark.

CHAPTER 16

Lillian Hobbs carried an armful of paperbacks and gently placed them on the front table where Rosie had started setting up the new display. Rosie had another excellent idea, only Lillian's mind was off somewhere. How could she concentrate with a different media van driving by almost every half hour? It was much more exciting than her regular view of the gray, bleak headstones peeking up over the brick fence from the Center Street Cemetery.

This morning they had served half a dozen out-of-town reporters while watching *Good Morning America* on their new portable TV. Maybe it was only a matter of time before Diane Sawyer and Charlie Gibson showed up at their little coffee counter. In fact, Lillian was certain she recognized the reporter ordering a double espresso. She had seen him on Fox News, but she just couldn't remember his name.

She sorted through the books, keeping one eye on the front store window. Rosie had suggested they do a table display with murder mysteries, maybe even a serial killer novel or two. It certainly fit the current atmosphere, although a bit macabre, perhaps. Rosie considered it a business opportunity. Lillian worried that someone might find it offensive, until she realized that she would be able to showcase some of her favorite suspense-thriller authors.

For Lillian, so much of what she saw in real life reminded her of something she had read in a book. This mess at the quarry was no different. Besides that, it truly sounded like it had been concocted by the imagination of Jeffery Deaver or Patricia Cornwell. Fiction Lillian could grasp, like a puzzle with pieces waiting to be fit together or simply sorted through, usually leading to an exciting climax and a neat and tidy conclusion. Or if not neat and tidy, then, at least, one that made sense. Real life, however, wasn't as easy to figure out and oftentimes made no sense at all. Wouldn't it be nice if real-life situations could be summed up in a two- to three-page epilogue?

She stopped arranging the paperbacks and thumbed through the top one. She knew all the characters in this series by heart. Knew the major plots and the killers' MOs. She could even quote some of her favorite lines. But these murders out at the quarry were strange. Lillian shook her head. Truth really was stranger than fiction. She realized she was treating these brutal findings much as she did a new mystery novel—especially by a new and unfamiliar author. She found herself reading, looking for and gathering as many clues as possible and putting the pieces of the puzzle together. She had even started to create a profile of the killer, using images and details, personality traits and deviations she had learned from the masters. Yes, the masters, meaning Cornwell, Deaver, Patterson. Anyone else might think it silly, which is why she hadn't shared her findings with even Rosie. Instead, she casually pumped Rosie for information, any tidbits her husband, Henry, may have mentioned.

Lillian stacked the paperbacks, making a creative pyramid, then chose a half dozen to stand up, using some of the innovative new plastic stands she had convinced Rosie they needed. She sandwiched the stark white and ice blue of Dennis Lehane's *Mystic River* between the black and red of Jan Burke's *Bones* and the black-and-white, hard-to-find copy of *The Prettiest Feathers* by John Philpin and Patricia Sierra. This would be an excellent opportunity for her to prove to Rosie that her compulsive buys were wise financial moves, after all.

The store's front door chimed and she looked over her shoulder. Her brother, Wally, gave a one-finger wave. Lillian returned the wave, then stiffened when she saw Calvin Vargus following behind. Immediately, Calvin seemed to fill the store with his wide shoulders, thick neck and booming laugh. He patted Wally on the back, more of a slap with a hand that looked like a racket. Lillian returned to her display. She didn't want or need to know what the private joke was between the two of them. There was always something. And she hated watching her brother take Calvin's abuse. Of course, Wally would never call it abuse.

Her brother and his business partner had a strange relationship. Calvin had grown up to be a bigger and meaner version of the bully he was when the three of them knew one another in junior high school. Wally, the eternal nerd, seemed content, almost pleased to have the bully now on his side, despite the ramifications or the cost. Lillian gave her glasses a quick, nervous nudge and shook her head. She wasn't the only one who noticed the men's strange arrangement. Why else would they have been anointed with the nickname Calvin and Hobbs after the comic strip of an imaginative and sometimes strange little boy and his pet tiger? A tiger that came to life only in Calvin's presence.

Lillian Hobbs watched the regular performance of the bully and his willing patsy. Only today it wasn't just with distaste. Today she watched with embarrassment. Embarrassed that her brother was weak. Embarrassed that he didn't seem to mind. No, it almost appeared as if he enjoyed the attention, attention at whatever the cost. Why else would he put up with it? Or had it been all those years of training? All those years of growing up with a mother who bullied and praised, often in the same sentence.

Maybe it wasn't embarrassment she felt. Perhaps it was regret, regret that as the older sibling she should have also been her brother's protector. But how could she? It wasn't as though their mother had spared her from the same ritual. Lillian, however, had found solitude in books. She had learned how to escape to her own world of imaginary friends and fantastic places. But Wally. Well, he hadn't been so lucky. Funny how a murder could dig up such things. Dig up! Oh, dear, what a pun. But it made Lillian smile.

Calvin was bragging about how he had found the first body, bragging and telling. How many times had it been? And in only a matter of twenty-four hours. Yet, each time the story became more elaborate with new details added, ones he seemed to have forgotten in the original telling.

"I knew right away that she was dead," Calvin boomed to a new audience, waiting for every gruesome detail. "I could see that her fucking skull had been bashed in. There was blood all over. Still spilling out of the barrel. Buckets of it. Good thing ole Wally wasn't with me. He's such a wuss, he would have upchucked a week's worth of breakfasts. Ain't that right, Wally?" Calvin tousled Wally's hair with that huge hand that made Wally look even more like a child.

Lillian rolled her eyes just as she noticed her brother watching her. Despite his partner's abuse, Wally remained perched at his side by the coffee counter, with a stupid, lopsided grin.

"Our own coffee house entertainment," Rosie said, coming up beside Lillian and pulling out a couple of paperbacks from the shelf behind them.

"Should we ask them to leave?" Lillian asked, then felt her stomach flip when she realized Rosie might ask her to do it.

"Nah, don't bother. People are hungry for details. Look at them." She pointed to the growing crowd around Calvin and Wally. "Not such a bad thing for our little bookstore to be the place to come to for the latest gruesome details. It doesn't bother you, does it?"

"No, of course not. But won't Henry mind?"

"It's not Henry's store," Rosie said abruptly, and Lillian knew she shouldn't have said it. "Besides, maybe if they have someplace to go for information, they'll stop hounding Henry."

Lillian decided not to mention that it might be false or fabricated information from Calvin Vargus. She saw Rosie's face suddenly soften into a smile. The concern of the last twenty-four hours had already started to show in new lines around her friend's mouth and in her forehead. Whenever Lillian studied her partner's face, she was immediately reminded of how beautiful the woman had been. She could see the remnants of the high school prom queen. Rosie was still an attractive woman—even the lines made her face interesting, not marred.

Then Lillian realized what had softened her partner's expression. Her big, strapping, good-looking John Wayne of a husband had walked in the door. All the attention shifted to Henry as he fielded questions while trying to make his way to the coffee bar.

"I better go rescue him," Rosie said with a smile.

As she watched Rosie greet her husband, Lillian noticed her brother, Wally, sneaking out the bookstore's back entrance. And he hadn't even had his daily bear claw and glass of milk.

CHAPTER 17

Henry shoved his way past the cameras and yelling reporters. The pretty, little one with the thick glasses had
been following him everywhere. Earlier she had been at
the bookstore, waiting for him as if she knew that he
stopped by there every morning. Except now she had a
camera guy with her and the camera was rolling. He could
tell, because her thick, Coke-bottle glasses came off as
soon as the camera went on. He wondered how the hell
she had gotten into broadcast journalism with those things.

"Sheriff Watermeier, is it true there may be more
than a hundred bodies buried in the quarry?"

"A hundred bodies?" He laughed. Not an appropriate response, but this was ridiculous. "Let's hope not."

"What about the rumors that some of the victims have been cannibalized? Can you elaborate on that, Sheriff?"

This time Henry avoided rolling his eyes. "We'll try to answer some of your questions later today when we know more."

He kept walking, not looking back, despite the questions that continued and despite the clicks of shutters and the hum of video cameras. He knew he would need to address the media, and soon. Earlier he had gotten a call from Randal Graham, the assistant to the governor, and good ole Randal advised him that he needed to somehow calm things down a notch. According to Randal, the governor was tremendously concerned about the national media calling these the worst serial killings in Connecticut's history. Henry wanted to tell that weasel Graham that those reports were probably accurate, and if he wanted things toned down a notch maybe he should get his ass down here and tone them down himself. But, instead, he told the governor's assistant that he had things under control. So, in other words, he had lied.

The tall grass was slick with dew, glittering in the morning sun. Once he got into the mouth of the quarry he couldn't hear the reporters. The rocks and trees insulated the area. Henry took in the surroundings. The leftover, rusted conveyor system that hovered over Vargus and Hobbs's shiny yellow earthmover looked out of place in this sanctuary. It really was beautiful, giant stepping stones all the way up the mountain, sheltered by thick evergreens alongside yellow-and-orange-leafed oak and walnut trees. It only now occurred to him that the killer had chosen wisely when he made this his graveyard.

He stayed back from the commotion and watched Bonzado with his students unloading equipment from the shell of his El Camino. The three students—one woman and two men—looked like typical nerds with none of the flamboyance of their professor, who today wore a pink-and-blue Hawaiian shirt, khaki shorts and brown hiking boots. Henry managed a smile. He actually liked Bonzado. He trusted the kid, which was more than he could say about some of his own men. Most of these guys hadn't seen a bloodied body outside of a car accident. He knew he could depend on the police lab techs, but his own deputies were another story. As if on cue he saw Truman screaming at a reporter. Shit! Henry recognized the guy from NBC News. Wonderful! That would look great tonight on the *Nightly News* with Tom Brokaw.

This really was a fucking mess. Even Rosie couldn't put a positive spin on this one. What he needed was someone he could blame if things went south. Some expert that no one would second-guess. That certainly wouldn't be Dr. Stolz. He watched the medical examiner making his way through the reporters. He was dressed as if for court again in his suit and tie and expensive leather shoes. Shoes that would send him—yup, sure enough, Stolz slipped on the wet grass, almost losing his balance and ending up on his skinny little ass. Henry wiped at his smile, almost breaking out into a laugh when he noticed Bonzado doing the same.

His cell phone vibrated in his shirt pocket, and he grabbed it. Beverly had instructions to forward only the important calls. He hoped this wasn't Graham again. He should have put him on the nonimportant list.

"Watermeier," he barked into the phone.

"Sheriff Watermeier, this is Special Agent Maggie O'Dell with the FBI."

"I don't remember calling the FBI for help, Agent O'Dell."

"Actually, I think we might be able to help each other, Sheriff Watermeier."

"How do you figure?"

"I'm a criminal profiler and it sounds like you might have a serial killer on your hands."

Henry stopped himself from automatically shrugging off this unexpected offer, another in a long list of know-it-alls wanting a piece of the action. Maybe this was exactly what he needed. The local yokels would have a tough time arguing with him about bringing in federal assistance, no matter how uptight they were about outsiders. He did need some help. And this Agent O'Dell might come in handy if he needed a scapegoat.

"You said we could help each other. What is it you want from me, Agent O'Dell?"

"I'm looking for a missing person."

"I don't have a whole lot of time for wild-goose chases right now. I've got my plate full, if you know what I mean."

"No, you don't understand, Sheriff Watermeier. I'm hoping I'm wrong, but I think you may have already found her."

CHAPTER 18

Maggie slowed the rental car, wishing she had noticed the squeaky brakes before she left Bradley International Airport. She should have insisted on something other than the freshly washed white Ford Escort. She hated rental cars. They always looked good from the outside, but the insides couldn't conceal the last occupants. The Escort's last driver was a smoker with sweaty hands. Easy enough to fix by rolling the windows down, swiping a couple of wet napkins around and introducing some aromatic McDonald's French fries. But squeaky brakes were a whole other matter, especially since it looked like she would need them.

The winding roads that took her up made her as nervous as on the plunges down. And there seemed to be an abundance of them. A small detail both Watermeier and Tully had forgotten to mention when giving her directions. Although Tully's directions had sounded more like a lecture. She remembered thinking at the time that he really must miss his daughter, Emma, because he was treating her like a teenager on her first outing alone, certain that she would get lost without his step-by-step road assistance. She had stopped him once, saying she could pick up a map from the AAA. His scowl told her it would be wise to not interrupt him again.

Who would have guessed that, when it came to road-trip instructions, the same R. J. Tully who used scraps of paper—receipts, napkins, the back of a dry cleaning ticket—would become Mr. Anal Retentive? Actually, it made her smile. After two years of working together, he was finally feeling comfortable enough to take off the kid gloves and treat her like a true partner. She liked that.

She glanced at Tully's homemade map stretched out on the passenger side of the Escort and tried to find the spot according to Watermeier's instructions. Before she could find it on the map, however, she saw the water around the next turn. A sign identified it as McKenzie Reservoir, and immediately she saw the road, Whippoorwill Drive, that would take her over the water. It took two more climbs and one more plunge before she saw the commotion alongside the two-lane road. One of the lanes was clogged with black and whites, media vans, a mobile crime unit and several unmarked sedans.

A uniformed officer waved for her to continue on, and even as she pulled up and stopped beside him, he continued shaking his head.

"Keep moving, lady. Nothing to see and I'm not answering any of your questions."

"I'm with the FBI, Special Agent Maggie O'Dell." She handed her badge out the car window, but he stood with his hands on his gun belt, looking not the least impressed. She tried again. "I just talked to Sheriff Henry Watermeier a few minutes ago."

The officer pulled a walkie-talkie from his shoulder and took her badge, holding it up to the light as if making sure it was authentic. "Yeah, this is Trotter. I've got a woman in a rental, says she's FBI and that Sheriff Watermeier *just talked* to her." He spit out the words, as if he didn't quite believe them.

Through the static came a garbled question. Maggie couldn't make a word out of it, but Officer Trotter seemed to have no problem interpreting static. Without hesitation, he held up the badge again and answered, "A Margaret O'Dell."

There was a crackled response, and this time Maggie saw the transformation in Officer Trotter's face. He handed her badge back through the car window and politely showed her where she could park the car. "You'll need to walk to the scene," he told her, pointing to an overgrown dirt road she may not have noticed otherwise. "Sheriff Watermeier will be waiting for you at the perimeter." Then he was off to wave on the next passersby, tourists in a black Jeep Cherokee with Rhode Island license plates, checking out Connecticut's latest wonder.

She would have recognized Watermeier even without the uniform. He reminded her of John Wayne—the trimmer version from his earlier movies—with a sheriff's hat in place of the ten-gallon cowboy hat. No dusty kerchief at his neck. Instead, his collar was open and his necktie gone. His brown shirtsleeves were rolled up to his elbows and his hat was pulled low on his brow. When he saw her, he waited patiently, raising the crime-scene tape for her to crawl under. There was no smile, no introduction, no raised eyebrow at her appearance. He simply started in as though the two of them had been working together forever.

"We're still scouring the scene, so we haven't started opening any more barrels yet. We'll need to move some rocks to get to some of them. I don't want us jumping in and destroying evidence."

"Sounds like a good idea."

"This missing person—" he shot her a look of suspicion "—she's not someone that's gonna cause all hell to break loose, is she?"

"I'm not sure what you mean."

"I checked you out, O'Dell." He waited as if expecting her to protest. When she didn't, he continued, "My office isn't exactly in the Stone Age. We can do that pretty quickly."

"I'm sure you can, Sheriff Watermeier."

"Well, point being that I know you're out of Quantico. FBI's looking for a missing person, and I'm thinking that missing person must be someone important, right?"

"Every missing person we look for is important to someone, Sheriff Watermeier."

He stared at her and this time she thought she saw the beginning of a smile at the corner of his mouth. He didn't press the issue.

"You ever have a case like this?" He started walking, slowing down when he realized his long strides were keeping her a step behind him. "I mean, there's not some crazy bastard who's been doing this in other states, too, is there?"

"I did check, but nothing registered on VICAP."

"Dr. Stolz—" he pointed to a small-framed, balding man in a suit "—hasn't gotten to the autopsy yet of the woman we found yesterday. You can join us for that later, if you'd like. She's a mess, though. I'm not sure you'll be able to do a visual ID."

"I have some of her physical characteristics that might, at the very least, rule her out."

"Right now, the M.E.'s having a hell of a time. We're trying to figure out how the hell to contain the barrels that have cracked open. He's thinking we may need to set up some kind of temporary morgue out here. On the other hand, if we just pull them out…hell, who knows. My quick reference check said you'd been with the bureau for about ten years. Have you come across anything like this before?"

"There was a case in Kansas. I believe 1998 or '99, John Robinson."

"I think I remember that one. The Internet wacko, right?"

"Yes, that's right. He lured women via the Internet to his farm, killed them and stuffed their bodies into fifty-five-gallon drums." Maggie watched her feet. Rocks protruded out of the ground and were hidden by knee-high grass. "I didn't work that case, but if I remember correctly, I think the drums were found in a storage shed, so there wasn't as much risk of jostling things around as you're dealing with here. Do you have any idea how many barrels there are? And how many are filled with bodies?"

"Could be as many as a dozen barrels. Maybe more. Doesn't mean they all have dead bodies. But we've seen inside several of them. Weird crap, really weird." He tilted his hat back and wiped the sweat from his forehead. "In one, it looks like there's just a pile of bones, but in the other one…" He shook his head and pointed to the barrel he wanted her to see first. "In the other one, the body looks pretty well preserved. From what we can see. Either way, we've got one sick son of a bitch on our hands."

He stopped in his tracks and Maggie waited. They were about a hundred feet from the commotion. A group was hunched over a barrel that had been brought down from the rock pile. Close by, several crime-scene techs searched the area on their latexed hands and padded knees, working their grid over the rocky surface. Maggie was impressed with the sheriff's careful handling of the scene. Too often small-town law enforcement officers allowed unnecessary civilians within the perimeter. They couldn't see the harm in letting the mayor or a local city councilor take a look. What they considered a smart move politically—sheriffs were elected, after all—oftentimes ended up contaminating a crime scene.

Suddenly, Maggie realized Watermeier was waiting, as if weighing what he wanted to ask or tell her before they joined the others.

"I spent over thirty years with the NYPD, so I'm not a rookie to messes, okay?" He met her eyes and held them, waiting for acknowledgment—a brief nod from Maggie—before he went on. "My wife and I moved here about four years ago. She's part owner in a nice little bookstore in downtown Wallingford. The locals elected me because they wanted somebody with some real experience. We like it here…a lot. This is where we wanna retire in a few years."

He stopped to watch his men, looking around him as if to take count. Maggie crossed her arms and shifted her weight from one leg to the other. She knew he didn't need a response from her. And more important, she knew he wasn't finished. She waited.

Finally he looked at her, his eyes meeting hers again. There was something in them Maggie recognized. There was determination, frustration, a bit of anger, but what Maggie recognized was just enough panic—just a glimpse—to tell her that the experienced Sheriff Henry Watermeier was also scared.

"This is one fucking mess," he said, pointing to the barrel the group was focused on. "Whoever did this may have been doing it for years. I'm not gonna bull-shit you, O'Dell. Even if we don't find your missing person, I could use your help. I'm going to need it to find this goddamn psycho. I'm not a betting man, but if I were, I'd say he still lives around here. And if I don't find him and haul his ass in, I can kiss my dream of re-tiring in this community goodbye."

Watermeier waited for her response. But this time he avoided her eyes, looking, searching, assessing, all in an effort to downplay the enormous level of trust he had laid at Maggie's feet. Trust and confidence he had in-vested in a woman he was meeting for the first time, a woman who had insinuated herself into his investigation. Whether out of desperation or simple strategy, Maggie could tell this was not something a tough, independent sheriff like Watermeier did easily.

She turned toward the group surrounding the barrel, and simply told him, "Then I guess we better get to work."

Maggie didn't glance back for his reaction, but soon he was beside her, restraining his long strides so that they walked side by side.

CHAPTER 19

Henry introduced Special Agent Maggie O'Dell to the rest of the group and watched the casual exchange and assessment. Of course, Bonzado got the longest look. Bonz looked like some California surfer dude instead of a professor in that goddamn Hawaiian shirt. But the kid was brilliant in a humble, nonarrogant way, and despite his getup, he was good at magically attributing an identity to a pile of bones. But Henry already knew what Dr. Stolz, the medical examiner, was thinking. He had shot Henry one of those famous "what the hell?" looks when he first saw Bonzado. And now, without saying a word,

Henry could feel Stolz's scowl saying, "The feds? You brought in the fucking feds already?"

Stolz was probably worried that it was a direct reflection on his own competence. Actually, Henry didn't care what Stolz or any of the rest of them thought. He had learned a long time ago to live by one simple philosophy—CYOA—cover your own ass.

They had a body bag spread out under the lip of one of the barrels that had cracked open during Vargus's shake-up. Henry would just as soon load it up and have the poor sucker join the woman from yesterday at the morgue. But this was Stolz's call. He wanted to process the fractured barrels out here at the scene, worried that jostling around the fragile remains might compromise them. This process didn't look any more efficient to Henry. But again, he reminded himself, it was Stolz's call, Stolz's risk to take. In other words, Stolz's ass. He could only be concerned about one ass at a time, and right now it was his own.

All that could be seen of the corpse inside the barrel was the head and shoulders, a tuff of peppered gray hair and what looked like the lapels of a navy blue suit. Stolz and Bonzado, their hands covered in latex gloves, carefully groped inside, grabbing hold of anything solid that hopefully wouldn't rip or tear or crack. At the other end of the barrel, two of Henry's deputies held tight to a rope that had been secured around the cracked middle. They were ready to play a sort of macabre game of tug-of-war.

Henry handed Agent O'Dell a small jar of Vicks VapoRub. The smell would only get worse once they pulled the unlucky bastard out. But the agent declined with a polite "no thanks." Something told him it had nothing to do with her pretending to be tough. No, she really didn't need it. She was used to the stench of death, not that anyone could get used to that sour, pungent odor. There was something different about the smell of a human corpse, different from any other animal. He hated that smell. Had never gotten used to it and didn't want to. Yet, without taking a swipe of Vicks for himself, Henry dropped the jar into his pocket. He knew better than to offer any to Stolz or Bonzado. And Bonzado's students stayed back, probably at Bonzado's instructions, his way of assuring Henry that they wouldn't get in the way.

They started slowly easing the corpse out of the barrel and immediately there came a low, sickening noise, a sucking sound that made Henry cringe. This one was fresh. This one would be messy. Henry glanced at O'Dell. Maybe he hoped to see her cringe, show at least a twinge of discomfort. There was nothing like that. Anticipation, but certainly not discomfort. Hell, she had probably seen lots worse.

O'Dell stood maybe five five, had an athletic but slight frame and was a bit too attractive to fit Henry's stereotype of an FBI agent. But her self-assured manner revealed an air of confidence that put him at ease.

He had noticed it during their phone conversation, too. Confident, not cocky. Hell, he wouldn't have confided what he had if she had come off with that government-issued cockiness that seemed to run rampant at the federal level.

Maybe he was crazy to be putting so much trust and faith in someone he hardly knew, but Special Agent Margaret O'Dell would come in useful if things went south. Bottom line—he wasn't about to piss away a thirty-year career because of some psycho. O'Dell seemed nice enough, but if the governor came looking for answers, Henry needed to be ready. Hell, it wasn't such a bad idea to have someone else he could blame if answers didn't come quick enough.

"Hey, watch it," Stolz yelled at Bonzado as the corpse came loose from the barrel with what almost sounded like a pop. The lower extremities swung free. The M.E. lost his grip and the corpse slid out of their control, falling onto the body bag, the torso slamming hard against the rocks. It fell flat on its face with a hollow thud. And, as it hit against the hard surface, the top of the head cracked open.

"God Almighty," Stolz yelled again. "We're gonna need a better way to do this. We may have just given this guy a new head injury. How am I supposed to figure out what the killer did and what we did?"

Henry practically bit his tongue to avoid saying, "This was your idea." Only the second barrel and already Stolz's incompetence showed in his blatant con-tradictions. This only reassured him about his decision to bring in Bonzado and O'Dell, two outsiders to wit-ness and document any irregularities.

While the others backed away to regroup and rethink this archaic method, O'Dell came in for a closer look, kneeling on the rocks. Despite the fractured and now-open skull, the corpse appeared to have no other injuries, no mess. Even the navy blue suit had few wrinkles.

"This guy looks in good shape," Henry said.

"Too good a shape. I don't see any blood," Bonzado pointed out. He moved aside for Carl, who came in closer with a camera.

Bonzado's students now dared to come closer, the woman being the bravest of the group, looking over her professor's shoulder. Both of the male students looked as though they might be sick. The older guy limply held a camera at his side and didn't attempt to take a single picture. Maybe he was waiting for Carl to finish. Henry wondered if the two guys were having second thoughts about their choice of career.

"Nice suit," Carl said, setting aside his camera and pulling out a forceps to retrieve a stray thread from the back of the corpse's jacket.

"Doesn't look like the body has begun to liquefy." Stolz squatted on the opposite side of O'Dell.

"I think the skull's been cut open," she said, now on hands and knees.

"Probably sliced right open on these rocks," Stolz said.

"No, I don't think so. Take a look at this." O'Dell moved aside for Stolz to get a better angle, looking up at Henry as she did. For the first time he thought he noticed something in her eyes. Maybe that bit of discomfort he had been searching for earlier. "It looks like someone may have used a saw. Maybe a bone saw or even a Stryker saw."

"A Stryker saw?" Now Stolz seemed interested.

O'Dell got up and came around the rocks to peer inside the top of the skull. The flap that came loose hung over, like a lid or a dismantled toupee. O'Dell practically had her nose to the scalp when she said, "Whatever he used it's left very fine marks. There's no blade chattering."

"Blade chattering?" Henry asked, and glanced around at the others, noticing Bonzado giving O'Dell a look of admiration.

"It's sort of a technical term." It was Bonzado who jumped in with an explanation. "It's when a thin blade jumps slightly from side to side while you're using it. You know, like a hacksaw, especially when you're just starting to cut." Ever the professor, Henry thought, though the kid had a genuine desire to provide information. There was no intention to upstage anyone or condescend to anyone, not like Stolz might do.

"From what I can see," O'Dell continued, "I think the skull is empty."

"A Stryker saw? Empty? What the hell are you talking about? Are you saying the brain is missing?" Stolz shot up, stepping over the corpse to get to O'Dell's side.

Ordinarily, Henry would have laughed at the little man who rarely became animated or allowed an outburst of emotion. He usually confined his emotions to those famous facial expressions. He shouldn't be focused on Stolz. But focusing on Stolz's incompetence and his rising panic was a hell of a lot better than dealing with his own. This crap only got stranger by the minute.

"If you've got enough pictures, let's try to flip him and get all of him on the body bag," Stolz instructed.

Henry stood back. He hated to admit it, but he was starting to enjoy watching the little man get all worked up. Plus, Stolz had more than enough help with Bonzado and two of the students joining in. Even O'Dell had her jacket sleeves pushed up and was grabbing hold of a shoulder. This time the group wasn't taking any chances on having the corpse slip out of their control. They barely had the body turned and Henry's stomach took a plunge.

"Jesus Christ," he said under his breath, and everyone stopped, looking up at him, and then back at the corpse. "It's Steve Earlman."

"You know this man?" O'Dell asked.

Henry found the nearest boulder to lean on before his knees buckled. "Not only do I know him, I was a goddamned pallbearer at his funeral last May."

CHAPTER 20

Maggie could now see the tacks and pins holding Mr. Earlman's tie and jacket lapels in place. She lifted an eyelid and found a small, convex plastic disk in the eye socket, something morticians used to give definition to the eye area and to keep the eyelids closed.

"It looks like an autopsy incision," Dr. Stolz said, taking his glasses completely off and pocketing them.

"Can't be," Sheriff Watermeier said. "There was no autopsy."

"You're sure?" Maggie was back on her feet, inspecting the rest of the body while the M.E. poked at the flap of skull. The suit looked awfully clean, almost as if it had gone directly from the casket to the sealed barrel. "It certainly looks like a Stryker saw."

"It definitely was a bone saw of some kind," Stolz insisted.

"I know for a fact there was no autopsy," Water-meier said.

"How about surgery?" Adam Bonzado was beside Stolz now, on hands and knees, peering into the top of the dead man's head.

"No surgery," Watermeier answered quietly. "Steve died of an inoperable brain tumor."

Maggie glanced at Watermeier to make sure he was okay. She knew what it was like to discover a friend had been a victim of some heinous crime. Almost a year had gone by since she unzipped a body bag to find a friend of her own with a bullet hole in his forehead. She was sure she would never forget Special Agent Richard Delaney's empty eyes staring up at her. None of the law enforcement workshops and no amount of experience could prepare someone for that shock, that helplessness, that sick feeling in the bottom of the stomach.

Watermeier removed his hat. He wiped the sweat from his face with the sleeve of his shirt, despite what Maggie had noticed was a chill in the air now that the sun was disappearing behind the ridge of rock and trees. Watermeier put the hat on and this time pushed it back. Maggie surveyed the equipment the crime-lab technicians had carefully stacked out of the way on one of the boulders. Finally she saw a red-and-white water jug.

She reached and grabbed it, glanced at Carl and waited for his nod of approval. Then she unscrewed the top, took a long slow drink and, as casually as possible, handed the jug to Sheriff Watermeier as if handing it down the line. He didn't hesitate, took a generous swig and passed it on.

"Was it public knowledge?" she asked Watermeier.

He looked at her, knew she was addressing him, but his eyes drew a blank. "What's that?"

"Did Mr. Earlman tell people about the tumor? Friends, family, acquaintances?"

"Oh, yeah. He didn't hide it," Watermeier said. "But he didn't complain about it, either."

"Was there any public mention of it? Was it listed as COD in the obituary?"

Watermeier scratched his head, reaching under his hat. "I don't remember about the obituary, but almost everyone knew Steve. He owned the butcher shop in downtown Wallingford. Bought it from old Ralph Shelby years ago but still kept the name. Figured everybody already knew it as Ralph's. That was Steve. He was a pretty humble guy. And a good guy, fair and honest. Even after he got sick he was going in to work every day. Still did the custom cuts himself. After Steve died, the store closed. Someone bought all the equipment but didn't want to run the shop. It's some kind of knickknack shop now."

Dr. Stolz looked up at Maggie from his perch. "What exactly are you thinking, Agent O'Dell?"

"If it's not a surgery cut, it had to have been made postmortem, right?"

"Yes."

"Was his funeral an open casket?" she asked Watermeier, who now only nodded. "So it had to be after the funeral."

"Someone dug up his grave?" Henry asked, but from the look on his face, Maggie could tell he didn't really want to think about it.

"When and how would they able to do that?" Stolz said. "A sealed vault isn't the easiest thing to break into."

"Not all caskets are put into vaults," Bonzado offered. "Depends on whether or not the family wants to add that extra expense. If I remember correctly it's about $700 to $1,000."

"There's another possibility," Maggie said. "The body could have been taken before the casket was buried."

"You mean someone may have snatched the body right from the funeral home?" Bonzado said as he stood, brushing his knees clean.

His sartorial get-up was an odd uniform for a forensic anthropologist, even for a professor. Maybe not for an eccentric professor with muscular, tanned legs. As Maggie caught herself admiring Bonzado's legs, she also noticed his knees were covered with the rust-colored dust from the rocks and a green weed had latched onto the tops of his socks. It reminded Maggie to take a closer look at the dead man's clothes for any similar debris.

"If someone had access they could have made a switch," Maggie answered as she examined the suit, a lightweight wool, damp and sticky with what she guessed to be embalming fluid.

The skull cut had definitely been made after the body had been embalmed and prepared for its casket. There would be no way to hide leaking embalming fluid for an open-casket viewing without repairing the gaping hole, and the cutter hadn't felt the urgency to make any such repairs. Now that she got a closer look at the blue suit, she could tell there were no signs of green weed, no brown rock dust on the wool. The cut hadn't been made out here. In fact, other than the sticky embalming fluid, the suit looked clean.

"I helped carry his casket," Watermeier said, sounding quiet and far away. "It was heavy. He had to be in there."

Maggie glanced up at the sheriff. He rubbed his temple, not like a man puzzled in thought, but pressing hard—hard enough to wince—as if he wanted the image before him to disappear.

"I'm just saying we need to consider all the possibilities," Maggie said. "In any case, we should find out who had access to the casket and the grave. Maybe his suit might tell us more." She found Stolz watching and met his eyes, ignoring their skepticism and what she immediately recognized as a trace of suspicion. Not even an hour into the investigation and Stolz had already decided to label her an intruder. It didn't matter. She was used to it. "Usually funeral clothes are clean when a mortician puts them on a corpse, right?" She continued, "So anything the clothes came in contact with would have to be from the mortuary or a destination that came later."

Stolz simply nodded.

"We might find something on the suit, some debris from the killer like hair or fibers. He couldn't have done this without making contact with the body."

"He went to a lot of trouble just to take the brain. Maybe he sells parts to teaching colleges," Bonzado's female student suggested, as she helped Carl, who had been quietly collecting evidence that may have spilled from the barrel. The woman seemed overly anxious to help and held open a plastic bag while Carl dropped small particles in with forceps.

Maggie was impressed that Carl already had two bags in his other hand, one containing what looked to be a swatch of hair or fur and in the other, a small, crumpled piece of white paper.

"What is this?" She pointed to the crumpled piece of paper.

"Not sure," Carl said as he handed her the bag. "It's not a note, if that's what you were hoping. It's not even writing paper."

Maggie held it up, examining it in the sunlight. "Looks like a waxy texture."

"Getting back to more important matters," Stolz grumbled. "Like missing brains. Serial killers often take things, clothing, jewelry, even body parts." He looked from Bonzado and Carl to Watermeier and finally—lastly—to Maggie. "As trophies, right?"

"Yes, serial killers often do that. There's only one small problem here," Maggie said, stopping all of them, waiting for their attention. "Mr. Earlman wasn't murdered."

CHAPTER 21

Adam Bonzado helped Simon with the bags of sand-wiches and sodas, keeping an eye on his student. Ramona and Joe had literally dug into this project, but Simon... Well, it was hard to tell. His pasty complexion and quiet demeanor were typical. So when he volunteered to get lunch for the group, Adam knew it was Simon just being Simon, always the first to offer when there were errands that needed to be run.

They made their way through what seemed to be a growing crowd of reporters and cameras. Officer Trotter with the state patrol had the media trained to stay back behind the crime-scene tape, but that didn't stop the barrage of questions.

"Professor, Jennifer Carpenter with WVXB Channel 12. When will we have an official update?"

Adam recognized the attractive blonde behind the glasses.

"I'm not in charge, Ms. Carpenter. You'd have to ask Sheriff Watermeier."

"I've been asking Sheriff Watermeier. What exactly are you finding? And why are you hiding it?"

"We're not hiding anything," Adam said, and when she whipped off her glasses, he realized the cameraman behind her was now running film. Jesus! Just what he needed. Why hadn't he kept his big mouth shut? "We're simply trying to assess the situation. I'm sure we'll let all of you know what's going on as soon as we can."

He turned his back to them and headed for the quarry. Simon waited for him on the other side of the tree line.

"Vultures," he told his student, hoping for a smile.

"I think she likes you."

Adam glanced at him, expecting some smart aleck comment to follow. His students were always razzing him about being single. But Simon looked serious. Adam knew Simon was older than most of the other graduate students, having come into the program late. "Yeah? You think so? I'm not sure she's my type."

Now, Special Agent Maggie O'Dell was another story. From their first introduction Adam couldn't help thinking that if he did actually have a type, she would be in the running. Forget that the woman had amazing brown eyes and could make an FBI-approved navy-blue suit look official as well as make it come alive, the woman was smart. She actually knew what blade chattering was. Definitely a woman who could steal his heart. It had been a long time since any woman had gotten his attention enough for him to check out her ring finger.

According to his mother, it had been an abnormally long time. "It's not good for such a young man to be so alone," she would tell him at every opportunity. But after Kate he had chosen to be alone. Besides, how could he begin to fill the void that Kate had left? When she drowned it was as if she had taken him down under with her. Even now he couldn't think about her without remembering, without feeling her cold, lifeless body, without remembering all those hands trying to pull him away as he continued over and over to pump her chest and try to breathe life into her blue-lipped mouth.

Suddenly Adam realized Simon was staring at him, waiting for him.

"You okay, Professor Bonzado?"

"I'm fine." He turned back to the road, pretending to be distracted, then realized he had actually forgotten something. "What time do you need to get to your job?"

Simon checked his wristwatch. "Not until later this afternoon."

"You still have my keys?"

"Oh, yeah, sorry." Simon shifted the sandwich bags to one hand while he dug in his jeans pockets for the keys.

"You mind going back to the El Camino?"

Simon looked eager to please.

"There's a pry bar that might help us open up some of the barrels. You mind getting that?"

"No, not at all." He started handing the bags to Adam, making sure he had a grasp of everything. "Is it still under the seat?"

"I tossed it into the bed, but I bet it got shoved clear to the back when we loaded everything else."

As Simon headed back, Adam took a deep breath, hoping to wipe out the images of Kate he thought he had buried long ago. Henry waved at him, then met him halfway, rescuing several of the bags before Adam dropped them.

"Hey, everybody. Lunch," Henry yelled.

Adam watched the group stop, setting tools down and placing evidence bags in containers. They gathered around as if there was nothing unusual about sitting down to eat sandwiches and drink Cokes in the middle of a rock quarry surrounded by barrels stuffed with dead and rotting bodies.

"Where did you get these?" Agent O'Dell asked, unwrapping a sandwich.

"Vinny's Deli."

"Vinny's has the best sandwiches in Connecticut,

O'Dell," Henry told her, but Adam could tell she hadn't asked because it looked absolutely mouthwatering. If she had, she wouldn't be so interested in the white paper it had been wrapped in.

"This looks like the same stuff you found with Mr. Earlman," she said, looking at Carl.

"I think you're right."

"What the hell are you two talking about?" Henry seemed a little pissed off that they weren't paying attention to their sandwiches.

"This white, waxy paper," she explained, and now Adam remembered it. "We found something like this in the barrel with Mr. Earlman."

"Lots of people use this stuff, O'Dell."

"Actually, I don't think so, Sheriff. I've never seen this stuff on the shelves of your regular grocery store. I bet it's a specialty item."

"So what the hell are you two saying? That the killer has himself a sandwich while he's slicing and dicing his victims?"

Adam wondered if it was simply the exhaustion that had Henry's face flushed and his voice raised. Maybe the fall sunshine that heated up the rocks and caused the beads of sweat on his upper lip had taken a toll on the aging sheriff. Or was Henry's panic slipping out? So far he had almost appeared too calm.

Whatever it was, Henry was waiting for an answer, standing in front of O'Dell, towering over her. She didn't look the least bit intimidated by the big man, and instead ripped off a piece of the paper to stick in her pocket. Everyone else stood watching, waiting, as if for permission to return to their lunches. Adam couldn't figure out why Henry was suddenly being so tough on Agent O'Dell. After all, he had invited her into the investigation, hadn't he?

"You think this could be important?" Henry finally asked, his tone almost back to normal. He must have realized he couldn't rattle O'Dell so easily.

"When a killer uses something out of the ordinary like this it's often because he has it handy. It may be a way for you to track him down."

"A piece of paper?"

"Sometimes it's the simplest things that lead us to a killer. What we might otherwise think is an insignificant piece of evidence. A serial killer named John Joubert used a strange piece of rope. It had unusual fibers. I think it was made in Korea, not something just anyone would have around the house. He tied up his young victims with it. When they arrested Joubert they found more of the rope in the trunk of his car. The rope was something he had access to as a scoutmaster. He had plenty of it handy and he never considered that it might be something that would be used to finger him. Whatever this white paper is, I'm guessing this killer has plenty of it available to him."

"Okay." Henry still didn't sound convinced. "But what the hell is he using it for?"

"I need to see more of the victims, but my guess right now..." O'Dell hesitated, looking around the group as if deciding whether or not to share her opinion. "My early guess is that he's using it to temporarily wrap things."

"Things," Henry chided as if impatient.

"Yes, things like Mr. Earlman's brain."

CHAPTER 22

Maggie accepted the Diet Coke Sheriff Watermeier offered. She preferred Diet Pepsi, but knew this was a sort of peace offering. As the others finished their lunches, Watermeier sat down next to her on the boulder.

"When we finish later this afternoon, I need to take a minute and throw a bone to those media piranhas." He smiled, pleased with his own pun. "Then Stolz says he'll do the autopsy of the woman we found yesterday. That suit your time schedule?"

"Yes, of course."

He continued to sit quietly at her side, and she wondered if there was something more he needed to tell her, something more he wanted to share.

"It's beautiful here, isn't it?"

She glanced at him, surprised. That wasn't exactly what she expected from the rough-and-tough, ex-NYPD-turned-small-town sheriff.

She followed his eyes, taking it in for the first time since she had arrived. Maggie couldn't help thinking how quiet it was. The trees were still thick with splashes of orange and yellow with flaming red vines licking up the trunks. And the sky seemed so blue it looked artificial. Even the ankle-high grass was dotted with tiny yellow flowers.

"Yes," she finally agreed. "It is beautiful."

"Everybody ready?" Watermeier broke the momentary peace, standing suddenly as though he needed to snap back to attention.

They joined the others where Adam Bonzado and his students had brought down another cracked barrel. This time Maggie pulled her jacket up over her nose. Already the stench was overbearing and the pry bar had only broken the seal. Despite Bonzado's effort the drum's lid came undone bit by squeaky bit, reminding Maggie of opening a lid off a vacuum-sealed can of coffee.

"Man, oh man, this one is ripe," the professor said, and stopped, his hands still clenching the pry bar while he wiped at his face with the bottom of his shirt, revealing for a second or two rock-hard abs. Maggie looked away, realizing that this was the second time in only hours that she had taken notice of his physique.

The rest of them waited. No one offered to take over for the poor professor. Not any of his three students. The one named Joe kept a safe distance, while the woman, Ramona, seemed interested but cautious. The older student Simon, stood quietly, almost rigid with a trowel in one hand and a camera in the other, making no effort to use either. He seemed stunned or perhaps overwhelmed by the sight. Maybe it was the stench.

"Should we be cutting these barrels open?" Watermeier suggested.

"With what?" Stolz swabbed at his forehead, which had been constantly shiny with sweat. "Anything we use could contaminate what's inside more than it already is. Let's at least see what's in these barrels before we go hauling all of them away. I don't want a dozen barrels of garbage in my lab, Henry. Is that okay? Can we at least see what the hell's in them before we do that? I know it's time consuming and I know it's a pain in the ass."

"Whatever you want. That's your call."

"I never said—" But Stolz stopped as a mass of black flies swarmed out the small opening of the barrel. "What the hell?"

"Son of a bitch." Watermeier took a step back.

Bonzado hesitated for a second, then slammed the lid back down. "We should probably collect a few of these, right?" He looked to Maggie and then to Carl, who was already searching for a container.

"Ramona and Simon, could you give Carl a hand?"

The woman practically jumped to Carl's side, but Simon stood there as if he hadn't heard Bonzado.

"Simon?"

"Yeah, okay."

Maggie watched him set the trowel and camera down so slowly it seemed as if in slow motion. Perhaps Bonzado was expecting a bit much from his students, who had imagined their careers examining clean, fleshless bones in sterile, warm and dry laboratories.

Bonzado pried at the lid again and this time Carl and Ramona held the opposite corners of a makeshift net and caught several flies. Simon held the wide-mouth container for them to shake the flies into, slapping the lid on quickly. He handed the container back to Carl and returned to his previous stance, trowel back in one hand, camera in the other.

Now Bonzado proceeded, ignoring the rest of the flies. Finally, the lid came loose, thumping to the ground. More flies were freed and so was the smell, a sour pungent odor like rotten-egg gas. Maggie watched Joe and one of Henry's deputies hurry away. Joe didn't make it to the trees before he began retching. Even Watermeier and Carl backed away, the sheriff's hat now over his nose.

"Holy fucking crap," Watermeier said, his words muffled through his hat.

Maggie climbed onto the rocks, putting some space between herself and the smell, while attempting a look down into the barrel. "Anyone have a flashlight?"

Pry bar now tossed aside, Bonzado shuffled through his toolbox, setting metal clanking. Maggie couldn't help wondering if it was to distract attention from his nervousness. But when he reached up to hand her the penlight, she realized his sudden clumsiness was no disguise. His hand was perfectly still and he had no trouble meeting her eyes.

"How the hell would flies get inside?" Watermeier asked. "That barrel was sealed good and tight. Did they squeeze through the crack?"

"Possibly," Maggie said. "It's also possible the body was exposed to the elements for a while before it was stuffed inside the barrel." Maggie shot the penlight into the black hole and wished she could see more than the spots of lights. The afternoon sun cast shadows that didn't help matters. Swaying branches overhead created dancing shadows that almost made it look like there was movement down inside the barrel.

"But they couldn't have lasted that long," Watermeier insisted.

"They would have laid their larvae," Maggie said while concentrating on the spots of light showing pieces of torn fabric, a tangle of hair, maybe a shoe.

"Blowflies are pretty quick and efficient," Bonzado joined in. "They can sense blood from up to three miles away and be on a body before it's even cooled, sometimes before it's dead."

Maggie checked faces, but the pallor from moments ago was gone, no one wincing at the gruesome details the professor described. In fact, now everyone seemed ready.

"This one's gonna be a mess," Bonzado said, using another flashlight to take a look for himself into the barrel. "Lots of tissue already gone."

"Wonderful," Stolz said, slipping on his jacket against a breeze that suddenly came out of nowhere. Despite his insistence to open the barrels and make certain they did, indeed, contain bodies, he made no attempt to look for himself. "Let's load it up."

"This is interesting," Bonzado said, still examining the contents. "The back is facing up—at least I think it's the back. There's a strange pattern on the skin."

"You mean a tattoo?" Stolz became interested and Maggie came in for a look, too.

Bonzado's flashlight showed what looked like bright red welts crisscrossed into the corpse's back, at least what was left of the back. The flies had already devoured patches of tissue, though Maggie guessed the majority of their feeding frenzy was on the other side, starting in the moist areas first.

"It's just livor mortis," Stolz said as if it didn't matter. "She…or he died lying on something that had this pattern. All the blood settles. Jesus! This one smells." He backed away, disgusted and shaking his head.

"Henry, let's call it a day. I need to get back to start doing some autopsies."

"What about this other one?" Henry pointed to the dented barrel off to the side. Maggie hadn't seen the contents of this one. They must have opened it before her arrival.

"Give it to Bonzado." Stolz waved a hand over his head as he headed for the road. "It's nothing but bones. Not much I can do with that."

Maggie buttoned her jacket, also noticing the chill. The sun had begun to sink behind the mountain though it still seemed early. Bonzado and his students were preparing the barrel for transport as Henry gave directions and pointed to the clearing in the trees, the dirt path where the other vehicles had come in. That's when she noticed something flapping in the breeze, something white sticking out from under the discarded lid.

"Carl," she said, waving the tech over. "Take a look."

He squatted down by her side. "I'll be damned." He pulled out an evidence bag and forceps. Gently he tugged the torn white paper from under its trap while Maggie lifted the lid.

It was the same white, waxy paper.

Just then Maggie felt a nudge at her elbow. She turned to find a Jack Russell terrier ready to lick her hand.

"Speaking of burying things," Carl said, "if Watermeier sees that dog here again—"

"Goddamn it, Racine."

"Too late."

"What did I tell you, Racine?" Watermeier yelled at the old man hurrying down from a footpath in the trees. "You've got to keep that mutt the hell away from here."

"Sorry, Sheriff. He has a mind of his own sometimes. Come here, Scrapple."

But the dog was already sitting and leaning against Maggie's hand as she scratched behind his ears.

"Well, you convince him," Watermeier continued, "to stay the hell out of here, Racine. We can't have him dragging off evidence."

"I take it he's been finding scraps?" Maggie smiled up at the old man who seemed embarrassed and agitated, shifting from one foot to the other. Then she remembered what Tully had said about Detective Racine being from this area. "Racine? Do you have daughter named Julia?"

"I don't know," the man mumbled, and Maggie stood up, sure she must have misunderstood him.

"Excuse me?" she said.

"Yes, I do. Jules. Her name's Julia," he said, his eyes meeting hers though making an effort to do so. His daughter possessed the same blue eyes. He scratched his head, reaching up under the black beret. "That's right, Detective Julia Racine with the…with the D.C. police force. Yes, ma'am. That's my daughter, Jules."

CHAPTER 23

Luc Racine fumbled with the tangle of keys he found in his pocket. Scrapple waited impatiently, staring at the door as if that might help open it. He knew the terrier was upset with him. He had ducked several attempts Luc had made to pet him.

"I'm not gonna have you eating people, okay?" he told the dog for the third time. "Even if they are dead already." Only now Scrapple ignored him—not a flinch, not even a perk of an ear, no indication that he was listening—and he continued to stare at the door.

Luc would make it up to him. Surely there was something in the refrigerator besides sour milk. He sorted through the keys again, trying to concentrate, trying to remember. He used to be able to pull out the house key automatically without a second thought. These days it seemed to take all his deductive reasoning, or at least, all that remained.

Then as if in a sudden flash he remembered. He grabbed at the doorknob and smiled when it turned easily. He had stopped locking the door, afraid he would eventually forget to take the keys and lock himself out. Relief washed over him, so much so that he could feel a chill. It was becoming a typical response, his body reacting, first with surprise and disappointment then relief that the mind could still participate.

Losing his memory wouldn't be so bad if he didn't know it was happening. That was the worst part. Laboring over shoestrings, unsuccessfully looping worthless knots and all the while knowing that tying his shoes was once something he did without a thought, let alone without a struggle. Learning to tie your shoes. How hard could that be? Easy enough for a five-year-old. Easy. Right. Only now Luc Racine wore slip-on loafers.

But forgetting Jules's name. That was unforgivable. How could he have forgotten? He could hear what Julia would say to that, "You never forget the fucking dog's name, but you can't remember your own daughter's."

The house was cold, as if a window had been left open. Summer was certainly over. He didn't need to see the flaming red of the turning oak leaves. He could feel it in the evening chill, hear it after dark in the chirp of crickets.

He stopped in the middle of the living room. He stopped and looked slowly around. Something didn't feel right. It wasn't like last night when he couldn't recognize anything. No, something felt out of place. A clammy shiver swept through him. He felt the hairs on the back of his neck rise.

Coming back from the quarry he had gotten the same chill. He had followed the footpath, watching his feet so he wouldn't trip over the protruding rocks hidden in the tall grass. All the way back it felt like someone had been watching him. Not just Watermeier or one of the others making sure he left, but someone watching. Watching and following. He had heard twigs snap behind him. Thought it was his imagination, but Scrapple heard it, too, growling once, then putting his tail between his legs, his ears back and hurrying home. He barely waited for Luc, only slowing because the wuss of a dog counted on Luc as his protector. There was something wrong with that. Something backward. Weren't dogs instinctively supposed to be protective of their masters?

Now Luc checked around his own living room, looking for signs that he wasn't alone. He looked out the windows, checking for anyone hiding in the trees. His only assurance was that Scrapple seemed content, stretched out on his favorite rug. Luc hurried to the front door, turned the dead bolt, then made sure the kitchen door was bolted, too. It was probably all in his imagination, although he couldn't remember reading a thing about the disease causing hallucinations or paranoia. But then, how the hell would he remember reading about it when he couldn't remember his own daughter's name?

He shook his head, disgusted with himself. He stopped to check the meager possibilities for dinner, opening the refrigerator. There had to be something he and Scrapple could eat. He stared at the top shelf.

A twinge of panic rushed through him again. What the hell? Calm down, he told himself. It was nothing. Nothing at all. Nothing but his own stupid forgetfulness. And he grabbed the TV remote from the top shelf of the refrigerator.

"I've been looking all over the place for this."

CHAPTER 24

Henry told O'Dell she could follow him to the morgue. She probably thought he was being considerate. He really just wanted her beside him when they walked out of the quarry together, when the media piranhas attacked. He already knew Stolz wouldn't be any help. The M.E. seemed to have an allergic reaction to reporters and was long gone.

"So tell me, Agent O'Dell, from what you've seen, any ideas who I need to start looking for? And you can spare me the basics."

"The basics?"

"Yeah, white male, twenty-something recluse whose

mama abused him so now he doesn't know how to respond to a woman except with violence."

"How does Steve Earlman's mutilation fit into that profile?"

Damn! He'd forgotten about Steve, didn't even want to think about poor Steve.

"Okay, so let's hear your basics on this one."

"It's too soon to give you a physical description, except that yes, he is most likely a white male in his twenties or maybe early thirties. He drives an SUV or pickup or has access to one. He probably lives alone on an acreage outside of the city, but he lives within fifty miles of this quarry."

Henry glanced down at her, trying not to show his surprise or that he was impressed.

"This is all premature," she continued without him prompting her, "but just from looking at the place he chose to dump the bodies says a lot about him. Most serial killers leave their victims out in the open, some even display their handiwork. It's part of their ritual or, in some cases, part of their thrill to see others shocked by what they're capable of doing. This guy goes through a lot of trouble to hide the bodies. He didn't want them found. I'm wondering if he might even be embarrassed about what he's done. Because of that, I'm guessing he has a paranoid delusional personality, which means he'll feel threatened by us discovering his hiding place. He'll think we're out to get him, and it might make him do something irrational."

"In other words, he might screw up, and we'll be able to catch him?"

"He might panic and kill someone he thinks is out to destroy him. In other words, a panic kill. Yes, that could mean he screws up and leaves something behind for us to use to catch him, but it also means someone else could be killed."

"Not at all what I wanted to hear, O'Dell," Henry said, almost wishing he hadn't asked. He already had the governor up his ass. What the hell would happen if this madman started killing again? Jesus! He hadn't even thought of that.

As they got to the road, Henry noticed that the state patrol had arrived, two fresh officers to relieve Trotter and set up guard posts for the night. Earlier Randal Graham, the governor's gopher, had offered the local National Guard. All Henry could think of at the time was that the locals would panic if they started seeing the fucking National Guard moving in. This was bad enough. He didn't need to draw more attention.

"Sheriff Watermeier—" the media mongrels began the barrage as soon as he and O'Dell were in earshot "—what's going on?"

"How many bodies are there?"

"Is it true a serial killer is on the loose?"

"When will the victims' names be released?"

"How long has this been going on?"

"Hold on a minute." Watermeier raised one hand and

stopped O'Dell with his other by gently taking hold of her arm. She shot him a look, part surprise and part ir- ritation, just enough for him to know that this was not in her plans. He didn't care. What he did care about was retiring in a community that respected him. And that community damn well better think he was doing every- thing he could to protect it.

"I can't tell you any details, except to say that yes, there are fifty-five-gallon drums, sealed barrels that have been buried under some rock," he told them, slowing his words so that no one had an excuse to misquote him. "And yes, some of those barrels do have bodies inside. That's all I can say about that right now. But I will tell you that we have everything under control. We have ex- perts on the scene collecting evidence and we have—"

"But what about the killer, Sheriff?" someone from the back yelled, interrupting him. "You have a serial killer on the loose. What are you doing about that, Sheriff?"

Jesus! These assholes were hell-bent on starting a panic. Henry tucked his hat lower over his brow, as if to ward off further blows and hopefully to let them know he couldn't be goaded into their hysteria.

"We're working on that," he lied. It was only the sec- ond day. How the hell was he supposed to have a list of suspects already? "That's why we have Special Agent Maggie O'Dell here." He gave her a slight shove for- ward. "She's a criminal profiler with the FBI, up here from Quantico, Virginia. Her specialty is catching guys

like this. So you see we've got the very best working on
our team. That's all for now."

This time he grabbed O'Dell's arm to lead her out of
the crowd, Officer Trotter clearing a path for them.

"Have you brought in any suspects yet, Sheriff?"

"When will you give us more information? Like a
profile of the killer?"

"That's it, folks. That's all I have for today." He
waved a hand at them and continued to plow through,
shoving the cameras aside when they refused to move.

As soon as they were across the road, O'Dell
wrenched her arm from his hold and without a word
marched to her Ford Escort. He didn't care if she was
pissed. Tomorrow she would probably be long gone. All
she wanted was to find her precious missing person, and
there was a good chance the woman was waiting for
them in the morgue.

CHAPTER 25

Maggie waited, gloved hands at her sides, while Dr. Stolz unzipped the body bag. She was used to participating in autopsies. Her forensic and medical background had prepared her for doing everything from helping place the body block to taking fluid samples to weighing organs. But she knew when not to participate, too, and this was one of those times. Dr. Stolz had made that clear. So she waited, alongside Sheriff Henry Watermeier, still angry with him for blindsiding her, but anxious to have this trip over and done with.

She was trying to be patient despite her anger and her urge to help. She wanted to help clean the woman's

chest wound so they could see the incision, the punc-
ture marks, the rips and tears. There had to be multiple
ones to have caused such an eruption.

Stolz must have sensed her restlessness when he said,
"The chest wound is not the cause of death. Not as far
as I can tell from my preliminary exam." He began parting the long tangled hair, his gloved fingers carefully
splitting dried, bloody clumps to reveal a large crescent-
shaped wound to the side of the corpse's head. "I'm betting this is what knocked her lights out for good."

"There was an awful lot of blood in the chest area,"
Maggie said, trying not to contradict the doctor. "Are
you sure she wasn't just knocked unconscious?"

Stolz looked at Sheriff Watermeier and pursed his
thin lips as if showing him that he was purposely re-
fraining from what he'd like to say. Then he began spong-
ing the woman's chest, cleaning the wound, the mess. "If
he started cutting her immediately after he killed her,
there would still be a boatload of blood. Especially here
in the chest where there's some major gushers. And he
cut deep. May have even punctured the heart."

"Wait a minute. Deep wounds sound like fatal wounds,"
Watermeier said, which drew a scowl from Stolz.

"Not stab wounds." The medical examiner lifted skin
he had just cleaned. "She's cut open. Nothing pretty
about this handiwork, though. At least not as precise and
detailed as with Mr. Earlman."

"What did he remove?" Watermeier asked before
Maggie got the chance.

"I'll show you." Dr. Stolz began opening the wound with one hand and with the other flushed the wound with the sprayer hose attached to the side of the stainless steel table. "My first guess would have been the heart, maybe a lung. You know, stuff like the usual crazies take. But this one sort of defies anything I've ever seen."

With the wound now washed clean, Stolz pressed the mangled skin to the side and moved back for Watermeier and Maggie to take a closer look.

Watermeier stared, scratching his head, puzzled and not recognizing the scarred tissue. But Maggie knew immediately. And without getting out the photo Gwen had given her, Maggie also knew that this was not Joan Begley.

"I don't understand," Watermeier finally said, looking from Maggie to Stolz and realizing he was the only one in the dark.

"This woman must have been a breast cancer survivor," Stolz explained. "The killer took her breast implants."

Maggie had already prepared herself, had already planned what she would say to Gwen when she called with the news that her patient had been murdered. She should have felt relief. But for some reason she felt beginning panic instead. If Joan Begley wasn't dead, where the hell was she?

CHAPTER 26

Joan Begley woke to the sound of doves cooing. Or at least that was what it sounded like through the spiderweb in her brain. Her eyes felt matted at the lashes, stuck down with webs. Her mouth was cotton dry. But the cooing reminded her of summer mornings, waking up at Granny's dairy farm outside of Wallingford, Connecticut. A distant humming lulled her in and out of sleep. The breeze over her head felt and smelled like dew-laced grass, the fresh air wafting in from the meadow. Along with the breeze and the cooing came a feeling of contentment.

A click startled her awake. A click and then a low rumble of a motor coming to life. She sat up, her eyes flying open, her arms straining. It was the leather wrist restraints that renewed the panic, that brought her back to reality. Or rather brought her back to her nightmare.

She stared down at the restraints clamping her to the bed rails, and for a brief moment she thought she might be in a hospital. Had he taken her to a hospital? The room was dimly lit, darkness filled the huge windows. She looked around the area and could see walls made of sturdy timber, rafters of the same, more windows with thick glass, none of which were open. The breeze she had dreamed of was only the ventilation fan above the bed, the hum of a chest freezer in the corner. It looked like she was in a cabin or converted shed. As frightened as she was she had to admit this place had a warm and almost cozy feeling, despite the smell of disinfectant laced with, of all things, the scent of lilac.

Where in the world had he taken her? And why?

She looked around again, her vision still blurred, distorting the items on the shelves, elongating and swirling them like something out of a van Gogh painting. Maybe she was hallucinating. Yes, maybe this was all a dream, a nightmare.

She tried to think through the cobwebs in her brain. She needed to stay calm. No good would come from panic. And she didn't seem to have any energy left. She couldn't allow the panic to take control of her again, to exhaust her. Last night…or was it days ago? How could she be sure? He had drugged her. Asked in his polite tone that she drink a bottle of some concoction.

"It won't hurt," he had promised her in that little-boy voice that she had once found endearing. "It tastes like cough syrup."

But when she refused, she remembered how he grabbed her, shoving her into a headlock. She had been surprised by his strength, by his frenzy, by his…his madness. He had forced the liquid down her throat despite her clawing at him, despite her kicking and coughing and gagging. Yes, he had become a madman, totally out of control. Someone she didn't recognize, and certainly not the Sonny she thought she had gotten to know.

She began to cry, thinking about it. Why had he done this? Why had he brought her here? What did he intend to do with her? If she screamed would anyone hear her?

She looked around the room again. The door was certainly bolted even if she could escape her restraints. Now she noticed that there were leather bindings attaching her ankles to the bed rails, as well. She couldn't focus on that. She wouldn't panic. She would talk to him. Yes, they would talk. Where was he? Had he left her? What in the world did he intend to do with her? She knew he hadn't sexually assaulted her. If that wasn't what he wanted, then what was it?

As if trying to find the answer, she began examining the room. There were shelves with jars of all sizes, crocks with metal-clasp lids, plastic containers, bottles and gallon glass containers. Close to her bed was a table with a lighted aquarium, illuminated jellyfish floating along the surface. On the other side was another table with what looked like bowls made of bits and pieces of shells.

There were pictures on the wall. Black-and-white photos of a boy and his parents. She couldn't tell if the boy was Sonny. This was definitely someone's work space or hideaway. There was no need to feel frightened, she tried to convince herself. She could talk to Sonny. Yes, talk and see what he wanted from her.

She lay back down, feeling better. The pillows were so soft. He had gone to some trouble to make her comfortable, despite whatever drug he had forced down her. But even the drug had simply made her sleepy. No headache, no hangover. She would just wait. Eventually he would come in and they would talk. She could feel herself relaxing. That was when she saw the shelf above her head.

She bolted up in bed, straining against the leather and twisting to get a better view, making herself look despite a fresh panic and the urge to flee. On the shelf above her were three skulls, hollow eye sockets staring out at her.

Oh, dear God! Why? What was this place?

She tried to focus on what was in the jars across the room, but it was too far to see anything more than blobs. Then she stared at the jellyfish in the aquarium next to the bed. They were transparent, illuminated from the backlighting, floating on the surface. There was nothing else in the aquarium. No little rocks at the bottom, none of the colorful greenery. She pulled herself closer for a better look. Did jellyfish always float on the surface like that?

Then in the light she noticed that both jellyfish had numbers imprinted on their surfaces. A string of numbers like a serial number, some sort of identification.

"Oh, my God!" Suddenly, she recognized them from a visit she had made to a plastic surgeon. These weren't jellyfish at all. They were breast implants.

CHAPTER 27

Dr. Stolz didn't bother to hide his displeasure. Maggie saw the scowl he gave Sheriff Watermeier—it was the third or fourth one of the day, Maggie had lost count. The sheriff announced he needed to leave but that she was welcome to stay. For a brief moment she expected Stolz to forbid it. But how could he? Instead, he muttered something into his mask about outsiders. Maggie got the impression he didn't just mean her, but Watermeier, as well.

She wasn't sure why she stayed. The only reason she was here was to identify Joan Begley. Perhaps she hoped that this victim, this woman, might be able to provide some answers of where Maggie could start looking for Gwen's missing patient.

She watched from beside the stainless steel table. Her hands stayed in her pockets beneath the gown. It was an effort to keep them from helping, part instinct and part annoying habit. Already once she had reached for a forceps, stopping herself before Stolz could see.

He was slow. Slow but not necessarily meticulous. In fact, his movements seemed a bit sloppy, slicing here and there around the edges of the body cavity, reminding Maggie of a fisherman severing all the linings before gutting a fish in one swift scoop. It wasn't the usual reverence she was accustomed to seeing medical examiners use. Perhaps it was simply a performance for her benefit. At first she worried that he would use the less-popular Rokitansky procedure where all the organs come out at once—one block of the internal system—instead of the Virchow method where each organ was removed separately to be examined.

She watched him cut with his elbow bent, hand zigging back and forth, a strange, almost sawing motion. But then she was relieved to see his gloved fingers reach in and scoop out the lungs, one at a time. First the right lung, which he plopped on the scale, then he yelled over the utensil tray to the recorder on the counter, "Right lung, 680 grams." He dropped it into a container of formalyn and scooped up the left one. "Left lung, 510 grams. Color in both, pink."

Maggie disagreed. She wanted to mention that the left lung was not quite as pink as the right, but kept quiet. It wasn't enough to note. No signs of foul play, at least none that had affected the lungs. In the killer's mutilation to get at the breast implants, he hadn't even punctured the lungs. And there wasn't enough discoloration to indicate that the woman had ever been a smoker. The darker pink of the left lung may have only suggested that she had spent a good deal of her life as a city dweller.

Dr. Stolz picked up a needle and syringe off the tray, looked it over, then exchanged it for a larger one. He inserted the needle into the heart, drawing blood into the syringe. The heart showed definite signs of being punctured by the killer. Maggie could easily see a cut that didn't belong, next to the area where Stolz took his sample. Satisfied, he labeled the sample and set aside the syringe, but he didn't bother to remove the heart. Instead, he moved down to the stomach.

Maggie didn't let him see her impatience. Okay, so he had his own way of doing things.

Of all the incredible workings and mysteries of the human body, Maggie always thought the stomach to be one of the most whimsical of the organs. It resembled a small, saggy pink pouch. A simple and soft touch of a scalpel was usually all that was needed to slit it open, and Stolz, despite his bull-in-a-china-shop approach, handled this organ with a gentleness that surprised Maggie. He laid it on a small stainless steel tray of its own, slit it open slowly and carefully. Using just his fingertips, he spread back the walls. Then, reverting to his normal routine, he grabbed a stainless steel ladle and began scooping out the contents, pouring them into a small basin on the tray.

Maggie moved around the table for a closer look. Stolz didn't seem to mind. Now he seemed excited and anxious to share.

"Still lots here," he said, continuing to scoop and stir the contents, clanking the metal ladle against the metal side of the basin with each pour. "This might be our best estimate of time of death. Being in that barrel threw off too many of the other indicators."

So that was why he was so interested. Finally, something to show off his expertise.

"Is that green pepper?" Maggie asked.

"Green pepper, onions, maybe pepperoni. Looks like she had pizza. Lots still here, which means she was most likely murdered shortly after her meal."

"What do you think? Two hours?" Maggie knew that almost ninety-five-percent of food moved out of the stomach within two hours of being consumed. However, it wasn't an exact science, either. There were things that sped up digestion, just as there were things that slowed it, stress being a major factor.

"Not much has made it into to the small intestine yet," he said, his fingers back in the body cavity examining the coil of intestine. "I'd guess less than two hours. Closer to one."

"So the next question, can you tell whether or not it was frozen or restaurant style?"

He looked up at her with raised eyebrows. "The pizza? Why in the world would that matter?"

"If it was restaurant style, chances are she ate out that night. Maybe even with someone. We might be able to track where she was—and with whom—right before she was murdered."

"Well, that's simply impossible to know," he told her, shaking his head. "But—" he seemed to reconsider as he stirred the contents with what looked like an ordinary butter knife "—the colors, especially of the vegetables, seem brighter than normal, which from my experience could indicate that they were fresh and not frozen."

Maggie brought out a pocket notebook and jotted down the contents. When she looked back up, Stolz was staring at her, his arms folded over his chest. The scowl had returned and was now directed at her, the only person left to try his patience.

"You can't be serious?" he said. "You think the killer took her out for pizza first, then bashed in her head and sliced out her breast implants? That's absurd."

"Really? And why do you say that, Dr. Stolz?" It

was her turn to grow impatient with his questioning of her expertise, his distrust that an outsider might have an answer.

"For one thing, that would suggest it could be someone local."

"And you don't think that's possible?"

"This is the middle of Connecticut, Agent O'Dell. Maybe on the coast or closer to New York. This guy, whoever he may be, is using the quarry as a dumping ground for his sick game. My guess is that he lives miles away. Why would he risk dumping bodies in his own backyard?"

"Didn't Richard Craft do that?"

"Who?"

"Richard Craft, the guy who killed his wife and then put her dismembered body through a wood chipper." She watched Stolz's expression go from arrogance to embarrassment. "In the middle of a snowstorm, if I'm not mistaken, and not far from his home in Newtown. Newtown, Connecticut—isn't that just west of here?"

CHAPTER 28

Lillian sat quietly, listening in disbelief as Henry told her and Rosie about the bodies they had found so far. Of course, it was all confidential, and she knew there were things he wasn't telling them, couldn't tell them. When he came in earlier, his distraught and exhausted demeanor had been enough for Rosie to suggest they close the store early, something Lillian thought she would never hear her partner suggest. Now they sat, sipping decaf among thousands of the best stories captured in print, and yet Lillian couldn't help thinking Henry's story had them all beat. Forget Deaver and

Cornwell, this was something only Stephen King or Dean Koontz could concoct.

"Sweetie," Rosie said to her husband, keeping her small hand on top of his large one. "Maybe it's some drifter. Maybe this has scared him off."

"No, O'Dell says he has a paranoid personality. Usually those guys stick to familiar territory because they are paranoid. I've been trying to think of everyone I know who lives alone out on acreages in this area. But those I can think of don't seem like the type."

"The profiler says he lives close by?" Lillian wasn't sure why that made her heart skip a beat. Perhaps it made it all too real. She liked thinking about this case in terms of fiction.

"He's probably watching the news coverage every day, getting his kicks."

"But if he's paranoid, Henry, he's not getting kicks," Rosie said. "Wouldn't he be devastated that you discovered his hiding place? Maybe even ticked off?"

Henry looked at his wife, surprised, as if he hadn't expected her to hit the nail right on the head. But it seemed like common sense. You didn't need to be a rocket scientist or Sherlock Holmes to know this guy would be upset. Lillian added to Rosie's thesis, "Yes, very upset. Are you concerned that he might come after one of you?"

"That's what O'Dell suggested." He didn't look happy that someone else would suggest the same. "She said the guy might panic, but I don't think he would risk screwing up."

Lillian couldn't help feeling elated that she could have come up with the same idea the profiler had come up with. Maybe she was good at this. Who said you had to have life experiences to figure these things out, when all she had done was read about it.

"I'm guessing the profiler says he's a loner, a plain sort of man who goes about his business without much notice." She liked playing this game. She tried to remember some of her favorite serial killer novels. "Perhaps he's someone who doesn't draw much attention to himself in public," she continued while Henry and Rosie listened, sipping their coffee, "but ordinarily, he seems to be a nice enough guy. He works with his hands, a skilled worker who has access to a variety of tools. And, of course, his penchant for killing will most likely be somehow tracked to the volatile relationship he probably had with his mother, who no doubt was a very controlling person."

Now the pair was looking at her with what she interpreted as admiration or maybe amazement. Lillian liked to think it was admiration.

"How do you know so much about him?" Henry asked, but Lillian had been wrong about his look of admiration. It appeared instead to be laced with a hint of suspicion.

"I read a lot. Novels. Crime novels. Suspense thrillers."

"She does read a lot," Rosie said, as if she needed to vouch for her partner.

Lillian looked from Rosie back to Henry, who seemed to be studying her now. It caught her off guard and she felt a blush starting at her neck. She gave a nervous shove to her glasses and tucked her hair behind her ears. Did he really think she knew something about this case, about this killer?

"Maybe I should read more," he finally said with a smile. "I could probably crack this case faster. But I have to tell you, for a minute there you sounded like you were describing someone, someone you knew fairly well."

"Really?" she said, and tried to think of a character who might fit the bill. And suddenly her stomach did a somersault. She did know someone who fit her description, but it wasn't anyone in a novel. The person she had described could very easily be her own brother, Wally.

CHAPTER 29

It was late by the time Maggie got to the Ramada Plaza Hotel. She started to feel the exhaustion of the day. A tight knot throbbed between her shoulder blades. Her eyes begged for sleep. And she wondered if her mind was playing tricks on her. In the parking lot, while she unloaded her bags, she felt someone watching her. She had looked around but saw no one.

As she waited for the desk clerk—or rather, according to Cindy's plastic clip-on badge, "desk clerk in training"—Maggie tried to decide what she'd tell Gwen. After everything that had happened today, she wasn't any closer to knowing where Joan Begley was. For all she knew the woman was still here at the Ramada Plaza Hotel, lying low and simply escaping.

Maggie watched the desk clerk as she plugged in her credit card information. Hotel policy wouldn't allow them to give out Joan's room number. And Maggie didn't want to draw attention to herself or cause alarm by whipping out her FBI badge. So instead she said, "A friend of mine is staying here, too. Could I leave a note for her?"

"Sure," Cindy said, and handed her a pen, folded note card and envelope with the hotel's emblem.

Maggie jotted down her name and cell phone number, slipped the card into the envelope, tucked in the flap and wrote "Joan Begley" on the outside. She handed it to Cindy, who glanced at the name, checked the computer and then scratched some numbers under the name before putting it aside.

"Here's your key card, Ms. O'Dell. Your room number is written on the inside flap. The elevators are around the corner and to your right. Would you like some help with your luggage?"

"No thanks, I've got them." She slung her garment bag's strap over her shoulder and picked up her computer case, taking several steps before turning back. "Oh, you know what? I forgot to tell my friend what time we're supposed to meet tomorrow. Could I just jot it down quickly?"

"Oh, sure," Cindy said, grabbing the note and sliding it across the counter to Maggie.

She opened the envelope and pretended to write down a time before slipping the card back in, this time sealing the envelope and handing it back to Cindy. "Thanks so much."

"No problem." And Cindy put the card aside, not realizing she had just shown Maggie Joan Begley's room number.

Maggie threw her bags onto the bed in her own room. She kicked off her shoes, took off her jacket and untucked her blouse. Then she found the ice bucket, grabbed her key card and headed up to room 624. As soon as she got off the elevator, she stopped at the ice machine to fill the plastic bucket, and she padded down the hall in stocking feet to find Joan's room. Then she waited.

She popped an ice cube into her mouth, only now realizing she hadn't eaten since the sandwich at the quarry. Maybe she would order some room service. And as if by magic she heard the elevator ding from around the corner. Sure enough a young man clad in white jacket and black trousers with a tray lifted over his head turned the corner, walking away from her to deliver to the room at the far corner. She waited until he came back and saw her, before she slipped her key card into the slot.

"Darn it," she said loud enough for him to hear.

"Is there a problem, miss?"

"I can't get this key card to work again. This is the second time tonight."

"Let me try."

He took her card and slipped it into the slot, only to get the same red-dotted results. He tried again, sliding it slower. "You'll probably need to have them give you a new card down at the front desk."

"Look, I'm beat, Ricardo," she said, glancing at his name badge. "All I want to do is watch a little Fox News and crash. Could you let me in, so I don't have to go all the way back down tonight?"

"Sure, hold on a minute." He dug through his pockets and pulled out a master. In seconds he was holding the door open for her.

"Thanks so much," she told him. She was getting good at this. She stood in the doorway and waved to him, waiting for him to round the corner. Then she went inside.

Maggie's first thought was that Joan Begley must do quite well as an artist. She had a suite, and from first glance Maggie guessed that she hadn't been here for at least the last two days. Three complimentary *USA Today's* were stacked on the coffee table. On the desk was a punch card for a week's worth of complimentary continental breakfasts. Every day was punched except for Sunday. There was also an express checkout bill dated Sunday, September 14, with a revised copy for Monday and another for Tuesday.

Several suits and blouses were hung in the closet by the door. A jacket remained thrown over the back of the bedroom chair. Maggie patted down the jacket pockets and found a leather checkbook. She flipped it open, pleased to find Joan Begley kept track of her transactions. There were few since she had arrived in Connecticut. The first was to Marley and Marley for $1,000, listed as a "funeral down payment." There was one at the Stop & Shop with the notation, "snacks." Another at DB Mart, "gas."

The last entry was on Saturday, September 13. At first she thought nothing of it. The check had been made out to Fellini's Pizzeria with a notation, "dinner with Marley." She glanced at the earlier notation. Dinner with one of the funeral directors? Would they meet for dinner to discuss funeral business? Yes, that was possible. If it were something else, a date, perhaps, Mr. Marley probably would have paid.

Saturday, September 13. If Gwen was right, Joan Begley may have disappeared later that night. But obviously she had come back to the room or the checkbook wouldn't be here. Had she come back to change? Was Marley the man she was meeting again when she called Gwen?

She started to replace the checkbook when she thought about the autopsy. Whoever the poor woman was from barrel number one, she had been murdered shortly after having pizza, maybe at Fellini's. Maybe shortly after meeting someone, perhaps even the killer for pizza. Maggie slipped the checkbook into her own trouser's pocket.

She continued to survey the suite. A Pullman was spread open on the valet table. Two pairs of shoes lay tipped underneath where they had been kicked off. In the bathroom, various cosmetics and toiletries were scattered. A nightshirt hung on the back of the bathroom door.

Maggie stood in the middle of the suite, rubbing at her tired eyes. There was no doubt that Joan Begley hadn't just picked up and escaped to the shore or somewhere. Even if she had run off with some new man in her life, she wouldn't have left her things. No, it looked as if Joan had intended to come back to her suite. Yet it was obvious that she hadn't done so for several days. So what happened?

She looked around the two rooms again for any clues, and this time she remembered to check the notepad alongside the phone. Bingo! She could see some indentations on the top page. It was an old trick, but she found a pencil in the drawer and with its side, shaded over the top page of the notepad. Like magic the indentations in the page turned into white lines, forming letters and numbers. Soon she had an address and a time: Hubbard Park, Percival Park Road, West Peak, 11:30 p.m.

Maggie ripped off the page and pocketed it. She

stopped at the door for one last look. And before she turned out the light, she said to the empty room, "Where the hell are you, Joan Begley?"

CHAPTER 30

"Tell me about your illness," he said while sitting on the edge of the bed.

Joan had been asleep. It had to be the middle of the night. But when the light snapped on she woke with a jerk. And there he was. She had to squint to see him, sitting at the foot of the bed, watching her. Staring at her.

She could smell him, a combination of wet dirt and human sweat, as if he had just come in after digging in the woods. Oh, God! Had he been digging her grave?

"What did you say?" She tried to wipe at the sleep from her eyes, only then remembering the leather restraints. Alarm spread through her body. Her muscles ached. She strained to reach her face, to push the strands of hair from her mouth, noticing how very dry her skin had gotten, almost crusty at the corners of her eyes and mouth. Perhaps there were no more tears, was no more saliva inside her. Was that possible? Could a person cry herself dry?

She felt the fear already clawing at her. Felt his eyes examining her. Her stomach growled and for a brief moment she realized she was hungry. "What time is it?" She tried to stay calm. If she didn't panic maybe it wouldn't trigger the madman in him.

"Tell me about your disease, your hormone deficiency."

"What?"

"You know, the hormone deficiency. Which hormone is it?"

"I'm not sure what you're talking about," she lied, but she knew exactly what he was talking about. She had told him that a hormone deficiency was the cause of her struggle with her weight. She had lied, embarrassed to admit that it had only been a lack of self-discipline. Oh, dear God. What had her lies gotten her into? She glanced around the room, at the containers and the skulls above her. Is that what he wanted from her?

"Tell me what gland. Is it the pituitary? Or did you say the thyroid?" He continued in almost a singsong tone, as if trying to coax her into sharing. "You know the hormone that makes you fat? Or I guess it's the lack of a hormone, right? You told me about it. Remember? I think you said it had something to do with your thyroid, but I can't remember. Is it the thyroid?"

She looked over his shoulder at the jars that lined the shelves. There were a variety of shapes and sizes: mason jars and pickle jars with the labels scratched out and taped over with new labels. From a distance she could see only globs, but after recognizing the breast implants, she now realized these containers must hold other specimens, bits and pieces of human tissue. And now he was asking about her thyroid. Oh, Jesus! Was that why he had always been interested? Did he have a jar ready to plop it into?

"I don't know," she managed to say over the lump in her throat. "I mean, they don't know." Her lips quivered and she pulled the covers up over her shoulders as best she could, pretending it was because of the cold and not the fear.

"But I thought you said it was your thyroid?" He sounded like a little boy, almost pouting.

"No, no, not the thyroid. No, not at all." She tried to sound sure of herself. She needed to convince him. "In fact, they discounted the thyroid. Discounted it altogether. You know, it may just be a lack of self-discipline."

"Self-discipline?"

His brow furrowed—puzzled, not angry—as he thought about this. Maybe it was only the tinge of blue fluorescent light from the aquarium, but he reminded her of a little boy again. Even the way he was sitting, cross-legged with one foot tucked under himself, his hands in his lap, his eyes hooded with exhaustion and his hair tousled as if he, too, had just been awakened.

She wondered if he was trying to figure out how he might bottle her self-discipline, or rather lack of self-discipline. Would he try to find another answer? Then she caught a glimpse of shiny metal. Her empty stomach plunged. In his folded hands that sat quietly in his lap, he held what looked like a boning knife.

Her muscles tightened. Her eyes darted around the room. The panic crawled up from her empty stomach, on the verge of becoming a scream.

He had come for her thyroid. He planned to cut it out. Would he even bother to kill her first? Oh, dear God.

Then suddenly he said, "I never thought you looked fat at all." He was looking down at his hands and glanced up at her with a smile, a shy, boyish smile. It reminded her of the way he had been when they first met, polite and quiet with interested eyes that listened and wanted to please.

"Thank you," she said, forcing herself to smile.

"Sometimes doctors make mistakes, you know." He looked sad now as he stood up, and every nerve in her body prepared itself. "They don't know everything," he told her.

And then he turned and left.

CHAPTER 31

Wednesday, September 17

Midnight had come and gone, but the nausea had not.

He had an hour before he needed to leave. Today would be a long day. He had done these double-duty days before, hadn't minded, but not like today. Last night sleep never came, reminiscent of his childhood, when he waited for his mother to come in at midnight, administering her homemade concoction of medicine only to leave him with even more pain. Today he'd be forced to hide that same nausea, that relentless nausea that had lived with him day after day during his childhood. But he had done it before. He had survived. He could do it again.

If only he had taken care of her that first night like he had planned. He had even brought the chain saw with him, expecting to cut her up piece by piece, hoping to somehow find the prize. Instead, he had decided at the last minute to wait.

It was the wrong decision, a *stupid, stupid, stupid decision.*

He thought he could wait, thinking she'd tell him where her precious hormone deficiency resided, saving him a mess, because he hated messes. *Hated, hated, hated them.* And the chain saw was the messiest of all to clean. But here he was with an even bigger mess on his hands. Not only did he need to worry about those who wanted to destroy him, all those digging in the quarry, but now he needed to figure out a way to dispose of her body when he was finished.

He couldn't think about it now. He needed to get ready for the day. He needed to stop worrying or his stomach would make it impossible to get through this day.

He scraped the mayonnaise from inside the jar, the clank-clank of the knife against glass only frustrating him, grating on his nerves, which already felt rubbed raw. How could he function? How could he do this?

No, no, no. Of course he could. He could do this.

He spread the condiment on the soft white bread, slow strokes so he wouldn't tear it, taking time to reach each corner but deliberately not touching the crust. He unwrapped two slices of American cheese, laying them on the bread, making sure neither slice hung over the edge, again, not touching the crust, but letting them overlap in the center. Then carefully he cut the top slice of cheese exactly at the overlap and set aside the unneeded section.

He reached up into the cabinet, back behind the Pepto-Bismol and cough syrup, grabbing hold of the brown bottle his mother had kept hidden for years. He opened it, carefully sprinkled just a few of the crystals on the cheese, then replaced the bottle to its secret place.

He topped the sandwich with the other slice of bread, but not before slathering it with just the right amount of mayonnaise. Last, but most important, he cut away the crust, then cut it in two, diagonally, not down the middle. There. Perfect.

Perfect, perfect, perfect.

He wrapped his creation in white wax paper, putting it on a tray that already included a can of Coke, an individual-size bag of potato chips and a Snickers candy bar. It was the exact lunch his mother had packed for him every day of his childhood, or at least, every day for as long back as he could remember. The perfect lunch. Rarely a substitution. It always made him feel better, but this lunch wasn't for him. It was for his guest.

He smiled at that—his guest. He had never had a guest before. Especially not an overnight one. His mother would never allow it. And despite this being an accident, a mistake, a mess... Well, perhaps, yes, just perhaps, he liked the idea of having a guest. He liked having someone he could control for a change. At least for a little while. At least until he decided how to dispose of the parts he didn't need.

That was when he remembered. He might be able to use one of the freezers. Yes, maybe there was room for her in the freezer.

CHAPTER 32

Luc Racine sat in the second row of folding chairs. The first row was reserved but remained empty, so Luc had a perfect view of the coffin at the front of the room. Too perfect a view. He could see the woman's makeup-caked face with cheeks too rosy. He wondered if she had ever worn lipstick that deep a shade of red. It almost made her look as if she wore a mask.

Luc pulled out the small notebook and pen from his shirt pocket, flipped it open and jotted down the date. Then he wrote, "No makeup. Absolutely no makeup," and he underlined "absolutely." He kept the notebook out and glanced around.

Marley stood by the door waiting for someone coming down the hallway. Perhaps it was that girl reporter. Luc had seen her in the reception area when he came in. Thank goodness she didn't recognize him, but then she probably couldn't see without her glasses.

Marley was in what Luc called his funeral director position, shoulders squared, back straight, his hands coming together below his waist, folded almost reverently as if in prayer, but his chin was up, showing an amazing amount of strength and authority. And there was the look that went with the posture.

Luc had observed Jake Marley so many times that he could catch the transition process though it happened quickly, within a blink of an eye. The man was an expert. He could go from any range of facial expressions, whether it be anger with an employee, sarcasm or even boredom, then within seconds the man could transform his entire face into an expression of *complete* compassion and sympathy. Complete, but Luc knew complete didn't necessarily mean *genuine*. In fact, he knew Jake Marley's expression wasn't genuine. It was just a part of his job, a skill honed and perfected. One necessary for his profession, like a fine craftsman's eye for detail, or in Luc's case, like a mail carrier's ability to memorize strings of numbers. But there was something about this skill of Marley's that seemed… hmm…Luc couldn't remember the word. Sometimes he had trouble remembering the right words. He scratched his jaw, trying to remember.

Holy crap! He had forgotten to shave.

Then he glanced down at his feet—dad blasted! He still had his slippers on.

He looked back at Marley to see if the funeral director had noticed him. Maybe he could slip out the back. He twisted around in his seat. Shoot! This room didn't have another door. And now Marley was escorting two women in, directing them to the coffin. He gave Luc a slight nod of acknowledgment but nothing more. Marley's attention was, instead, on the two mourners, and Luc knew he didn't have to worry about Marley paying any more attention to him.

The elderly woman had artificial silver hair and big red-framed glasses that swallowed her small pigeonlike face. She leaned on her companion with every step. It was the companion who assured Luc he didn't have to worry about Marley. The woman wore a tight-fitting blue suit that accentuated her full figure in all the right places. She wore her long dark hair pulled back to reveal creamy, flawless skin.

Yes, she would have Jake Marley's full attention. She already had his hand on her lower back as he escorted them to the front of the room. Luc wondered if Marley was imagining his hand a few inches lower. Of course, he'd never slip. He was one smooth operator. Luc had observed him many times. Just as he had caught the sudden subtle face transformations, Luc had also watched Marley smooth talk and literally handle the pretty ones with a touch on the arm, the half pat, half stroke of the shoulder, the hand on the lower back. Luc had seen all of Marley's moves.

Maybe the women found it comforting, Luc told himself. Marley wasn't obnoxious about it. He wasn't a bad-looking guy, either. Sort of plain, but put him in one of his five hundred dollar black suits and the guy seemed to ooze strength, comfort and yes, authority. And women seemed to love guys with authority, especially when they were at their most vulnerable.

Luc watched the two women now at the casket, gazing at their loved one, whispering to each other as if not to wake her.

"Her hair looks beautiful," the older woman said, then added, "She wouldn't have worn that color of lipstick."

Luc smiled. See, he knew it wasn't her shade. He flipped his notebook open again and jotted down, "No whispering. Make people talk in normal tones."

The young woman glanced back at Luc and smiled. Her eyes were puffy, though she wasn't crying anymore. He smiled back and gave her a nod. In his notebook he wrote, "No crying allowed. And maybe some cheerful music. None of this…this funeral home music."

He tried to remember what kind of music he liked and drew a blank. Surely he could remember a particular song or maybe a singer. How could he not remember music?

Just then he noticed the two women whispering again, only this time the older woman was looking back over her shoulder at him as the young woman said something to Marley. There were talking about him. Wondering who he was. Why they didn't recognize him.

Time to leave.

He got up and took his time shuffling through the long second row of chairs. By the time he got to the door he heard one of them say something about bedroom slippers and realized that yes, they were talking about him.

Luc made it to the end of the hallway, out the door and down the street. Still no Marley. Of course, he wouldn't leave that beautiful brunette. So Luc took a moment to catch his breath and scratch in his notebook, "Bedroom slippers. Bury me in my bedroom slippers. The blue ones, not the brown ones."

He flipped the notebook closed and put it and the pen in his pocket. In the reflection of the store window he saw a man watching him from behind, from across the street. Was it Marley? He didn't want to turn around to look. Didn't want the man to know. He stood still, pretending to look at the knickknacks in the store that used to be Ralph's Butcher Shop. He looked between the hanging wind chimes and colorful wind socks, the same area where the rows of salami used to hang. He looked for the man's reflection and couldn't see it. Luc stole a quick glance over his shoulder. The man was gone.

Luc stared at his feet, at the slippers that he couldn't

remember putting on that morning. Had there even been a man following him? Or was he really just imagining things?

CHAPTER 33

Maggie moved her room service tray aside, snatching one last piece of toast. She glanced at her watch. She had plenty she needed to do today, places to go, people to talk to. Adam Bonzado had tracked her down first thing this morning, inviting her to his lab at the university to take a look at one of the victims. He seemed under the impression that she was officially on this case. Maybe Sheriff Watermeier had even told him so. She wasn't sure why she was considering it. Most likely it wouldn't help her find Joan Begley. Except that his lab was at the University of New Haven, the same university where Patrick was.

She glanced at her watch again and dug out her cell phone. She had been putting this off long enough. She punched in the number from memory.

Gwen answered on the second ring as if she was expecting the call.

"It's not her," Maggie said without stalling, then waited out her friend's silence, letting it sink in.

"Thank God!"

"But she is missing," Maggie said, not wanting Gwen to misunderstand. She shoved aside a file she had thrown on the hotel desk. She opened it, but only to retrieve a photo. A photo of Joan Begley that Gwen had given her last week.

"Tell me," Gwen said. "Tell me whatever you've found out."

"I was in her hotel room last night."

"They let you in?"

"Let's just say I was in her hotel room last night, okay?" She didn't have the patience this morning for a lecture from her friend, the same friend who had managed to finagle someone into telling her Joan Begley had missed her flight. "It looks like she's been gone since Saturday. But I don't think she just left. Her things are scattered around the room like she intended to come back."

"Is it possible he may have talked her into running off without her things?"

"I don't know. All her cosmetics? And her checkbook? You tell me, Gwen. Is she the type who would do that?"

There was silence again and Maggie used it to examine the photo. The photographer had interrupted Joan Begley, making her look up from a metal sculpture, her welding hood's protective glass mask pushed up, revealing serious brown eyes and porcelain-white skin. In the background were framed prints, bright splashes of red and orange and royal blue, beautiful explosions of colors with black streaks and slashes through the middle. And in the reflection of the glass, Maggie could almost make out another image. Sort of ironic. A portrait of the artist with a self-portrait of the photographer.

"No," Gwen Patterson finally answered. "She's not the type who would run off and leave her things. No, I don't think she would do that."

"I'm going to need your help, Gwen." She hesitated again, making sure she had her friend's attention. "Now's not the time to be holding back any client-patient confidentiality."

"No, of course not. No, I wouldn't do that. Not if it was something that might help find her."

"You said you had an e-mail from her that mentioned this man she may have been meeting. You said she called him Sonny, right?"

"Yes, that's right."

"Can you forward that e-mail to me?"

"Sure, I'll do it as soon as I get off the phone with you."

"I talked to Tully earlier. He's going to see if he can get into Joan's apartment."

"Can he do that?"

"She's been gone long enough to file a missing persons report. I want him to look around her place. Maybe see if she has a computer and if he can get into her e-mail. We need to find out if there's anything more about Sonny. If possible, Tully'll be going over later today. Would you be able to go over with him?"

More silence. Maggie waited. Had Gwen even heard her? Or had she asked too much?

"Yes," she finally said, and this time her voice was strong again. "I can do that."

"Gwen, one other thing." Maggie examined the photo again. "Did Joan ever mention a man named Marley?"

"Marley? No. I don't think so."

"Okay. I'm just checking. Call me if you think of anything."

"Maggie?"

"Yes?"

"Thank you."

"Thank me when I find her. I'll talk to you later, okay?"

She barely clicked off and the phone started ringing. Gwen must have forgotten something.

"You remembered something?" Maggie said in place of a greeting.

"Agent O'Dell, why the hell am I seeing you on TV?"

It wasn't Gwen. It was her boss, Assistant Director Kyle Cunningham. Damn!

"Good morning, sir."

"It says a rock quarry in Connecticut. I thought you were supposed to be in your backyard and I see you're profiling a case in Connecticut. A case I don't remember assigning you to."

"I'm here on personal business, sir. It was a mistake yesterday when Sheriff Watermeier said I was profiling this case."

"Really? A mistake? But you were there at the quarry?"

"Yes. I stopped by to check on—"

"You just stopped by? O'Dell, this isn't the first time you've just stopped by, but it better be the very last time. Do you understand?"

"Yes, sir. But they may actually need a profiler. This certainly has all the signs of a serial—"

"Then they need to request a profiler. Perhaps their own FBI office has someone available."

"I'm already familiar with—"

"I believe you're on vacation, Agent O'Dell. If you have personal business in the area, that's on your own time, but I better not see you on TV again. Do you understand, Agent O'Dell?"

"Yes, sir. I understand." But there was already a dial tone.

Damn!

She paced the room, stopping to watch the morning traffic down on Pomeroy Avenue and Research Parkway. She checked her watch again. There was still time for one stop. She swung on her jacket, slipping her key card into the pocket, and grabbed her notebook with directions already scrawled inside. She started out the door when she hesitated. What would it hurt? She went back to her computer case, unzipped the pockets until she found it. Then without giving it any more thought she shoved the envelope into her notebook and left.

CHAPTER 34

Lillian did something that she had never done in all the years she had owned the bookstore—she called Rosie and told her she'd be late. Now as she sat in her car looking at the old house where she had grown up she couldn't help wondering if this was a mistake.

The entire place looked worn and run-down, from the peeling paint on the other buildings to the rusted old cars deserted in the yard like some graveyard for unwanted vehicles. There were a few she didn't recognize, added since her last visit, alongside the old panel station wagon, the one that had been first to be exiled after their mother's death. Somehow it had seemed inappropriate for either of them to use it without her permission.

Lillian stared out her own car window, her hands still on the steering wheel as she tried to decide whether to stay or leave. How in the world did her brother, Wally, live out here? Why did it not bother him to do so? That was something she had never understood. All those years growing up here and wanting, needing to escape. She couldn't imagine staying here, living here and not remembering, not being haunted by those memories. But Wally didn't seem to mind.

She tried to hold on to the courage, the determination she had started the morning with. She tried to imagine herself as one of the sleuths in the many mysteries she so enjoyed. She tried to go back to last night when she was putting pieces of the puzzle together and coming up with theories and ideas that even Henry admitted were exactly what the FBI profiler had come up with. And if all else failed, she needed to at least put to rest her nagging suspicion that Wally had anything to do with those bodies they were finding stuffed into barrels. If anything, maybe he was covering something up for Vargus. Yes, that would make sense. That was something Wally would do.

By the time she stepped up to the front door, she was having second thoughts. Yet, she reached under the nearby flowerpot for the spare keys. She wasn't sure why he bothered to lock the door. What could he possibly have that anyone would want? But that was Wally.

Always suspicious of others. Always paranoid that someone was out to hurt him.

The house smelled musty, almost as if it had been closed up and unused except for the pungent smell of burnt food, quickly contradicting her initial impression. He had piles everywhere. Piles of newspapers and magazines and videotapes. But the kitchen looked spotless. No dirty dishes in the sink. No crusted pots and pans on the stove. No trash in the corner. She couldn't believe it.

She should check the refrigerator. She braced herself and opened the refrigerator's freezer, ready to wince. Henry had mentioned missing body parts but hadn't elaborated. She wasn't sure what she might find. But there was nothing unusual. Some frozen pizzas and hamburger patties. What did she expect? What in the world was wrong with her?

She shook her head and glanced into the laundry room off the side of the kitchen. This looked more familiar, piles of dirty clothes on the floor in no order of separation, such as whites from darks or delicates from heavy duty. She turned back to the kitchen when she noticed a white T-shirt crumpled and tossed into the corner on top a black trash bag.

This was silly, she told herself. She needed to get to the bookstore. She was getting carried away, lost in her imagination as usual. But she went to the corner and picked up the T-shirt, gasping as she unfolded it. It was caked and crusted and reddish-brown. And Lillian was convinced that it was blood. Her hands were shaking as her mind tried to reason it away.

Wally got nosebleeds as a child all the time. He probably still got them. He was always complaining about some ache or pain. The man was not healthy. Of course, he probably still got nosebleeds.

"Lillian?"

She jumped at the sound of his voice at the door, dropping the T-shirt and turning to find him scowling at her.

"What the hell are you doing here?"

"I was looking for you," she lied, immediately recognizing what an awful liar she was. For someone who lived inside her imagination, she should be better at coming up with stories.

"You never come out here."

"I guess I was feeling nostalgic. Maybe a little lonely for the old place." The lies only got worse. Even she wouldn't believe them. "Can I be honest with you, Wally?"

"That would be a good idea."

"I was looking for…I wanted to see if I could find…that old blue vase Mom had."

"What?"

"Yes, that blue ceramic one. Do you remember it?" Now, this was good. She could see that she had him trying to remember. "It was the one Aunt Hannah gave her."

"I don't know why you want that now." But the suspicion was gone from his voice. "I think it's up in the attic. I'll go see if I can find it."

He was a good guy. A good brother despite everything their mother had put them through. He couldn't possibly have done any of the things Lillian had imagined in her overzealous imagination. It simply wasn't possible. But as she heard him on the stairs, Lillian plucked the bloodied T-shirt up from out of the corner and stuffed it into her handbag.

CHAPTER 35

Washington, D.C.

R. J. Tully paced in front of the brick apartment building, his hands in his pocket jingling change. He made himself stop. Leaned against the handrail and glanced up at the dark clouds. Any minute now they would surely burst open. Why didn't he own an umbrella?

In his younger days it had been a macho thing. Men didn't use umbrellas. Now as the breeze turned chilly and he lifted his jacket collar, he decided staying dry was more important than being macho. He remembered Emma telling him once that there was a fine line between being macho and being a dweeb. When had his fifteen-year-old daughter become so wise?

Tully checked his wristwatch and searched the sidewalks and street. She was late. She was always late. Maybe she'd decided she didn't want to be alone with him. After all, they had done a good job avoiding that since Boston.

Boston...that seemed like ages ago. Then he saw her, walking a half block up the street, black trench coat, black heels, black umbrella and that silky strawberry-blond hair, and suddenly Boston didn't seem so long ago.

He waved when she finally looked his way. One of those wide, open-palmed, counterclockwise waves, like some idiot directing traffic. Something like a total dweeb might do. What was wrong with him? Why did he get all nervous around her? But she waved back. There was even a smile. And he tried to remember why they had decided to forget Boston.

"Sorry I'm late," Dr. Gwen Patterson said. "Have you been waiting long?"

"No, not at all." Suddenly he easily discounted the twenty minutes of pacing.

The building superintendent had given him the security code and key to Apartment 502, but he failed to mention the open freight elevator they needed to take up to the loft. Tully hated these things, metal gates instead of doors and nothing to hide the cables or muffle the groan of the ancient hydraulic system. None of it seemed to faze Dr. Patterson.

"Have you ever been to her apartment before?" he asked, offering chitchat to fill the silence and take his mind off the screech of a pulley in need of a good oiling.

"She had a show about six months ago. I was here then. But that was the only time."

"A show?"

"Yes. Her loft is also her studio."

"Her studio?"

"She is an artist."

"Oh, okay. Sure, that makes sense."

"I'm surprised Maggie didn't tell you that."

Tully thought she sounded almost pissed at O'Dell. He had to be mistaken, and he studied her profile as she watched the number at the top, indicating each floor as they ground past the levels. He decided to leave it alone.

He would have known soon enough about Joan Begley's profession. The loft looked more like a studio than living quarters, with track lighting focused on pedestals of sculptures and walls of framed paintings. In the corner, piles of canvases leaned against easels and more pedestals. Some of the canvases were filled with bright colors, others were whitewashed, waiting their turn. Chrome shelves held clusters of supplies, brushes still in jars of purple-green solution, paint tubes with missing caps, soldering tools and what looked like drill bits, alongside pieces of twisted metal and pipe. Interspersed among this mess were miniature clay figurines, thumbnail models of their larger finished counterparts. The only signs of living were an overstuffed sofa with matching pillows that tumbled onto the hardwood floor and in the distant corner a kitchen separated by a counter with empty take-out containers, discarded bottles of water, dirty tumblers and a stack of paper plates.

"Looks like she may have left in a hurry," Tully said, but was wondering how someone could live in the middle of her work space. He knew he couldn't.

"You might be right. She seemed very upset about her grandmother's death."

"So you spoke to her before she left."

"Just briefly."

Tully ignored the art stuff, a challenge in itself, and began searching for a desk and computer. O'Dell had given him a list of things she needed him to check out.

"Where the heck did she keep a computer?" He glanced back at Dr. Patterson, who stayed at the wall of paintings, looking with a tilted head as if she could see something in the random splashes of paint. Tully could never figure out art, despite his ex-wife Caroline having dragged him to gallery after gallery, pointing out social injustices and brilliant interpretations of individual pain and struggle where Tully could see only blobs of black paint with a mishap of purple splattered through the center.

"Do you have any idea where she may have kept her computer?" he asked again.

"Check the armoire."

"The armoire? Oh, okay." The cherry wood monstrosity took up almost one wall, and when Tully began opening doors and drawers it grew, spreading out into the room with swiveling shelves and sliding hideaways and, yes, a small laptop computer that seemed to be swallowed up inside.

"Do you know if this was her only one?"

Dr. Patterson came over and ran her fingertips over the armoire's surface, almost a caress.

"No, I think she had a couple of them. She liked the mobility of laptops. Said she could go to the park or coffee shop."

"So she may have had one with her in Connecticut?"

"Yes, I'm sure she did. She e-mailed me from Connecticut."

He opened its lid, carefully, touching it on the sides with the palms of his hands, purposely not disturbing fingerprints or adding his own. Then he used a pen to press the on key.

"I should be able to get into her e-mail with a few tricks. It may take a while," he said, as he brought up her AOL program. He hesitated when the screen asked for a password. "I don't suppose you could save me some time. Any idea what she may have used as a password?"

"She wouldn't have used her name or any derivative of it." She stared at the screen and Tully thought he had lost her attention again when she added, "Try Picasso.

I believe it's one 'c' and two 's's. He was her favorite. She used to say she was a whore to Picasso and his work. You may have noticed some of his blue-period influence in her paintings and the cubism influence in her sculptures. Especially her metal sculptures."

Tully nodded, though he wouldn't know cubism from ice cubes, and keyed in P-I-C-A-S-S-O, again using the tip of his pen. "No go."

"Hmm…maybe his first name, then."

Tully waited, then realized she thought he knew this. Geez! He should know this. If ever there was a time to impress her, this would be it. What the hell was it? She wasn't helping. Was it a test? He stole a glance her way only to discover that her eyes had been distracted again, her face with the expression of someone lost in thought and trying to find the answers in the wall of paintings. And so even Tully's flash of brilliance was lost on her when he finally keyed in "Pablo."

"Nope. Pablo doesn't work, either," he announced, perhaps a bit too proud for someone who had just keyed in the wrong password. He waited. He glanced up at her again and waited some more. Finally he stood up, stretching his back, towering over her.

"I know what it is," she said suddenly, without turning her eyes from what looked like an anorexic, pasty self-portrait, a nude with the metal frame cutting her below the emaciated breasts. "Try Dora Maar," she told him, spelling it slowly while he keyed in the letters.

"Bingo." Tully watched AOL come to life, announcing, "You've got mail." "How did you know that?"

"Joan started signing some of her paintings as Dora Maar. It's complicated. She was complicated. That one," Patterson pointed out, "reminded me."

"Why Dora Maar?"

"Dora Maar was Picasso's mistress."

Tully shook his head and muttered, "Artists." He clicked on the New Mail. Nothing had been opened since Saturday, the day Joan Begley supposedly disappeared. He clicked on Old Mail. One e-mail address stood out from the rest because there were so many, appearing every day, sometimes twice a day, but stopping the day she disappeared.

"This could be helpful," he said as he opened one of the e-mails from the Old Mail queue. "She has quite a few from someone with an e-mail address of Sonny-Boy@hotmail.com. Any idea who that might be?"

"That's what Maggie and I are hoping you'll be able to find out."

CHAPTER 36

Joan felt sick to her stomach.

She had been famished, devouring the food he brought her earlier. Perhaps she had made herself sick, eating too fast. She had even been embarrassed. Here he was holding her captive, possibly hoping to slice out her thyroid at any moment, and she couldn't wait to wolf down the cheese sandwich and potato chips. But she had always taken solace in food. Why would a time like this be any different?

Her wrists and ankles burned from a night of trying to pull and twist out of the restraints. Her throat felt raw and her voice had gone hoarse from her yells and screams for help. Where was she that no one could hear her? And if Sonny didn't kill her, would anyone ever find her? No one was probably even looking for her. How pathetic was that? But true. There was no one in her life who would miss her if she disappeared. No one who would notice. All that hard work, losing weight and making herself look good, and for what? When it came right down to it she was still alone.

All along that had been her greatest fear, that she would lose all the weight and still not be happy. Oh, she certainly tried. Over and over again she tried, expecting happiness to arrive with the next man she met. And now she met plenty of men, each time hoping this one would somehow make her feel special, complete. And each time they left her feeling more empty and miserable.

It was something that Dr. P. had warned her about. That she could make a wonderful-looking package who would attract men just like she had always desired, but that someone would still be miserable on the inside.

Damn! She hated when Dr. P. was right, because yes, she was still miserable, but now she no longer had the extra weight to blame. Before, she could fall back on that excuse. If she couldn't attract a man, it was because of her weight. If she had no friends, it was because of her weight. If she wasn't a successful artist it was because no one wanted a contract with a fat artist.

She had transferred her tendency to find comfort from food to trying to find it in men. Maybe she could try explaining that to Sonny the next time he stopped by.

Would that stop him from trying to slice out her hormone deficiency?

Oh, God! What had she done?

Suddenly her stomach felt as if she were being sliced in two. She tried to curl up to stop the pain but the restraints wouldn't let her. This pain was not from eating too fast. Could it be food poisoning? Had the mayonnaise in the sandwich gone bad? Now every muscle in her body tensed as she cringed against the cramp that turned her stomach inside out. What was happening to her? She had never felt like this before.

Finally the pain eased. She began to relax. Maybe it was from the panic. Maybe she just needed to stay calm. But not a minute later, her entire body braced itself for a second wave of cramps. And that's when she knew Sonny had poisoned her.

CHAPTER 37

Maggie let Jacob Marley lead her to his office, down the hallway to the rear of the funeral home. Each time he attempted to place his hand on the small of her back she found a way to make him remove it, either by turning toward him or simply stopping short. She recognized the tactic as a leveling tool, a way for him to gain the upper hand. She couldn't help thinking that it was probably an occupational hazard. Maybe it worked with his clients, not the dead ones, of course, but the ones who would be vulnerable and making the spending decisions.

Now she watched as he offered his office's guest chair while he took a seat on the front corner of his desk where he would tower over her. That was when Maggie decided there was something about Jacob Marley she didn't like. What was worse, there was something about him she didn't trust.

She remained standing, pretending to be interested in the black-and-white photos that took up one wall, photos of a small boy, presumably young Jacob, an only child, with his mother and father.

"What is it that I can help you with, Maggie? You don't mind if I call you Maggie, do you?"

"Actually, when it's official business I prefer Agent O'Dell, thank you."

"Official business." He attempted a laugh, but it ended up sounding like a nervous cough. "That sounds serious."

Before she could bring up Joan Begley, he asked, "Is this about Steve Earlman?"

She had forgotten about the town butcher and only now realized Marley and Marley may have been the funeral home that hadn't managed to bury him. Or at least, not keep him buried. She leaned against the wall, studying Mr. Jacob Marley. She guessed him to be in his early thirties, a plain-looking man with a weak chin and narrow eyes, but in the expensive black suit and sitting high on the corner of his desk, he looked in control and poised. And he was concerned about Steve Earlman.

"I know it hasn't been released," he continued, "but rumor is that Steve's body showed up in one of those barrels. It's true, isn't it? That's what you're here to check on, right?"

He was fidgeting, swinging one foot. Marley didn't look like the type of man who allowed himself to perspire, and yet if she wasn't mistaken, there were beads of sweat forming on his upper lip. Now Maggie was curious. What exactly was Jacob Marley worried about?

"I really can't go into any details," she told him. "But if that were true, what explanation could there be for something like that happening?"

Maggie still believed the killer had access to the body before it made it out to the graveyard. Perhaps he had sneaked into the funeral home after hours. Had there been a break-in that Marley failed to report? Was that what had him worried?

"We buried him in a vault," he said, then quickly added, "the family requested a vault. You can see for yourself." He picked up a folder from his desk, handing it to her.

It was Steve Earlman's file with copies of his funeral arrangements and an itemized invoice. Marley had pulled it. He had been waiting for this visit. He was worried about something and it wasn't poor Steve Earlman's corpse.

She flipped through the file, not sure what she should be looking for. The charges looked standard. No extravagances stood out. And yes, there was a charge of $850 for a vault, not just a vault but something called a "Monticello vault."

"Our vaults are sealed tight," he continued. "They're guaranteed against cracking or seepage."

"Really? Has anyone ever complained?"

"Excuse me?"

"Has anyone ever asked for their money back?"

He stared at her then finally laughed, this time a loud, hearty, rehearsed one. "Oh, goodness, no. But that's a good one, Maggie."

"Agent O'Dell."

"Excuse me?"

"I really would prefer if you called me Agent O'Dell, Mr. Marley."

"Oh, sure, of course."

Maggie searched the rest of the documents in Steve Earlman's file.

"Actually, I was curious about another client of yours. I understand you worked with Joan Begley to make arrangements for her grandmother's funeral. Is that right?"

"Joan Begley?"

This seemed to throw him off completely.

"Yes, of course, I worked with Joan last week. We finished the last of the paperwork on Saturday. Was there a problem?"

Jacob Marley seemed more surprised than concerned this time.

She wanted to ask about their dinner out at Fellini's. She wanted to ask him if he knew she was missing. But the look on Marley's face answered her questions. Whatever hope she had that Jacob Marley may have had something to do with Joan Begley's disappearance, Maggie knew that hope was squelched by the look of total confusion and surprise. Jacob Marley was hiding something, but it didn't have anything to do with Joan. Instead, it was probably right in front of her inside this file.

Marley's phone began ringing. He grabbed the receiver. "Yes?"

What should she be looking for? What was Marley nervous they would find?

"I'm with someone right now," Marley said into the phone, unable to hide his irritation. "No, I won't be able to pick up the body for at least another hour. Is Simon working today? Good. Send him when he gets in."

He hung up the phone and turned back to Maggie. "Worst part of this job is that we always have to be on call and keep some strange hours."

"Yes, I suppose it would be very unpredictable," Maggie said, flipping through the pages. Then she noticed something that caught her attention. If she remembered correctly, Calvin Vargus was one of the men who had discovered the first body at the rock quarry. "You contract out with Calvin Vargus and Walter Hobbs to dig the graves?"

"Yes, that's right." He shifted his weight and the other leg began swinging this time. "They have the equipment to do it."

"How long have they been doing it?"

"Oh, gosh—" Marley folded his arms over his chest "—I think as far back as when Wally's father ran the business and he contracted with my father. So it goes back a ways. My father was a very loyal man, working with the same people for years." He pointed to one of the photos on the wall, a portrait of the older Marley, looking somber as if ready for a funeral. "People felt the same way about him, too, God rest his soul. Even now when I try to do something different, make a few changes here and there, I can't seem to do it without someone telling me, 'That's not the way Jacob Marley would do it.'"

Suddenly it struck Maggie. Maybe she was wrong after all. "Your father's name was Jacob, too?"

"Yes, that's right."

"So you're a junior?"

"Yes, but please, I really hate being called Junior. Anything but Junior."

CHAPTER 38

Tully let her wait on him. She had insisted. It was the first time he had been inside her brownstone. The first time he had been invited. By default, of course, he reminded himself, but still, an invitation was an invitation.

She had decided they would be more comfortable here than at Joan Begley's loft. There, she had been distracted. Tully had noticed her walking, stepping lightly, quietly, reverently. He knew Joan Begley was a client of Dr. Patterson's, but he didn't have to be a profiler to guess she had also been somewhat of a friend. Or if not a friend, then someone Dr. Patterson genuinely cared about. There was a connection. Even he could see that, feel that.

He studied her face while she poured the coffee into mugs, preoccupied with the task, and so it was safe to study her. He sat at the counter that separated her living room from her kitchen—a spic-and-span kitchen with hanging utensils and pots and pans in more sizes and shapes than Tully could think of uses for. Here, among her own things, she looked less vulnerable than she had at Joan Begley's. But even here, she still looked…it was hard to explain. She looked tired. No, that wasn't right. She looked…sad.

"Cream or sugar?" she asked with only a glance over her shoulder.

"No, thanks. I take it black." He knew before she reached for the cream that she would pour a healthy dollop of it into hers, making it look like milky chocolate. Cream, but no sugar. And if available she preferred a café mocha.

The realization startled him. These days he couldn't remember what color socks he had put on in the morning—hopefully they at least matched. And yet, here he was remembering how Dr. Gwen Patterson took her coffee.

"So you think Maggie's right? That this Sonny has something to do with Joan's disappearance?"

"He sends her e-mails every day that she's in Connecticut, obviously every day after they met. Sometimes two and three a day. Then all of a sudden they just happen to stop on Saturday, the day she disappeared. Too much of a coincidence, don't you think?"

"But from the e-mails we read, they sounded like friends, confidants. He didn't sound like someone who would want to hurt her."

Her cell phone interrupted them and Dr. Patterson managed to grab it before the second ring, like someone expecting news, any news.

"Hello?" Then her entire face softened. "Hi, Maggie," she greeted her friend. "No, I'm okay. Yes, I did meet Tully at Joan's apartment. Actually, he's here. No, here at my brownstone." She listened for a few minutes then said, "Hold on." She handed him the phone. "She wants to talk to you."

"Hey, O'Dell."

"Tully, can you tell me anything about Sonny?"

"Well, we were able to get into her e-mail."

"Already?"

"Dr. Patterson figured out the password. There're daily e-mails from this guy, but we were just talking about that. They sound pretty chummy, in a friendly way, not a romantic way. Right?" He looked at Gwen for her agreement. "But here's the thing. His e-mails stop the day she disappeared."

"Can you track him?"

"I've got Bernard working on it. So far it looks like he uses a free e-mail account and there's no customer profile on him anywhere that I can find. I'm betting he uses a public computer. Probably the local library or maybe one of those cafés that have computers available."

"Have you talked to Cunningham today?"

"No, he's in meetings all day. Why?"

"He managed to get out of a meeting long enough to call me."

"Uh-oh. You're busted?"

"Not sure. Look, Tully, I just don't want you getting into trouble for helping me out on this."

Tully glanced up at Dr. Patterson. She stood on the other side of the counter, sipping coffee and watching him, thinking he was focused on listening to O'Dell when he couldn't take his eyes off of her.

"Tully, do you hear me?" O'Dell was saying in his ear. "I don't want you getting into trouble over this."

"Don't worry about it, O'Dell."

CHAPTER 39

He fixed her soup, hearty chicken noodle. It was just canned—that's all he had—but it smelled good even after he had dissolved the crystals in it. She'd never notice the tiny white residue. Especially after he crumbled saltine crackers into it.

He placed the small bottle back behind his mother's secret stash, her array of "home remedies" that included molasses and honey and vinegar alongside cough syrup and plenty of children's aspirin. The brown bottle contained the magic crystals she insisted would make him well. It wasn't until after she was gone, her control over him broken only by death, that he discovered the brown bottle with the real label hidden underneath an old expired prescription. The real label simply read in bold, black letters, "Arsenic." He had kept it just as he had found it, realizing that some day he might need that kind of control over someone. And he had been right.

He found her sitting at the window, exactly where he had left her with the restraints now wrapped around the chair. She stared out at the woods through the tempered glass. He had specially ordered and installed the custom-made glass himself. Thick and unbreakable, it allowed a view and let the sunshine in, but on the outside it simply looked like a mirrored solar panel for heat. It provided an excellent work environment— sunny and cheerful, yet private and quiet, protecting his specimens.

She looked up at him. This time her hand didn't move, though he could see the red welts on her wrists where she must have fought the leather restraints again. And then he saw the scratches and grooves in the chair's arm. She had ruined the wood. She had done it on purpose. His mother's chair, a Duncan Phyfe he had re-upholstered himself, and she had ruined it by rubbing the buckles of the leather restraints into the wood.

He felt the anger rising but it came with bile, threatening to back up from his stomach. He could taste it. No, no. He couldn't be sick. He wouldn't. He mustn't think about the chair. No anger. He couldn't afford to make himself sick.

He placed the tray on the table next to her and avoided looking at the scarred chair arm.

"You must be hungry," he said, as he pulled up a stool from his workbench.

"I don't feel so good, Sonny," she mumbled. "Why are you doing this?"

"Why? Why? Because you must be hungry," he said in a singsong voice, a fake happy voice he had learned so well from his mother. "You ate all of your sandwich but that was hours ago."

"Can't we just talk for a while?" she insisted. And he thought her voice sounded whiny. He hadn't noticed before how whiny her voice was.

He scooped up a spoonful of soup and held it in front of her, waiting for her to open her mouth. She only stared at him.

"Open wide," he instructed.

She continued to stare.

He brought the spoon to her lips and began to wedge it in, but she kept her lips pursed tight. Suddenly she jerked her head away to the side, so abruptly that she almost knocked the spoon out of his hand and did end up spilling it on his shirtsleeve.

He tasted the bile again. Oh, God! He couldn't be sick. He felt his face grow hot. But he scooped up another spoonful and held it in front of her again.

"Come on, now, you have to eat."

She turned her head slowly to look at him, this time the glaze clearing a bit, revealing her defiance.

"Not until we talk."

"Look, we can do this the easy way or the hard way," he told her, continuing to keep his happy voice, despite the turmoil brewing in his stomach. "Now, open up."

He brought the spoon to her lips again, but this time she raised her restrained hand just enough to knock his elbow. It spilled all over his trousers. He'd have to change before work.

He rose slowly to his feet, taking his time to roll up the soiled sleeves of his shirt. A difficult task when his hands were shaking and his fingers were balling up into fists. He could feel the transformation, a lead-hot iron stabbing into his guts. And he could see the transformation in the way she looked at him. Whatever drugged courage had possessed her was gone now. She struggled against the restraints, kicking at the chair legs and smacking the ankle shackles against the wood, leaving more grooves in the precious wood.

"I guess you've chosen to do this the hard way," he said through gritted teeth. This time he left the spoon on the tray, and he picked up the bowl of soup.

CHAPTER 40

West Haven, Connecticut

Maggie wasn't sure what she was doing here. There were other places she needed to check out, coincidences she needed to follow up on. Like Jacob Marley Jr. and whether or not anyone called him Sonny. Or if Wally Hobbs's contract to dig graves for the funeral home had anything to do with Steve Earlman not staying buried. Not to mention the address she had found imprinted on Joan Begley's hotel notepad, and whether or not it was the meeting place for a rendezvous that may have been her last. There were plenty of places where she needed to look for answers and she wasn't sure this was one of them. Yet, here she was at the University of New Haven.

The aroma filled the classroom laboratory. Maggie thought it smelled like beef broth. And annoyingly good. Professor Adam Bonzado stood over the industrial-size stove, lifting the lids of several steaming pots, stirring one with a wooden spoon before replacing the lids and turning down the gas flame. Today he wore a purple-and-yellow Hawaiian shirt with blue jeans and high-top sneakers. His plastic goggles were down around his neck, sharing swing space with a paper surgical mask. He glanced at her over his shoulder. Then did a double take, surprised to see her.

"You're early," he said.

"I didn't have as much trouble finding the campus as I thought I might. Would you rather I go wander and come back?"

"No, no, not at all. I've got lots to show you." He checked the pots one more time and turned to give her his attention. "Welcome to our humble lab." He waved a hand over the area. "Come take a look."

Maggie let her eyes take in the shelves of specimen jars and vials, odd assortments and sizes, some makeshift baby-food jars alongside bell jars and pickle jars with scientific labels covering the name brands. From a corner came the soft whirr of a dehumidifier. The room felt cool, and beneath the aroma of soup broth there was a trace of cleaning supplies, perhaps a hint of ammonia. The countertops were filled with microscopes and a scattered, strange collection of tools, from an impressive jawlike clamp without teeth to small forceps and an array of every sized brush imaginable.

In another corner were two huge plastic bubbles. Maggie guessed they were odor hoods. She could hear the quiet wheezing of ventilation fans from inside the contraptions that reminded her of old-fashioned beauty parlor dryers. The contents below, however, quickly dispelled that image. In the double sink underneath the two hoods Maggie could see skeletal remains, soaking in what appeared to be a sudsy solution. A hand stuck up out of the foam as if waving to her, most of the flesh gone.

And then there were the tables, six-foot-long tables, three of them between the aisles, a fleshless village of skulls and bones. Several skulls stared back at her. Others, too wounded to sit up, lay with hollow sockets staring at the wall or gazing at the ceiling. The bones were a variety of sizes and shapes and pieces, as well as colors. Some were sooty black, others creamy white, some dirty gray and still others a buttery yellow—butterscotch came to Maggie's mind. Some were laid out carefully as if reconstructing a puzzle. Others were tangled in cardboard boxes at the edge of the tables, waiting to be sorted, waiting to tell their story.

"Let me finish this, okay? Then I want to show you a few interesting things I've discovered."

Bonzado put on a pair of latex gloves, then put another pair over the first. He pulled the plastic goggles and mask in place, then grabbed what looked like an oven mitt and lifted the lid off one of the pots. He waited for the steam to clear, then took an oversize wooden spoon and began fishing out what looked like chunks of boiled meat and fat and carefully placed them into an open, waiting plastic bag.

"We save as much of the tissue as we can," he explained, raising his voice to get through the mask in what sounded like a practiced tone, perhaps his teaching voice. "These bags are great. They're like 4.5 mil thick so we can heat-seal them, make them airtight and throw them in the freezer. Plus, they can go directly from the freezer to a boiling pot or the microwave."

Maggie couldn't help thinking he sounded like a chef on one of those cable cooking shows.

"The periosteum is what takes the longest to remove," he said, holding up a long thin piece of what looked like gristle. "I'm sorry—" he looked at her over his goggles "—I hope I'm not being condescending. You probably know all this stuff."

"No, no. Go on. I'm quite sure there's a thing or two I don't know." The truth was, despite all the time she'd spent hanging around the FBI's crime lab to pester Keith Ganza, she had never been to an anthropological lab, least of all, a teaching one. The surroundings fascinated her. And Bonzado's enthusiasm and style were far from condescending. He simply seemed excited to share. His excitement could be contagious.

"We try to get all the way down to the bone," he continued while he filled one plastic bag and then another. "Usually using some dishwashing detergent. My personal preference is Arm & Hammer's Super Washing Soda," he said, holding up the container and sounding like a commercial, "and a good long, slow boil. That usually does the trick. But this stuff takes forever."

"The periosteum?"

"That's right." He smiled at her, another practiced response for his students, but practiced or not, Adam Bonzado's smiles always seemed genuine, even to a trained FBI profiler. "All our bones are covered with it. It's this tough fibrous material. I tell my students that a really gross comparison is when you eat barbecue ribs and there's that tough part that sticks to the ribs. You know the stuff I'm talking about?"

She simply nodded.

"That's the pig's periosteum."

This time she rewarded him with a smile and he seemed pleased, all the while she was thinking she probably wouldn't be eating barbecue ribs any time soon. It surprised her that little things like that would make a difference, considering what didn't bother her. But to this day she still couldn't eat anything Keith Ganza offered her from the small refrigerator he kept in his lab. Maggie looked at it as a good sign. A sign that she hadn't grown so jaded she could eat a tuna salad sandwich after it had shared a shelf with human body tissue.

"I'll let these others boil," he told her while he heat-sealed the two newly filled plastic bags and crossed the room to place them in the freezer. He stopped at the sink to pull off the gloves and wash his hands. He reached for a small bottle of what Maggie could see was vanilla extract, dabbing some onto his hands and rubbing it in. Then he started removing his goggles and mask, but hurried back to the stove when one of the pots started boiling over.

He lifted the lid and grabbed a clean wooden spoon to stir. He turned down the flame and then absently scooped out a spoonful and brought it to his lips, blowing on it before he did the unthinkable—he took a sip from the spoon.

"What the hell are you doing!"

He glanced at her, then quickly back at the stove and pot before his face flushed with embarrassment. "Oh, jeez! I'm sorry. I didn't mean to freak you out. It's my lunch." But her look mustn't have convinced him, so he scooped up more as evidence, showing her what she could now identify as carrots, green beans, maybe some potatoes. "It's just vegetable beef soup. Really." He fumbled around the countertop and finally held up the can. "See. It's just soup. Campbell's. Mmm-mm…good."

CHAPTER 41

"I guess I get so used to being around this all day, I forget. Sorry about that," Bonzado apologized for the third time. "Let me make it up to you. How 'bout I take you out to dinner?"

"You don't have to do that. Really. It's not a problem. It just surprised me, is all."

"No, really, I insist. There's a place called Giovani's close to the Ramada."

"Okay, if you insist."

"Now, let me show you some stuff." He finished peeling off the mask and shoved the goggles up atop his head, messing his hair and not caring. Finally he returned to his enthusiastic self. "On to our body-snatcher case."

"Body snatcher?"

"That's what the kids are calling him. Actually, I think that's what they're calling him in the news media, too. You have to admit, it has a ring to it. Don't you FBI types nickname your killers?"

"I think everyone watches too much TV." But it was true. They often did give killers nicknames. She remembered some of her most recent ones: the collector and the soul catcher. But it wasn't a matter of policy or even morbid name-calling. Perhaps it came out of a need to define, maybe a need to understand and control the killer. Body snatcher seemed appropriate. Appropriate but too easy.

Bonzado waved her over to a table where freshly cleaned bones lay on a white drop cloth.

"This is the young man from barrel number three." The numbering was one of those things that unfortunately had come from necessity. She had watched Watermeier request the number be painted onto the barrel and its lid. And now she saw that all the paper tags with strings attached to each of the skeletal remains were also given the number three.

"Young man? How can you tell?" This was one of the barrels that she hadn't seen inside. The one Stolz had said was a bunch of bones. She wondered if there could have been enough tissue to indicate sex, let alone age.

Bonzado picked up what Maggie recognized as a thigh bone, or the femur. She did, after all, have a medical background, not that bones had been a favorite subject.

"At birth there are several places where there is an epiphysis, or a separate element, separate pieces of bone that throughout childhood and into young adulthood end up getting larger and slowly ossify…or rather, it eventually joins or unites. The end of the femur is one of those places. Right here—" he pointed "—at the knee. Can you see the slight separation? It's just a groove now, sorta looks like a scar on the bone where the growth has occurred. In adulthood it disappears."

He bent over the bone so that his forehead almost touched hers, his elbow brushing her side. For a brief moment his closeness distracted her. She seemed suddenly and acutely aware of his scent, a fresh deodorant soap perhaps with a subtle hint of aftershave lotion, despite being surrounded by the ghastly odors of the lab.

"Do you see it?" he asked again.

She quickly nodded and shifted her weight to put some distance between them.

"Now, because the groove hasn't totally disappeared, I'd say he was a young adult, between eighteen and twenty-two, maybe twenty-three or twenty-four at the oldest. Sometimes with adolescents and young adults it's difficult to determine sex, but this was definitely a young man. You'll notice his bones are thick, the joints are knobby, the skull has a square jaw and a low, heavy brow."

"Which means this killer has chosen a forty-some-thing-year-old woman, an elderly man who had already been dead and embalmed, and a young man. What about the fourth barrel? The one with the waffle pattern imprinted on the back? Do we know anything more about that victim?"

"Not much. Stolz faxed me the head wound, only because I asked. It's a woman. He's having a tough time determining age."

"Most serial killers choose a particular type of victim. Ted Bundy even went as far as choosing young women with long, dark hair, parted in the middle. This guy is all over the place. There doesn't seem to be a pattern to the victims he chooses."

"Oh, I think there is a pattern. But not the kind we're used to seeing. That's why I think you'll find this interesting." Bonzado put down the femur and reached for its pair or a part of what was once its pair. This one looked like it had been sawed above the kneecap. "Take a look at the end of his right femur." He handed it to Maggie and she examined the bulbous growth of bone or cartilage that stuck out at the end. Part of it had been sawed away as well.

"What is it?"

"It's probably been there from birth. I'm guessing it was some form of bone spur. Maybe it's a progressive disorder that they may have been waiting to remove or correct after he finished growing. This part on the femur would have been a small part of the problem so it's difficult to tell. He probably would have had a limp. I'm not sure how pronounced a limp. Depending on what shape the tibia and fibula is in I could probably tell you more."

"But let me guess," Maggie said. "You can't tell me because that part of his leg is missing, right?"

"I'm afraid so. That's your pattern. The first woman's body was missing her breast implants, right? And the old guy had a brain tumor and the killer took the brain. This kid's bum leg must have been what the killer wanted. The barrel was sealed when we found it. As far as I can tell, everything else is here." He indicated the tabletop with the man's skeletal remains stretched out and in place.

"Even the woman with the waffle pattern on her back from livor mortis," he continued. "Stolz hasn't been able to figure it out yet because the maggots made a mess of her, but I bet he finds something, some imperfection or deformity missing. That's got to be our connection. He wants to remove the deformity. Maybe he's a perfectionist? Maybe he feels like he's cleansing the earth of imperfections."

He stopped and waited. She could feel him watching her, gauging her response. "So there's your victimology. That's what they all had in common. It can't be coincidence, right?"

"No, you're right," she said. "I don't believe in coincidence. But there's something else they all had in common."

"What's that?"

"They all knew the killer."

CHAPTER 42

R. J. Tully cleared away the dirty dishes, putting them in the sink, and wiped up the crumbs. He pulled out the laptop computer and set it on the kitchen table, connecting the power cord to the outlet and the cables for Internet access. The lid showed a trace of dusting powder, otherwise the lab guys had been tidy, quick and efficient.

Bernard was still trying to track down the e-mail address, though it looked like Tully had been right. SonnyBoy used only public computers. They had tracked him back to the Meriden Public Library and the University of New Haven. At this rate they might never be able to identify him or narrow down a user profile. It looked like he used this address strictly for chat. There were no accounts, no member profiles, no credit cards or online purchases. Nothing except dead ends.

Tully accessed Joan Begley's AOL account, using the password and going through her file cabinet. He read the e-mails that hadn't been opened yet, but saved each, clicking on "Keep as new" just in case someone else was checking them, too.

Harvey jumped up from under the table, startling Tully. He had forgotten the dog was there. Within seconds he heard the front door unlock. This dog was good.

"Hi, Dad," Emma said, coming in the front door, her friend, Aleesha, her constant companion, following.

"You're home early," he said, trying not to sound as pleased as he was feeling. These days he barely saw her and that was only in passing.

"We thought we'd study here tonight. Is that okay with you?"

She had already thrown her armful of books on the sofa and squatted down to hug Harvey's thick neck. She laughed at her friend, who had to move or risk getting swatted by the dog's tail.

"You can pet him," she told Aleesha, who seemed to be waiting for permission. "Could we order a pizza later for dinner?"

She let Harvey lick her hand while she looked up at Tully. He thought he saw something in his daughter's eyes—a sparkle, a glint—something that he hadn't seen in a very long time. And that was pure and unadulterated happiness.

"Sure, sweet pea. But only if I get to have some."

"Well, duh, of course you get some. Especially since you're paying for it." She rolled her eyes but was still smiling.

If only he had known that all it took to make his daughter's eyes sparkle was the simple lick and wag of a dog. Who'd ever have guessed? Teenaged girls—he'd never be able to figure them out.

Sometimes it didn't surprise him so much that Emma was almost sixteen as much as it surprised him that he was supposed to be the father of a sixteen-year-old. What did he know about teenaged girls? He had no experience in this category. The father of a little girl, now, that he could handle. He was good at protecting, providing and admiring, but those all seemed qualities his teenaged daughter considered lame.

"Come on, Harvey." Emma called the dog from the hallway. "Watch him, Aleesha," he heard Emma tell her friend as they went back to her bedroom. "This is so cool. He lies at the foot of my bed like he's watching out for me. And those big, sad brown eyes. Aren't they the best?"

Tully smiled. Evidently protecting and admiring were annoying characteristics in a father, but prime qualities for a dog. Was he being replaced in his daughter's life? Better by a dog than by a boy.

He went back to Joan Begley's e-mail. O'Dell had said that the rock quarry killer may be paranoid and delusional. She suggested that he hid the bodies because he didn't want anyone to see his handiwork, unlike some serial killers who put the bodies on display to show their control, their power. So this killer, according to O'Dell, got what he wanted from something other than torturing and killing his victims. There may be no gratification in the actual kills for him. If she was correct, the killing was only a means to the end result, what O'Dell called his trophies. But if this was the same man who had taken Joan Begley, what did he want from her?

Tully scanned the contents of one of SonnyBoy's e-mails to Joan Begley. He sounded genuinely interested and concerned about her. Yes, it might be necessary to lure the victim, get her to trust. But this seemed more than that.

The e-mail read, "You need to let yourself mourn. Let yourself be sad. It's okay, you know. You don't have to be embarrassed. No one will think of you as being weak."

Did SonnyBoy connect with his victims in some way, actually feel for them? Or perhaps feel sorry for them because of their imperfections? Was it part of his game? Or was Joan Begley different?

Tully wondered if O'Dell was right. If on some level, the killer hid the bodies because he was embarrassed by what he was doing. Could that be? A killer embarrassed by his need to possess these deformities that others had? Perhaps even embarrassed that he must kill? Was that possible? It would make sense that he started out with people who were already dead. According to O'Dell, there was an old guy with a brain tumor who had been embalmed and buried. Maybe SonnyBoy started with the dead and worked up his courage. Or maybe his need to possess what they had finally overrode any qualms he may have had about murder.

Tully sat back and stared at the computer screen, the last e-mail that SonnyBoy had sent Joan Begley still open on the screen. Just how paranoid and delusional was good ole SonnyBoy? Tully was tempted to find out.

He probably should check out his theory with O'Dell. Probably shouldn't do anything silly or reckless. And yet, what did he really have to lose? Maybe O'Dell was rubbing off on him. Maybe she was a bad influence on him, tempting him to stray from his by-the-book approach.

He scooted the chair closer to the table. His fingers hovered over the keyboard. What the hell. He hit the reply icon, which brought up Joan Begley's response screen. Before he could change his mind he typed in the message and hit the send icon. What if SonnyBoy did have Joan Begley, bound and gagged? Or what if he had already killed her? Then wouldn't he be surprised to receive an e-mail from her, even if it was just one word:

"Why?"

CHAPTER 43

Maggie left Bonzado's lab. It had been another warm day, but crispness filled the air as the sun began setting. She walked across campus, trying to enjoy the sights and smells of fall despite her mind flipping over the puzzle pieces Bonzado had added. She pulled out her cell phone as she checked the directions she had scrawled in her notebook. The building had to be close by. As she dialed, she looked around, wondering if perhaps it was on the other side of campus.

"Dr. Gwen Patterson."

"Gwen, it's Maggie. A quick question. Does Joan

have anything wrong with her, like a physical handicap of any kind?"

"A handicap? No, not at all. Why?"

"I'm still trying to figure out if there's a connection between her disappearance and this rock quarry killer."

"But you said none of the victims matched Joan's description."

"Okay, now is not the time to worry," she said, hearing the panic in her friend's voice. "I'm just wondering if it's possible he may have taken her. You have to be upfront with me, Gwen. This is no time for secrets."

"Secrets? You think I've been keeping secrets about her?"

"Maybe not secrets, but something she may have told you in confidence."

"I've told you everything that could possibly help find her."

"Are you sure?"

"What's this about, Maggie?"

"The rock quarry killer has been taking…pieces from his victims. Imperfections. Deformities."

"Like what?"

"One woman's breast implants were missing. There's what looks to be a crippled leg bone missing from another. And a man's brain with an inoperable tumor was also taken. But if Joan didn't have any physical deformities or any disease, I don't think we need to worry that she was taken by this killer."

She pulled the envelope from her notebook, fumbled with the index card and double-checked the address. How could she not find this place? Gwen still hadn't responded.

"Gwen?"

"There may be something, Maggie. Joan's lost a lot of weight in the last two years, but when she talks about it she sometimes tells people her weight problems were due to a hormone deficiency."

"What do you mean, a hormone deficiency? You mean a problem with her thyroid?"

"Yes."

"Okay, it may be time to worry. I'll call Sheriff Watermeier as soon as I get back to Meriden."

"Where are you now?"

"I'm sort of taking care of some personal business."

"You're finally going to see him?"

"No, I'm not in Boston, Gwen. I'm not seeing Nick Morrelli. I'm not sure I'll be seeing him ever again."

"Actually, I didn't mean Boston. I meant West Haven."

Maggie almost tripped over the curb. She had never told Gwen about her brother. "How did you know?"

"Your mother asked for my advice before she gave you his name and address last December."

"You've known all along? Why didn't you say anything?"

"I was waiting for you to tell me. Why didn't you tell me, Maggie?"

"I suppose I was waiting, too."

"Waiting for what?"

"Courage."

"Courage? I don't think I understand. You're one of the most courageous people I know, Margaret O'Dell."

"We'll see how courageous I am. I'll talk to you later, okay?"

She dropped the phone into her pocket and was ready to give up—so much for courage when she couldn't even find the place. Then she saw the sign pointing to Durham Hall. She stared at the building, hesitating. What the hell. She was here. It was silly to not go in.

She stopped at the front desk where a brunette with a nose piercing and pink eye shadow held an open textbook in her lap, a phone in one hand and a bottled water in the other.

"I know it'll be on the exam. He only mentioned it about a thousand times." She looked up at Maggie and without putting down the phone, asked, "Can I help you?"

"I'm looking for Patrick Murphy."

The girl glanced at a sign-out sheet on the corner of the desk. "He's out until late this evening, but umm… You know, I think he's working. You might be able to catch him there." She pointed across the street.

At first Maggie wasn't certain where she meant. Then she saw it, Champs Grill. A job to work his way through college, of course. It was one of the details she didn't have in any of her files.

Champs Grill smelled of greasy fries, was dark and noisy and smoky with tall-backed booths, all packed with students. Maggie found a stool at the bar and began her search, looking out into the dining area and watching the waiters, wondering if she would be able to recognize him. And if she did, what would she say? How did you tell someone you'd never met before that you were his big sister? Maybe she should have sent a Hallmark card first. Didn't Hallmark have a card for every occasion?

She saw a tall, dark-haired waiter at the corner table, laughing with the group as he took their order. Did his profile look familiar? He seemed to be the one making them all laugh and Maggie smiled, remembering how her father had been able to make her laugh so hard it hurt. She hadn't laughed as hard since. So many of her memories of her father were overshadowed by his death. Instead of remembering his jokes and his hugs, she woke up in the middle of the night able to smell the scorched scent of his flesh, despite all the efforts the funeral home had made. Instead of remembering that medallion he had given her to wear for protection, one that matched his, all she could think about was that his hadn't protected him when he ran into the inferno, only to be carried out a hero.

She fingered her own medallion now, though she kept it under her blouse. There were memories she needed to allow, reminders that didn't need to be painful. She watched the waiter in the corner and she wondered if Patrick even knew who his father was. Had his mother shared that with him? Or had that been part of the bargain Maggie's mother had made with his mother after their father's death?

"Can I get you something to drink, ma'am?" she heard the bartender ask.

"A Diet Pepsi, please," she said, when what she really wanted was a Scotch. She turned just enough to glance at him.

"Would you like that with a twist of lemon?"

"No, I really don't—" She stopped in midsentence, staring at the bartender as if she were seeing a ghost. She *was* seeing a ghost. It was as if she were looking at her father, the exact same brown eyes, the same dimpled chin.

"No lemon?" he asked, smiling at her with her father's smile.

"No, thanks."

She tried not to stare while he tossed ice into a glass and poured her soda, setting it in front of her.

"It's a buck fifty, but no hurry. There's free refills on soda."

She seemed to have been rendered speechless and could only smile and nod. He left her to serve others and she watched, feeling like a voyeur, studying his every move, mesmerized by his hands, the long fingers. He wore his hair the same, a pronounced cowlick giving him few choices.

After three refills and a detailed rundown of the weather she finally left, needing to get back to Meriden to meet Bonzado for dinner. She hadn't had the guts to introduce herself. Hadn't been able to come close, and yet as she got into her rental car she couldn't help feeling like she had found something, something she had lost a long time ago and didn't realize was missing until now. And she knew she would be back.

CHAPTER 44

Luc stared at the pot on the stove. He couldn't have left it there. He had stopped cooking after he set fire to a skillet of sausages and hash browns, left on and forgotten until he smelled the smoke. From then on, he ate cold stuff, cereal and milk, sandwiches.

The pot's lid was still hot. He couldn't remember bringing out the huge roasting pot. He glanced around the kitchen. Nothing else seemed out of place. He checked the back door—closed. Kitchen windows were closed. Was it possible someone had been in here? Maybe he hadn't imagined someone following him. There had been someone hiding in between the trees.

Someone watching. And the footsteps. He had heard footsteps. And the reflection in the old butcher shop window of a man across the street, watching one minute and gone the next. Had that not been his imagination playing tricks on him?

He stared at the pot again. He would never have used such a huge pot. He could fit a small pig in the thing. It overlapped onto two burners. He didn't even remember owning a pot that big. Why would he need one that large?

Someone had to have left it. Why would they leave it on the stove? Why would they do that? Unless someone wanted to confuse him. Freak him out. Unless.... someone wanted to scare him.

Suddenly, Luc broke out in a cold sweat. His shirt stuck to his back. His heart began to pound against his rib cage. He glanced around the room again. Panic grabbed hold of him. His head jerked back and forth as he searched. His pace quickened. He moved into the living room, stumbling and rushing and searching.

And then the panic broke loose and he began to yell, "Scrapple. Scrapple, come here, buddy. Come, Scrapple. Where are you?"

Hot tears streaked down his face and he wiped at them with his shirtsleeve. He felt like he'd throw up. He could barely stand as he climbed the stairs, his knees going out halfway up. He fell and slid down several steps, smashing into the wall with a shoulder. He tried yelling again but his throat seemed clogged. A whine was all that came out, startling and panicking him even more because he didn't recognize the sound that came from within him. It sounded like a wounded animal.

He lay on the steps, unable to stand on knees that refused to hold him up. His cheek lay against the cold wooden step. His body shook. He couldn't control the convulsions. Was this part of the disease? He wrapped his arms around himself, hugging himself as best he could in the stairwell. He brought his knees up to his chest and buried his face, trying desperately to stop the nausea and chill. He could still hear the screech, the whine, that awful cry coming out of his mouth.

Then suddenly he felt a nudge. A cold nudge. Slowly he lifted his head. Slowly he forced his cheek off the step. Immediately, he was met by a wet tongue in his face.

"Scrapple. Scrapple, goddamn it, why don't you come when I call you?" He grabbed the dog around the neck and pulled him against him and held him so tight the dog began to wiggle and whine. But Luc only held on tighter.

CHAPTER 45

Maggie watched Sheriff Watermeier stomp around Luc Racine's small kitchen, examining the calendar on the wall, the ratty towel hanging from the drawer handle, the dirty dishes in the sink. Watermeier seemed to be interested in anything and everything other than the human skull submerged in its own broth. The large pot on the stove still felt warm to the touch.

Adam Bonzado suggested Luc come with him outside for some fresh air, but not before Bonzado poured a glass of water and gulped it down. Then he poured another glassful, this time, Maggie knew, for Racine, and followed the old man out the back door.

"He's really shaken up by this," Maggie said.

"Of course he's shaken up," Watermeier answered with almost a snort. "I'd be shaken up, too, if I had a chunk of someone simmering on my stove and couldn't remember putting it there."

"You think he did this and just can't remember?"

"His damn dog has been digging up pieces for months now. Who knows what Racine has kept for souvenirs and what might be under the fucking front porch." He noticed Maggie's skepticism. "What other explanation is there?"

"Wasn't Racine one of the men who found the first body?"

"Sure was. And he didn't waste any time getting on TV to talk about it. This is probably another attention-getter for the sorry son of a bitch."

"He claims someone's been following him."

"Yeah, and next week he'll probably claim to be Abe Lincoln."

"Has he done this sort of thing before?" Maggie was growing impatient with Watermeier's sarcasm.

"What? Boiled up fucking skulls?"

"No. Has he done anything eccentric to get attention in the past?"

"Not that I know of. But you know the old man has Alzheimer's, right?"

"Yes, I'm well aware of that," she said calmly, but it was becoming more and more of an effort. "From what I know about Alzheimer's, it doesn't usually manifest paranoia."

"What exactly are you saying, O'Dell? You think someone's following him around, sneaking into his house and leaving him little presents like this to freak him out?" Watermeier crossed his arms over his chest and leaned against the counter as if challenging her. He made the small kitchen seem smaller. Even his size-twelve work boots took up too much room.

"What if the killer saw Mr. Racine on TV? What if he believes he's to blame for discovering his little hiding place?" She paused for Watermeier's response, but he was waiting for more, still unconvinced. "We talked about this killer being paranoid and delusional. Remember?"

"Yeah, I remember. You also said he might come after anyone he thought was out to get him, to destroy him. But why choose Racine to screw with? Why not Vargus? He's the one who really discovered the barrels."

"From what we can tell, this killer bashes in his victims' skulls from behind and then hides their bodies. We're not talking about a killer with a lot of arrogant false courage. If you were him, would you go after the strong, young burly construction worker or the old man with early-onset Alzheimer's disease?"

"You also said that he could panic. That he might kill again."

"Yes. And I think he may have taken the woman I'm looking for, Joan Begley. She may have driven to Hubbard Park to meet him Saturday night."

"Hubbard Park?"

"I found a note in her hotel room with Hubbard Park, West Peak and 11:30 written on it. The time fits with when she was last heard from. Could you check the park?"

"For her car?"

"Yes. Or her body."

Maggie could see Watermeier's eyes narrowing. He shifted his weight and leaned against the counter again, only this time he looked like he was seriously considering what she had said.

"You know I was with the NYPD for more than thirty years?"

The question startled Maggie. Watermeier was looking somewhere over her head, out the window, maybe watching Bonzado and Racine. Maybe. And although he hesitated, she knew he wasn't waiting for an answer.

"I've seen a lot of weird crap in my time, O'Dell." He glanced at her, then the eyes went back out the window. "It was my wife, Rosie's, idea for us to move out here. I didn't like it much at first. Her idea that I run for sheriff, too. I didn't like that at first, either. Too goddamn slow of a pace. Then 9/11 happened. I lost a lot of old buddies. In one day. Gone."

He scratched at his jaw, but this time he didn't look back at Maggie. "I could have been with them that day.

And I would have been gone, too. Just like that. I ended up spending weeks there…there in that mess. Rosie hated it, but she knew it was something I had to do. I kept going back week after week. Had to. Had to help find my buddies. It was the least I could do.

"We kept searching every stinking day, as if we'd rescue them though all we'd find were scraps, bits and pieces. Thirty years on the force and I thought I'd seen it all. But there wasn't anything could prepare me for that mess. Faces melted off. A foot left in a laced-up boot. A severed hand still gripping the melted impression of a cell phone. I've seen a lot of crap, O'Dell. So this," he said, nodding at the roasting pot on the stove, "doesn't shock me. Neither does anything we've found in those barrels.

"But the difference here—" and now he looked at Maggie, making sure he had her attention "—this here I'm being asked to explain. Like there *is* some fucking explanation. I'm expected to figure this out. And then I'm expected to stop this asshole."

Maggie wasn't sure what he wanted her to say. Was she supposed to tell him it'd be okay? That, of course, they'd find the killer? That she already had a more detailed profile drawn up in her mind? That her profiles were always right? She wasn't even sure they could protect Luc Racine.

Adam Bonzado came in the back door, checking over his shoulder. Racine stayed seated on a bench on the stone terrace, his Jack Russell on his lap. The two of them stared out at the pond, the dog's head turning and following the geese as they flew overhead, but Racine continued to stare straight ahead.

Bonzado looked at Maggie and then Watermeier. "Mind if I take that back to the lab?"

"Help yourself. Stolz's not gonna be much help with this one. I need to get one of the techs to bag the roaster. O'Dell here thinks it might have the killer's fingerprints." There was no sarcasm in Watermeier's voice this time.

"What about the old man?" Bonzado asked the sheriff.

"What about him?"

"You have anyone to stay with him tonight?"

"My guys are pulling double duty as it is. I can't be asking—"

"I'll stay with him tonight," Maggie said, surprising herself with the offer almost as much as she surprised the two men.

CHAPTER 46

Agents did it all the time—looked out for one another, covered one another's backs. Oftentimes that extended to one another's families. But Detective Julia Racine was with the District Police Department, not the FBI. And although she and Maggie had worked a couple of cases together, they were far from friends, tolerating each other as colleagues. Detective Racine had climbed the career ladder by breaking rules that stood in her way. She could be reckless at times, ruthless at others. But last year in a park rest room in Cleveland, Ohio, Julia Racine had stopped Maggie's mother from slitting her own wrists. Maggie didn't like owing favors. She owed Julia Racine. It seemed appropriate that she pay her back by protecting her father from a killer. Besides, Maggie sort of liked the old guy. He was nothing like his daughter.

She brought a tray out to him where he continued to sit and stare despite the fact that the landscape he seemed so interested in was disappearing into the night shadows. He had refused to go back into the house until the skull was removed and the smell of boiled human flesh could no longer be detected. Maggie had left the stove's ventilation fan on High and opened all the windows that weren't painted shut. She honestly couldn't smell it anymore, but Luc said he could.

"I made us sandwiches," she told him as she set the tray on the bench between them. Other than milk and juice, the cold cuts, mayonnaise and bread were all there had been in the refrigerator.

"I'm not hungry," he said with barely a glance at the food. Then he went back to what looked like a vigil, sitting straight-backed as if on alert and listening for something out of the ordinary. Instead there were only crickets chirping and nocturnal birds calling out to one another. Scrapple sat on Luc's lap, previously content but now interested in the tray of food, wiggling enough to get his owner's attention. Luc reached over and pulled off the edge of some ham for the dog, instructing him,

"Chew it. Don't just swallow." But the dog gulped and waited for more.

"So I wasn't imagining things. He was in my house," he said without looking at Maggie.

"Yes."

It seemed a relief to him. Had he honestly believed he had imagined it? He even took a bite of the sandwich for himself and then pulled off another piece for Scrapple.

"But why? Why's he picking on me?"

"You and Calvin Vargus intruded on his private hiding place. He might simply be doing the same to you."

"Do you think he wants to hurt me? You know, like those others?"

Maggie looked for signs of fear, but now he seemed more interested in eating.

"He might just want to scare you," she told him, but she wasn't convinced. She wasn't convinced the killer wasn't still hiding in the shadows, watching despite Sheriff Watermeier's men having checked the premises.

"I think I saw him," Luc said matter-of-factly, but it made Maggie sit up.

"Where? When?"

"Yesterday. Maybe the day before. Just his reflection in a store window as I passed. I kept hearing footsteps...you know, following me, slowing when I slowed. Stopping when I stopped."

Maggie tried to contain her excitement, letting him tell at his own pace, but she was impatient. He had already put the half-eaten sandwich back down and was staring into the dark again.

"What did the reflection look like?" she asked.

Luc was quiet and she thought he might be trying to remember, to conjure up the image. After a while, she asked again, "Luc, what did the reflection look like?"

He turned to her, his eyes darting back and forth before meeting hers when he said, "I'm sorry, who did you say you were?"

CHAPTER 47

Tully couldn't be sure what her reaction would be, but he knew Dr. Patterson might be easier on him than O'Dell would be. Or at least that was his excuse for calling her, asking if he could run something by her. He could have told her about it over the phone or shown her by forwarding it to her e-mail, yet when she suggested that he stop by her brownstone again, he didn't hesitate.

She opened the door to greet him with bare feet, but still wearing her skirt and silk blouse, her usual business attire, only without the jacket and with the blouse untucked, as if she had just gotten home.

"Come on in." She left him and headed back to the

kitchen where a pot was on the stove, emitting wonderful aromas of garlic and tomato. "Have you eaten? Because I haven't and I'm starved for the first time in days."

"Smells great," he said, not wanting to admit that he had filled up on pizza with Emma and Aleesha.

"It's nothing fancy. Just some spaghetti and marinara sauce."

Tully checked her expression, wondering if perhaps this was some gesture, some reminder. Last year in Boston he had taken her to a small Italian restaurant, where she had shown him how to twirl his spaghetti correctly onto his fork in what he remembered to be an almost erotic experience. Or at least it had been for him.

While he looked for signs that she might also be remembering that evening, Gwen Patterson gave the sauce a quick stir, then starting slathering butter on a loaf of what looked like fresh bread. She wasn't even paying attention to him. No, he must be wrong about her wanting to remind him of Boston. What an idiot he was. She had said she wanted to forget about it. She meant it. Why was he still thinking about it?

"Can I help?" he asked, taking off his jacket and putting the briefcase with his laptop computer on the kitchen counter.

"There're some romaine hearts in the colander." She pointed to the sink. "Would you mind pulling them apart for our salad?"

"Sure, I can do that," he said, rolling up his shirtsleeves. Pulling apart hearts for a salad? Sure, he could do that, feeling relieved to recognize romaine hearts as lettuce. Why didn't he pay more attention to these kinds of things and what they were called—romaine hearts and Picasso…Pablo Picasso? Maybe it was time that he did. If he could figure out who Britney was, what raves were and that the ingredients of wet included PCP and embalming fluid—which by the way, he had told Emma if he discovered her doing any drugs she would be grounded until she was thirty-five—then certainly he could figure out what made up the world of Gwen Patterson. Although Emma had already informed him that Britney was so like yesterday.

"Nice job, Agent Tully." She came up beside him with bottles of vinegar and oil. "I have the bread in the oven and the sauce on simmer."

She sprinkled the lettuce with the oil and vinegar, gently tossing it, then topping it with some freshly grated parmesan and black pepper. It smelled wonderful, and Tully felt proud for having had a bit part in its creation. How did she make this all look so effortless? Lately it seemed an effort for him to put his takeout on regular plates rather than eat it right out of its plastic containers.

"Let's put this in the fridge," she told him. "And while we wait for the spaghetti, you can show me what you've got."

Tully took out the laptop computer, opened it and turned it on.

"If the killer and this Sonny is one and the same person, then I'm almost certain he's the one who has Joan. He says some weird stuff in a couple of his e-mails to her."

He kept an eye on her, wondering if it was such a good idea to talk about her patient and what this killer may have in mind for her. She looked pale, maybe just tired.

"You sure you want to talk about this?" he asked.

"Of course. It's a case. I offered to help. And it might help us find Joan." She pointed to the wine rack at the end of the counter. "Would you mind opening a bottle?"

He checked for a red wine, pulled one out and showed her the label for approval, but she was handing him the corkscrew and reaching for wineglasses. What kind seemed of little consequence.

"Let's go back a step. Maggie said he's been taking parts from his victims," she said, looking as if she was trying very hard to be her normal professional self, though the color hadn't yet returned to her face. "But why? This doesn't seem like the regular sort of trophies that serial killers take."

"Yes," he said, "this is different."

"Is he on a mission to rid the world of those with deformities or imperfections?"

"I thought of that, but then why not show off his handiwork? Usually killers on a mission want to show off what they've done. This guy hides what he's done.

Not just hides the victims but goes through a lot of trouble to stuff them in barrels and then bury them under tons of rock never to be found."

"Sort of overkill?" she said, then smiled. "Bad pun, sorry."

Maybe the wine was working. The color was returning to her cheeks. He filled her glass again.

"But it's exactly what I'm thinking. Why the overkill? I think he's embarrassed of what he's doing." He waited for her reaction. He wanted to know what Gwen Patterson, the psychologist, thought.

"Hmm…interesting."

"In fact, I don't think he gets much enjoyment or gratification from the killings. Don't get me wrong, I still think he gains something from killing besides just getting the pieces he wants. He might feel some sort of control, but again, I'm not sure it's from the actual killing as much as it is from simply possessing those pieces. Does that make sense?"

"What does Maggie think?"

He picked up his own glass of wine for the first time and took a drink. "I haven't talked to her about this yet."

"Really? Why not?"

"I wanted to run it by you first." He could tell from the look she gave him that she didn't buy that. "Okay, I haven't talked to her about it yet because I did something. And I'm not sure she's going to be very happy with me."

Now Dr. Patterson planted her elbows on the counter, leaning into him as if ready to share in his secret. "And just what did you do, Agent Tully?"

"I sort of pulled a Maggie O'Dell."

She smiled. "Oh, heavens, she's already a bad influence on you." She sipped more wine. "What did you do?"

He pulled the laptop closer and clicked on the AOL icon. "I sent him an e-mail."

"You sent Sonny an e-mail? That doesn't sound so unforgivable. Actually it sounds very much like something Maggie would do."

"I'm not so sure about that. Because I sent him an e-mail from Joan Begley."

He waited for her reaction. She sipped her wine, watching him over the rim of the glass. Finally she said, "You think she's dead, don't you?"

He could almost feel the blood drain from his face, replaced by embarrassment, embarrassed that, yes, he had given up on Joan Begley. Especially if Sonny was the rock quarry killer. And the e-mails that Sonny and Joan exchanged in the days preceding her disappearance had convinced Tully that Sonny had taken her and most likely had killed her.

"Let me show you some of their e-mail correspondence," he said in answer to her question. "And then you can tell me what you think."

He brought up the file on the laptop's screen and she came in behind him to look over his shoulder. Maybe it was the effect of the wine, because suddenly Tully found it difficult to concentrate on the computer screen. As Dr. Patterson read over his shoulder all he could think about was how good she smelled, a subtle soft scent like fresh flowers after a spring rain shower.

"It sounds almost like he's jealous of Joan's struggle with her weight," he said.

"Jealous?"

"He sees it as a reason for her to get sympathy, to draw attention."

"And you think that he's jealous of his victims' imperfections, their deformities?"

"Exactly. Here he tells her that he wishes he had a reason for people to feel sorry for him. In this one—" he scrolled down to find it "—he confides that as a child he had awful, terrible stomachaches and his mother never believed him. He says, 'She gave me medicine but it only made me sicker.' He tells her that's when he gave up on telling people about his own aches and pains because nobody believed him. He reminds me of a hypochondriac."

Tully felt her hair brush against his temple as she batted it out of her face in order to read the computer screen. He tried to focus. What was it he was saying? "So, anyway, I got to thinking, what if he had all these stomachaches, maybe he still gets them but the doctors have never found anything. Maybe the doctors even start telling him all his aches and pains are simply in his head, in his mind. But he sees people around him—a guy who has an inoperable brain tumor, a woman who's survived breast cancer—and he sees them getting sympathy or at least having justification for their aches and pains. He wants justification for his ailments, too. Maybe he wants it so much he decides to take it from others, cuts it out of them. By keeping these things for himself, these deformed pieces that have drawn sympathy for others, by possessing them he gains strength, control."

She came around to the other side of the table and sat down to look at him. He worried she was about to say he was way off base. But instead she said, "So he has no reason to keep Joan alive?"

She didn't wait for his answer. She didn't need it, having come to the same conclusion. She got up and went to the stove, busying herself with the sauce they had allowed to simmer for too long. "I can't help but feel partly responsible," she said, surprising him with what sounded like a confession.

"Responsible? Why in the world would you feel responsible?"

"Sounds silly, doesn't it?" And she laughed, running a hand through her hair, a nervous trait he had noticed long ago. She seemed to do it whenever she was feeling a bit vulnerable, as if she had revealed too much and needed to remind herself to *not* let her hair down so much.

"No, it doesn't sound silly. I'm just not sure why you

would feel responsible. You had no way of knowing Joan Begley would come across this killer when she went to Connecticut."

"But I should have been available that night when she called. If only I had called her back… She needed me and I wasn't available."

"And if you had been available?" He came into the kitchen, leaning against the counter. "It may not have changed things. It was still her choice."

She turned to meet his eyes, and he was surprised to find them moist with emotion. "She was asking for my help, asking me to talk her out of it." She wiped at her eyes and looked away, now trying to hide a flush of embarrassment.

"You're forgetting something, Doc."

"What's that?"

"It was still her choice to be there. A choice she was responsible for, not you. Didn't they teach you that in counseling school?"

She met his eyes again and tried to smile, but it looked like an effort to do so.

"Sometimes," he continued, putting aside every fiber in his brain that was yelling at him to stop while he was ahead, "it's not such a bad thing to give yourself a break. You can't be responsible for every patient." And without listening to his head, he stepped closer until he was wrapping his arms around her and pulling her gently against his chest.

He leaned down and kissed her hair. When she

seemed to respond, moving closer into him, he kissed her neck. She pulled away just enough to offer him her face, and he didn't hesitate. He kissed her like he had been wanting to kiss her ever since Boston.

Again, she pulled away just enough to whisper in his ear, "Stay with me tonight, Tully."

His body had already begun to say "yes" when common sense struck him like a hammer. He held her tight, nuzzling her neck as he told her, "I can't. God, I wish I could, but I can't."

She pushed away from him and he could see not only embarrassment but hurt. "Of course," she said in that professional tone that she retreated to in order to distance herself from the embarrassment. "I'm sorry. I should have never—"

"No, you don't understand."

"Of course I understand." She was at the stove, whipping the marinara sauce. "I didn't mean to step over the line."

"I think I'm the one who stepped over the line first."

"It doesn't matter, I shouldn't have suggested—"

"Gwen, stop. I can't stay because of Emma."

Now she looked back up at him and he watched the realization sweep over her face, the sting of rejection slip away.

"Otherwise…well, otherwise we certainly wouldn't even be standing here discussing it."

"But maybe we should discuss it."

"No, absolutely not," he said, holding up a hand to stop her. "And that's why I better leave right now. Because I don't want to give us a chance to discuss it to death, to talk ourselves out of it before there's anything to talk ourselves out of." He started packing up his case without looking at her.

Finally ready, he grabbed his jacket off the back of a chair, pulled it on and then returned to where he had left her, at the kitchen counter. "I like psychoanalyzing killers with you, but I don't want to psychoanalyze this. Whatever this is right now, can we just go with it for a while, first?" But before she could answer he kissed her again, a long deep kiss that, when he was finished, left her without an answer.

CHAPTER 48

He liked shopping at this time of night. The aisles of Stop & Shop were practically empty. The rage was still brewing inside him, threatening to dislodge the nausea, but there was no one to notice if he had to dart to the rest rooms or abandon his cart and leave the store suddenly. Which reminded him, he needed to stock up on more of the chalky crap.

Ever since leaving the library he'd felt a tingling in his hands and a weakness in his knees. He turned around to see if anyone was watching, if he was being followed. There was someone out to destroy him. But how did they know? How did they get his e-mail address?

At first he thought it might be the old man. But now he was convinced it had to be that nosy reporter. That bitch! He should have known she would be a problem. She was following him. He had seen her several places, snooping around. He had almost bumped into her yesterday, and she looked through him as if he didn't exist. Had she been pretending that she didn't know anything? No, she knew something. Why else was she everywhere he went?

And now was she playing games with him, sending him e-mails and pretending to be Joan. It had to be that reporter. *It had to be. Had to be.* But how did she know? How did she know he had Joan? Had the old man told her something? Had he seen him taking Joan that night in Hubbard Park?

He had to keep calm. He had to breathe. He would take care of his enemies, all in good time. He just needed to stay calm. He tapped his pocket, making sure the folded piece of paper was there. While at the library reading his e-mail he looked up the TV station's address and phone number. Some receptionist told him Jennifer Carpenter wouldn't be in until ten-thirty. That he could call back after the eleven o'clock news if he wished to speak with her. Speak to her? Well, yes, maybe he did wish to speak to her. Maybe he would ask her why she was following him. Why she was harassing him.

He searched the shelves, trying to relax, trying to concentrate on his shopping. He chose several jars of jelly. The twelve ounce would work fine. Then he noticed a large jar with olives. He hadn't seen these before. He picked it up to examine it, thirty-two ounces and a nice wide mouth with a screw-on lid. He put it into his cart next to the cans of soup and loaf of white bread. Mayonnaise. He remembered he was out of mayonnaise. If only it came in a larger jar, and now they were selling it in sixty-four-ounce plastic containers. Plastic just wasn't sufficient.

He tried to get his mind off the e-mail, off the rage it had made him feel. It was *stupid, stupid, stupid* to play games with him, to pretend to be Joan Begley. She was out to destroy him. They were all out to destroy him. That old man. Even that FBI agent. He didn't trust any of them. They were all out to get him. But they couldn't. No, they couldn't destroy him. Not if he took care of them first.

That made him smile. Yes, one by one he would take care of his enemies. They had discovered his dumping ground, but he could find other places. That made him feel back in control.

He started down a new aisle. Someone said the old man had Alzheimer's disease. He hated the way they had said it, like it was something that they were supposed to feel bad about. Like they felt sorry for the poor old guy.

He wondered what it looked like. What would something like Alzheimer's disease look like? Did it make parts of the brain shrivel up? Did it discolor it in any way? He wouldn't mind seeing that, taking a look.

Last time a large pickle jar had worked just fine, and he started to look for a similar one. Yes, Steve Earlman's brain fit perfectly in a large pickle jar and so would Luc Racine's.

CHAPTER 49

Luc heard something. A noise had awakened him. He propped himself up on one elbow, glancing at Scrapple sprawled on his back, feet in the air at the end of the bed. Either he was imagining things again or his dog was totally useless as a watchdog.

He listened, trying to hear over the thumping of his own heart. Maybe it was only the FBI woman downstairs, Julia's friend. He wasn't used to having anyone else in his house. Maybe he just wasn't used to the normal noises that came along with having someone else in his house. She had promised not to call Julia. He hoped she kept her promises. He didn't want Julia worrying about him. He didn't want her running home just because she felt sorry for him. He didn't want her—

Holy crap! Something moved inside his closet. The night-light in the wall socket made it difficult to see. He squinted. The closet door was open about a foot. He never left his closet door open, always made certain it was closed. And now he could see a shadow inside. Yes, someone was inside his closet. Oh, Jesus! The guy had never left. He was standing inside Luc's closet. Standing there, waiting. Probably waiting for Luc to fall fast asleep.

He eased himself back down into the pillows, pretending he was going back to sleep but positioning himself so he could see the closet door. He listened again, only this time it was impossible to hear anything. His heart thundered in his ears and his breathing seemed hard to control. He had to think. What did he have close by that he could use as a weapon? The lamp? It was plugged into the wall and too small. His eyes darted around the room—looking, searching for something, anything—always returning to the shadow. Did it move again?

What the hell was wrong with Scrapple? The dog stayed on his back with not so much as a snort, let alone a growl. How could that dog have not sensed this guy?

Maybe a baseball bat. Yes, he used to have one around. A ball, a bat and a glove. He and Julia still hit it around sometimes. Who was he kidding? That was ages ago. No telling where the damn bat was now.

The FBI agent was downstairs. How could he get her

attention? Could he sneak out of the room? But not without Scrapple. The dog might be worthless, but no way would he leave him here.

Then he saw the top knob of the baseball bat sticking out from under the bed. Yes, he had kept it here. He let his hand dangle over the edge of the bed. Shoot! He couldn't reach it. He glanced back at the closet door. Was it opened a little more? Oh, Christ, was he coming out now? This was no time to hesitate.

Luc jumped out of bed. He slammed his knee into the dresser with a bang that woke up Scrapple. But he grabbed the baseball bat and ran to the closet door, not stopping, not waiting, snatching at the doorknob and pulling it open as he raised the bat. He delivered several strong death blows, smashing the shadow to the floor. It took him a second or two before he realized he had just bludgeoned the only suit he owned, the one he had recently picked up from the dry cleaners and hung in his closet, left in the plastic wrap. He had wanted to be sure the suit was clean and pressed and ready one day for his own funeral. And now it was a crumpled mess on the floor of his closet, after threatening his life.

Luc sat on the edge of his bed, petting the now alert and confused Scrapple, waiting for the shaking in his hands to stop. How ridiculous had he become? What the hell was wrong with him? He wasn't only losing his memory but perhaps his mind, as well.

Then he heard a noise from outside. A muffled thump that sounded like it came from the back of the house. And this time Scrapple heard it, too.

CHAPTER 50

It had been a long time since Maggie had slept any-where and heard the howls of coyotes in the distance. But as she tried to get comfortable on the lumpy old sofa, she thought she heard Luc upstairs. It almost sounded like he was moving furniture around. After his blank episode earlier, Maggie wasn't sure she wanted to go up and find him, indeed, stacking pieces of furniture on top of one another like a sleepwalker unaware of his actions.

No, that was ridiculous and she immediately ad-monished herself. Alzheimer's didn't manifest itself in totally absurd behavior. At least not that she knew of, but then what did she really know about it? She wished she hadn't promised him that she wouldn't call Julia. Racine needed to know if her father's life might be threatened. Maybe the old man simply wouldn't remember her promise. Or perhaps she could get him to call his daughter himself.

She watched the shadows of branches outside the window dancing on the ceiling. Luc had night-lights plugged into the sockets all over the house. In a weak moment, he had mentioned being afraid that one day he might forget how to switch on a lamp and be forced to sit in the dark. What an awful feeling it must be to know that could happen. She couldn't imagine what it must feel like to realize that pieces of your memory, even the basic pieces, had begun to crumble. Or to not have any memories at all. She thought about Patrick again, wondering what, if anything, he knew about their father.

Her own memories, especially of her childhood, of losing her father and growing up with an alcoholic, suicidal mother, those awful memories were burdens she thought she could live without. But earlier today, remembering some of the good ones made her realize that she was cheating herself. What if she were like Luc, not able to sift and select, not having control over what went and what stayed... What an awful feeling that must be. And yet, she had been allowing herself to remember only the awful things when she, in fact, had a choice.

Maggie decided she would go out tomorrow and buy some timers for Luc's lamps. Also some of the longer-lasting light bulbs. Maybe another lamp or two. She couldn't keep him from forgetting how to turn on a light, but she could be damn sure he wouldn't be left in the dark.

She heard him coming down the steps and she sat up. Before he got to the foot of the stairs she could see his elongated shadow carrying something over his shoulder and the little terrier following close behind.

Oh, Jesus! Was he, indeed, sleepwalking? And she tried to remember, were you supposed to wake a sleepwalker or leave him alone?

He rounded the corner and she recognized a bat hoisted on his shoulder in ready-to-swing mode. Instinctively, she bolted for her Smith & Wesson. As she whipped it out of its holster, she saw him putting his finger to his lips and whispering, "Someone's outside."

Maggie decided the old man must be sleepwalking or perhaps imagining things, the result of stress from an outrageous day. That was until she saw the shadow of a man pass by the front window.

She put up a cautionary hand to Luc and waved him away from the windows. The terrier growled but was sticking close by his owner. Maggie made her way to the front door, keeping her revolver nose down and close to her body. She worked the locks open, slowly, quietly. She looked back at Luc, making sure he was out of the line of fire. Then without hesitation, she flung the door open and stuck the Smith & Wesson's nose in the face of the shadow just as it stepped into the porch light.

"Jesus, Bonzado. What the hell are you doing here?"

CHAPTER 51

She startled him so badly he dropped one of the bags, scattering groceries across the wooden porch floor.

"I didn't think you'd both be down for the night. I guess I didn't think it was that late. Did I wake you?"

"You scared the living daylights out of us. What the hell are you doing?"

Maggie watched him pick up cartons and cans. She looked back at Luc and worried that he had blanked out on her again. He stood there, bat in his hands, staring at Bonzado, as if deciding whether he needed to use the bat.

"It's okay, Luc," she told him. "It's just Professor Bonzado. Do you remember him from this afternoon?"

"Why is he back?" Luc wanted to know. "Why is he out wandering around in the dark?"

"Good question," she said, now turning back to the professor.

He looked up at her, still down on his hands and knees retrieving several cans that had rolled underneath the porch swing. "I wasn't out wandering around in the dark. I was just coming up to the door, and before I could knock you jammed a gun in my face."

"What are you doing here, Adam?" she asked again.

"I noticed Mr. Racine didn't have much in his refrigerator. I thought I'd bring out some staples. I really didn't think you'd be asleep already. It's not even ten. And—" he got to his feet and opened one of the other bags, pulling out a small white box "—I wanted to bring you some dessert, since our dinner sort of got canceled."

"You should have called first." It was difficult to stay angry with him when he seemed genuinely determined to please them.

"I tried calling you. Your cell phone must be off. And I didn't know Mr. Racine's phone number."

"I'm sure directory assistance could have given it to you." Maggie wouldn't let him off the hook. She didn't like how quiet Luc continued to be. Finally, he came out on the porch to help Bonzado, taking one of the bags and looking inside.

"I don't cook much anymore."

"I figured as much. So I bought some deli meats and cheeses, some bread, and several different kinds of cereals and milk. Oh, and some Pop-Tarts. They're pretty good cold. You don't even have to put them in a toaster. Really. You'll have to try 'em."

The two men came in past Maggie, and Bonzado glanced at the revolver she hadn't holstered yet, then looked up at her and smiled. "Jeez, you're tough on a guy for just wanting to bring you a little cheesecake."

"Did you say cheesecake?" Now he had Luc's full attention and enthusiasm.

"That's right. None other than chocolate almond from the Stone House." Bonzado followed Luc into the kitchen.

Maggie shook her head. But before she closed the door she stepped out onto the porch. Why hadn't she heard Bonzado's El Camino or, at least, seen his headlights? She saw the vehicle parked up the driveway, away from the house. Odd that he didn't pull in behind her rented Escort.

As she turned to go back inside, she heard another vehicle's engine, beyond the trees, back on Whippoorwill Drive. She could hear it but couldn't see it. She stepped off the porch into the dark, straining to see through the branches, trying to follow the low, soft rumble of an engine.

The reason she couldn't see the vehicle was because

it had waited until it was almost out of sight before it turned on its headlights. And then it was quickly gone, the taillights disappearing around the first curve.

CHAPTER 52

Joan couldn't look at the tray of food he left on the bedside stand. She couldn't eat it. She wouldn't eat it. Whatever he was putting in her food made her insides feel as if they were being slit open. He didn't even need to use the leather restraints anymore. She couldn't leave the bed if she wanted to. Instead she spent what felt like hour after hour curled up in a fetal position trying to ward off the pain.

She no longer thought about talking him into releasing her. She no longer dreamed about escaping the cabin. She only wanted to escape the pain. Maybe he would finally kill her. Yes, why didn't he just kill her and get it over with? Instead, he kept bringing her food. The

smell of the soup alone reminded her of her body's reaction to it. And already her insides burned. The nausea had never left. For hours it continued, like being
seasick on a cruise and not being anywhere near land.
She couldn't think about it, nor could she feel anything
else. So when he sat down next to her and started showing her his collection, she could only stare right through
him and pretend to be interested.

He was the little boy again, excited and anxious, as if
bringing his show-and-tell projects to share with her.
Each one more hideous than the next and threatening to
make her vomit, though there couldn't possibly be anything left inside her stomach. She tried not to think about
the blobs as pieces of human beings. She tried not to think
about the fact that he had taken them from their owners.

He was showing her something in a large jar with a
white lid. She refused to look closely, not allowing her
eyes to focus on what appeared to be a dirty yellow glob
of fatty tissue.

"This one was a surprise," he told her, holding it up
at her eye level. "I knew an alcoholic's liver would look
abnormal but this…" He was smiling and explaining it
as if it were a prize he had won in some competition.
"They say a normal liver has the same texture and color
as calf's liver. You know, like you can buy at the super-
market. Actually, I can't imagine anyone wanting to eat
calf's liver. That's just gross." He turned the jar slowly
around as if giving her a full view. "See, the alcohol
causes that discoloration."

He got up to put the jar on one of the top shelves, and Joan hoped the presentation was over. He came back, stopping at the food tray. Oh, dear God, she couldn't handle him force-feeding her again. She simply couldn't survive another spoonful. But he left the bowl and picked up the brown paper bag that he had brought in with him on the tray. He sat down beside her and took another jar out of the bag. It looked like an ordinary twelve-ounce jelly jar. But it didn't look like jelly. The liquid was clear, like in the other jars. And like the other jars, something was floating inside.

"This is my newest acquisition," he told her, twirling it in front of her. Then he finally held it still and so close to her face that she couldn't avoid recognizing the two floating, bright blue eyeballs. "Amazing, isn't it, that these couldn't see except with really thick glasses."

CHAPTER 53

It was after midnight.

He threw the mop in the corner, only getting angrier when it started an avalanche of gardening tools. He emptied the bucket down the floor drain, holding his breath while he sprayed at the vomit, yellow mucuslike chunks that looked all too familiar from a childhood of buckets kept by his bedside. He was tired of her being sick all the time.

Yes, he had planned it. Yes, he had wanted her to be sick. He wanted her to see how much control he had over her. He wanted it and yet it still repulsed him. He should have made her clean up her own mess. Clean it up like his mother had made him clean up his messes.

He should have been feeling strong and in control, especially with his newest acquisition. Instead, his own stomach ached despite gagging down half a bottle of the chalky crap. That stupid so-called medicine promised to prevent his nausea. He could no longer count on it. Why didn't it work? Why was everything and everyone working against him?

He wanted Joan Begley to see, to understand what control he had. He wanted her weak and helpless. It had worked all those years for his mother. She had maintained control, first over his father and then over him. Why couldn't it work for him? But he hated the mess. *Hated, hated, hated it!*

He grabbed a meat cleaver from the workbench and slammed it into the wooden surface. Raised it and sent it into the wood again. Another chop. Another and another.

He shoved the meat cleaver aside. The wooden bench had plenty of cuts and slits, splinters and raw wounds from other angry bouts. It had been his father's workbench and had been pristine until the day he died. Yet he had taken his father's precious workbench, his workshop, his escape, and turned it into his own escape. And it had been an excellent escape. The only place he allowed his true emotions to come out. It had become his secret vault, protecting and absorbing and withstanding all the hurt, the pain, the anger, as well as the feeling of victory and sometimes even providing him with a sense of control.

He turned and leaned his back against the bench, allowing himself to take in the sights and smells of the magic workshop. The smells he loved: fresh sawdust, gasoline and WD-40—remnants of his father's hideaway and smells that reminded him of his father—were, unfortunately, long ago replaced by the smells of his own escape: caked blood, rotting bits of flesh, formaldehyde, ammonia and now vomit. The only one of that list that bothered him, that repulsed him, was the smell of vomit.

He admired his father's collection of tools, a strange and dazzling assortment hanging on the wall by pegs and hooks in organized rows. He had added the old meat hooks, boning knives and meat cleavers that now hung next to crescent wrenches, pry bars and hacksaws. Otherwise, he kept the wall of tools exactly the way his father had left it, paying tribute to the painstaking organization by cleaning and replacing the items after each use. So, too, had he kept the handy vises attached to the workbench in the same spots, along with the bone saw and the huge roll of white butcher-block paper resting in its own contraption with a sleek metal blade, sharp enough to slide through the paper with only the slightest touch of the fingertips.

In the corner was an old, battered chest-size freezer, gray scratches in the enamel like wounds and a low, constant hum that sounded like a cat purring. It had also been his father's, used back then for premium cuts of meat and trout or bass from infrequent fishing trips. After his father's death, he began using it as his first container, before he knew how to preserve his treasures. Quickly it filled up. Now it was one of several, with one next door and another at the house.

The shelves on the back wall were his addition, too, as were the vials, mason and jelly jars, crocks, glass tubes, plastic containers, fish tanks and wide-mouth bottles. All were immaculately clean, waiting to store his prizes. Even the cheap, store-bought pickle jars sparkled, not a trace of their brand labels left to block the view.

The top shelf held his own proud assortment of tools, shiny scalpels, X-Acto knives and blades, forceps, stainless steel probes and basins in different sizes and shapes. Most he had stolen one by one from work so that they wouldn't be missed.

Yes, he was proud of his workshop. Here, he felt in control. Despite the smell of her vomit turning his stomach, here, he never got sick. This was where he cut out other people's pain, their abnormalities, their deformities, their bragging rights, and kept them for himself.

All through his childhood his sickness had been so obscure. He could never point to a bum leg or heart defect or a precious tumor and say, "See, this is what makes me sick to my stomach." Had he been able to do so, they wouldn't have dared to doubt him, to whisper about him in hospital corners, to suggest he "get counseling."

They wouldn't have dared to laugh at him and point and snicker when he asked to be dismissed from class. They wouldn't have dared to call him weak and silly. If only he had had one cancerous tumor, one deformed limb to point to, they wouldn't have dared call him anything but brave and strong, a little soldier instead of a whiny brat.

These people with their claims to pain made him angry, made him jealous, made him crazy with envy. They could complain all they wanted and no one told them to buck up and shut up. And they didn't even realize the priceless treasures they possessed. Fools. All of them fools.

And so he cut them, slicing out that which made them different, made them special, that which gave them the right to complain and brag. He cut out their prizes and made them his own. It gave him power. It gave him control.

That's what he needed to do with Joan Begley. He needed to do exactly as he set out to do in the beginning. That was the only way he could gain control over her. But what would he use?

He examined the tools and scratched at his jaw. He wasn't even sure what it was that Joan possessed. Where would a hormone deficiency be located? Was it in the pituitary gland? That would be on the underside of the brain. He might need a drill and the bone saw. Or perhaps it was the thyroid gland, which would be a simple slit of the throat. Although, it could be one of the adrenal glands. Where the hell were they located? Somewhere over the kidneys, perhaps? He grabbed the illustrated medical dictionary off the top shelf and began flipping pages.

As he browsed the index, his fidgeting fingers found a boning knife, the curved blade razor sharp. And suddenly, he found himself hoping it was the thyroid. In fact, he thought he remembered her mentioning the thyroid. Yes, that would be good. After cleaning up her vomit over and over again, he wouldn't mind slitting Joan Begley's throat.

CHAPTER 54

Thursday, September 18

"**Y**ou don't have to fix breakfast for me, Mr. Racine," Maggie said, but her mouth was already watering from the aroma of hash browns and sausage sizzling in one skillet while Luc prepared another with scrambled eggs.

"No, no, I want to. God! I miss this." He splashed some milk and fresh ground pepper into the scrambled eggs, stirring and flipping with the expertise of a short-order cook. "I don't get to do this anymore. I don't trust myself to shut off the stove." He glanced back at her. "I'm only telling you so you'll keep an eye on things and make sure that I don't leave something on. Would you do that, please?"

He kept his back to her. Maggie knew it was not an easy thing for him to ask. She wondered if that was the real reason he wouldn't let her call Julia. Did his daughter know that he was deteriorating?

"Sure. Is there anything I can do to help?"

"Nope. Got the table all set." He looked around. "Maybe some orange juice. I noticed your friend brought some last night." He opened one cupboard door, then another and one more before grabbing two glasses to hand to her. This time he couldn't hide the slight flush of embarrassment. "I think he likes you."

"What?"

"The professor, he likes you."

This time she felt a slight flush. She found the juice and poured. "We're working on a case together. That's all."

"What? You don't like him?" He glanced at her over his shoulder.

"No, I didn't say that. It's just that I guess I haven't thought about him that way."

"Why not? He's a handsome young man. I noticed you're unattached."

"I don't know why not. I'm just…I'm not…" She realized that she sounded like some tongue-tied teenager. She wasn't sure why she thought she needed to explain it to him. "I'm not looking right now. My divorce was just finalized. I'm not ready to start another relationship."

"Oh, okay." He glanced back at her. "Sorry, I didn't mean to stick my nose in your business." He started cleaning the counter. "I like you. You remind me of Julia. I guess I miss her."

"I was thinking about that, Mr. Racine. I think—"

"I wish you'd call me Luc."

"Okay, but I was thinking maybe you should call Julia. I think she would like to know. Actually, I'd feel better if she knew."

He was putting away what he didn't use, sliding the egg carton back into the refrigerator and wrapping up the leftover sausage.

Maggie stopped him. "Where did you get this?" She pointed to the sausage he rolled tight into the white butcher-block paper.

"This? It's scrapple. I think they call it that because it's made from pork scraps," he said, misunderstanding what she meant and unwrapping the sausage to show her. "My wife was from Philadelphia. That's where they have the best. This stuff always reminds me of her. Partly why I named my best buddy Scrapple." He glanced down at the dog who, as if on cue, sat up to beg for a piece of his namesake. "Can't find it around here, though." Luc continued wrapping the sausage. "Last winter I had Steve Earlman make it for me out of some pork shoulder. He did a pretty good job, too. I think you'll like it."

Maggie wondered if Luc knew they had found Steve at the quarry. He had been to the site enough times he may have heard the rumors. Maybe he couldn't remember. Once again, she was reminded of that white paper that kept showing up. What was she missing?

"Luc, what did they do with the butcher shop when Steve passed away? Didn't he have any sons or daughters to keep the shop open?"

He scooped up hash browns, sausage and scrambled eggs, dividing the bounty between their two plates. It looked wonderful and she followed him to the table, bringing their juice.

"No, Steve never married. A nice guy, too." He pulled out a chair for her, waiting for her to get comfortable before he took his place. "It was sad to see the shop close. I remember hearing that someone bought all the equipment at the estate sale. I thought maybe whoever it was would keep the shop open or start a new one, but I guess not."

"Do you remember who bought all the equipment?"

Luc stared at her, his forehead furrowed in thought, the frustration playing in his eyes. "I should know that."

"It's okay if you can't remember. I was just curious."

"No, I should know. It was somebody I know."

Maggie's cell phone started ringing from the other room and Scrapple, who had taken his begging place under the table, now began to bark.

"Scrapple, that's enough. Hush."

"Excuse me. I need to get that," Maggie said as she hunted for her jacket, following the sound of the ringing. Finally. "Maggie O'Dell."

"O'Dell, it's Watermeier. I'm at Hubbard Park, the West Peak. We found something. I think you'll want to see this."

CHAPTER 55

Adam Bonzado pulled the Polaroids from his shirt pocket. He took another long, studied look, then slipped them back into the pocket. It probably wasn't a good idea to have the photos out while he rummaged the shelves of the local hardware store.

He was trying to get Maggie O'Dell off his mind. It didn't help matters that he still felt like a complete bonehead. First the soup incident and then waking her and Racine up last night. Not only waking them up but scaring them. Although Maggie didn't look that scared behind the barrel of her Smith & Wesson. He smiled at the memory. He liked that she could take care of herself. He didn't like having her almost blow off his head, though.

Sometimes he worried that his mother was right. That he spent too much time with skeletons and not enough time with real people. His students, according to his mother, didn't count.

"Why can't you go out like normal boys," his mother usually began her lecture that included something about dating nice girls. "You don't even go to a ball game with your brothers anymore."

But he liked his work. Why should he have to make excuses about that? And besides, most women were immediately turned off when they learned what he did for a living. No, the truth was he hadn't wanted anyone else after Kate. He buried himself in his work instead. It took his mind off that empty void.

So here he was again, burying himself in work to get his mind off Maggie O'Dell. What better way to do that than at a hardware store armed with a handful of Polaroids and a mission to add to his tools-of-death list.

Dr. Stolz had given him Polaroids of the victims' head wounds, all administered to the back top of the skull. Even the young man's skull Adam had in the lab, as well as the one he had plucked from the boiling pot at Luc Racine's, seemed to have been dealt similar deathblows.

He went down the aisle of hand tools, searching, paying close attention to the end of each tool. Ball-peen hammer, no. Bolt cutter, no. Then there were pliers.

Adam scratched his jaw, always amazed at the assortment. You had your long-nose locking pliers, jaw, diagonal, duckbill, slip joint, Arc joint, groove joint.

Jesus! Forget pliers.

Drive sockets: metric or standard. Screwdrivers: Phillips, slotted or torx. Wrenches: crescent, adjustable or pipe. The bolt clamp looked promising or maybe even the steel bar clamp. Woodworker's vise, no. Level, no.

"Hey, a mini hacksaw," he said, picking up the contraption. "For all those hard-to-reach joints when you're in the middle of dismembering a body."

"Can I help you, sir?" A clerk appeared at the end of the aisle.

Adam immediately put the mini hacksaw back as if he had been caught. He wondered if the clerk had heard him. The kid looked like he spent more time down in his family's basement rec room than in his dad's garage. In fact, he looked like he belonged in an electronics department, selling Game Boys and DVD players, not drills or circular saws, let alone hand tools.

"Is there something in particular you're looking for, sir?"

"Yeah, but it's one of those things that I'll know when I see it. You know what I mean?"

The clerk stared at him. No, he didn't know what he meant. "Like for a special project or something?"

Adam smiled. He wondered what the kid would do if he told him about his tools-of-death list. Or better yet, if he showed him the Polaroids and asked him to help find the tool that cracked open the skull and left that triangle mark. Instead, he said, "Yeah, I guess you could say that."

"Okay, then. Let me know if you change your mind."

"Thanks, I will."

Adam started down the next aisle. This one was full of bars. Yes, this was more like it. There were pry bars of every shape and size. Some of forged steel construction, others with black oxide coating to prevent rust. He read the labels below each: "easy, comfortable rubber grip" and "lowprofile claw for more leverage." There was one called a "gorilla bar." Another, the "wonder bar." An I-beam, a double-end nail puller, a gooseneck and a wrecking bar. This was crazy.

Then he saw it. The angle looked right. The size looked right. He slipped out the Polaroids again for a quick glance. Yes, this was it. The end of the double-end nail-pulling pry bar looked like the impressions left in the skulls.

Adam picked up the pry bar and turned it in his hands, examining it at every angle and getting the feel of it. It weighed more than it looked. He tried to hold it the way he imagined the killer had held it up over his head. He tried to imagine how he would swing it. It wouldn't require much force. A bit of a twist and the heavy, hooked end could crack a skull quite nicely.

He lifted it higher, getting ready to reenact a deathblow swing when he noticed the clerk at the end of the aisle. And he was watching. This time he looked…oh, perhaps *concerned* was an understatement.

"I think I found what I was looking for," Adam said, bringing the tool back down without any more fanfare. "And it's even on sale." He pointed to the tag, smiled and retreated down the other end of the aisle.

He waited in the checkout line, tapping the pry bar into the palm of his hand. Suddenly, it occurred to him that this pry bar was exactly like the one he kept in his El Camino.

CHAPTER 56

Henry watched from the top of the ridge. They almost had the car out of the trees, enough of a hood showing that he could tell it was a late model sedan. Jesus! What a mess. Why was it that when it rained it had to fucking pour?

He found himself wishing it was some poor drunk bastard who drove all the way up and simply lost control and went over the ledge. He wished it could be that simple. He had driven up here only to prove O'Dell wrong. But now he couldn't help wondering if they had just found Joan Begley.

He saw O'Dell leave her rented Ford Escort back behind the Meriden police blockade. They had the chain-link gate closed, padlocked and guarded down below at the entrance, but still it was a bit crowded up here along the winding road to the top of the peak. He waved to Deputy Truman to let O'Dell by.

"You found her?" she asked before he could say anything.

"I was standing here hoping that it was some drunk who took a wrong turn," Henry confessed, leaning on the wooden guard rail.

They stood quietly side by side, watching the tow truck cable pull the car up over the rocks and brush, listening to the scrape of metal against tree bark.

Finally, when it was on level ground, Deputy Charlie Newhouse yelled at him from the tilted smashed-in front of the car, "No one's inside, Sheriff."

"Jesus! I don't need this crap. Run the license plates." But even as Henry said it he could see the rear one was missing.

"Front plate's missing," Arliss said.

"So is the rear," Watermeier told him.

"You suppose it's stolen?" Charlie asked.

"Better give the boys a call to bring out a mobile unit." Henry walked around to the front, trying to get a look inside through the demolished windshield.

"Sheriff."

O'Dell was still at the back of the car, waiting for him. When he walked around she pointed to the trunk, where a small piece of fabric had gotten caught and was sticking out.

"Shit!" he mumbled, and felt the tightening in his chest. "Charlie, reach in there and pop the trunk, and try not to touch too much."

When no one moved, Henry looked up to find his two deputies and the tow truck operator staring at the trunk of the car.

"Charlie," Henry said again.

This time the deputy obeyed, but when the trunk snapped open Henry found himself wondering, once again, why the hell he hadn't retired six months ago.

He pushed the trunk wide-open and everyone remained motionless, wordless as they stared at the small body of a woman curled up inside. Henry noticed immediately that her wrists weren't bound. Neither were her ankles. But then there was no need. The back of the head faced them, a mess of blood and tangled hair where she had suffered what had to be a deathblow. It had cracked her skull open, an impact of force that seemed overkill for such a small woman.

"You suppose it's her?" he asked O'Dell.

"Hard to tell. All I have is a photo. The head wound definitely looks familiar."

"Yeah, that's what I was thinking." Henry swiped at his eyes. Jesus! They hadn't fished all his victims out of the barrels yet and here was another one. "Arliss, call

Carl and have him bring the mobile crime lab. And Dr. Stolz, too."

"I think they're probably out at the rock quarry, sir."

"I know where they probably are. Call them and tell them to get their asses over here."

"Sir? You want me to tell them that exactly?"

Henry wanted to throttle the kid. Instead he said, "Charlie, would you—"

"I've got it taken care of, Sheriff."

Henry noticed O'Dell just standing there, staring as if she couldn't believe it, yet she was the one who suggested he search the area. He moved in for a closer look, leaning into the trunk and under the lid without touching anything. He examined the area around the woman for signs of anything that may have been left. Anything to tell them whether or not this was the missing Joan Begley. Maybe he even hoped the weapon accidently got tossed in or dropped inside. But there was nothing. From this angle he could see the side of her face and there was something familiar about her. Yeah, she looked familiar but he hadn't seen O'Dell's photo of Begley.

He gently touched the woman's shoulder, moving her only slightly to get a better view. But what he saw made him jerk away.

"Holy crap!" He bashed his head on the lid of the trunk. He stumbled backward, slipping and almost losing his balance. Almost falling down.

The others stared at the back of the woman again, trying to see what had spooked him.

"It's that TV reporter," he said, out of breath and hating that his chest felt like it would explode. "That one who's been following me around everywhere."

"What are you talking about?" O'Dell said, stepping in closer to the trunk but waiting for him.

He rolled his shoulders and brushed his hands on the sides of his trousers as if to prepare himself. Then he leaned into the trunk as little as was necessary. He hesitated for only a second before he laid his hand on her shoulder again.

"He took her fucking eyes," he said, moving her enough for them to see her face. Just enough for them to see the hollow sockets where her blue eyes had once been.

CHAPTER 57

Maggie could hear her cell phone beep, warning her that the battery was low and reminding her that she had forgotten to charge it last night.

"Tully, I'm probably going to lose you pretty soon, so give me the bottom line. Were you able to find out anything by going through Sonny's e-mails?"

"He talks about getting sick a lot as a kid and his mother giving him medicine that only made it worse. Dr. Patterson suggested—okay now, this could be a long shot, but I think I agree with her—that he may have been the victim of Munchausen's syndrome by proxy. Are you familiar with that?"

"You think his mother purposely made him sick so that she could get attention?"

"Yes, exactly. Dr. Patterson is talking with the local hospital. She's hoping her credentials might get someone to check hospital records for maybe five to ten years ago."

"Could you check another name for me? Jacob Marley. See what you can find on him."

"Jacob Marley?"

"Yes, he's the funeral director. I think Joan Begley had pizza with him the night she was taken. It may have been exactly like he told me, a business dinner to wrap up funeral details, but when I visited him yesterday he seemed nervous and guilty about something. And he's a Junior who hates to be called Junior."

"If he's the funeral director he would have had access to Steve Earlman's embalmed body."

"Yes, he seemed too prepared to talk about that. But he doesn't fit the killer's profile. And now you're telling me I need to be looking for a hypochondriac who's also a paranoid delusional maniac because his mother made him sick on purpose? That should be easy to spot."

"Very funny, O'Dell. I'm trying to help you."

"I know you are. Sorry. It's just frustrating." She slowed the car, taking on more winding curves. "We just found another body."

"Oh, jeez. Do you know if it's Begley?"

"No, it isn't her. It may have been her rent-a-car. They're still checking it out. It was a local reporter with bad eyes."

"Let me guess, he took the eyes?"

"Yes. And he stuffed her in the trunk of a car. I worried that he might do this. He probably got paranoid that she was following him, but according to Watermeier she's been at the rock quarry every day and hounding *him*."

Her cell phone beeped again.

"I'm going to lose you, Tully."

"I'll call if I find anything on Marley. Oh, and I'll have Dr. Patterson call you if she finds anything out from the hospital."

"The thing is it could take too long. If Joan Begley is still alive I have a feeling she won't be much longer. This last kill means he's getting panicky. And all we seem to have right now are too many missing imperfections, a whole lot of coincidences and some white, waxy paper from a butcher shop."

"Butcher-block paper?"

"Yeah, I guess that's what it's called. I'm guessing he has tons of it and uses it to wrap and temporarily store the body pieces. I keep thinking it's got to mean something, but what? Any ideas?"

"I'm just wondering where you buy that stuff."

"Well, not at the local Stop & Shop. We already checked."

"Didn't you say Earlman was a butcher?"

"That's right."

"Any sons?"

"No, I already thought of that. His shop closed when he died. Someone bought all the equipment but didn't continue the business." She almost drove through a red light, braking hard and drawing a honk from the driver behind her. Why hadn't she thought about it before? Luc had said that someone bought all the equipment. "Why would you buy all the equipment if you weren't going to have a butcher shop? Doesn't that seem a bit odd?"

"I don't know. You should see the crazy stuff people buy and sell on eBay all the time."

"And how do you know what people buy and sell on eBay?" Another beep from her phone. "My battery really is running low, Tully. Before I go, two things—how's Harvey? He's not driving you crazy, is he?"

"Not at all. In fact, I think you may have to bribe Emma in order to get him back."

"Don't you dare let her get attached to my dog, Tully."

"Might be too late."

"Second, how's Gwen doing?"

There was silence and she thought she had already lost him when he finally said, "I think she's doing okay."

"Will you do a favor for me and please check on her?"

"Sure, I can do that."

"Thanks, Tully, and tell Emma she does not get my dog."

"O'Dell, one other thing." This time she could hear his tone change. "Cunningham asked me about you."

Maggie felt her muscles tighten.

"He wanted to know if you mentioned anything to me about your vacation," he continued, sounding serious, almost apologetic.

She knew Tully was a straight-shooter. He'd never lie, especially to Cunningham, and now, she had probably gotten both of them in trouble.

"What did you tell him?" she asked, gripping the steering wheel in preparation for his answer.

"I told him the truth, that you said something about daffodils." Then he hung up before she had a chance to respond.

She smiled and pulled the car into a parking lot, trying to get her mind back on track and off a possible reprimand. Somewhere she had a city map, besides the one Tully had drawn for her. It was just a hunch, but then what else did she have to go on? She needed to find the county courthouse. She needed to find out who had bought all that butcher shop equipment, including what might have been rolls and rolls of butcher-block paper.

CHAPTER 58

Henry started to head out to the rock quarry, had almost gotten there when he decided to go back to downtown Wallingford. He needed a strong cup of coffee, but mostly he just wanted to stop in at the bookstore and see his wife. After the media got hold of this latest development there was bound to be a frenzy, especially with the latest victim being one of their own. He was beginning to believe he and Rosie could kiss goodbye the idea of retiring in this community.

He took the back roads, winding around the edge of the city with the car window rolled down. He drove slowly, trying to suck in the fresh air, trying to relax enough so that the tight fist, that nagging ache in the middle of his chest, would let up. It'd serve him right for being so lax about taking—or rather not taking—his blood pressure medicine. Here he had escaped being with his buddies on 9/11 only to get a fucking heart attack while driving through the Connecticut countryside.

He drove by St. Francis Cemetery, curving around the hill, when he noticed a man hurry behind one of the tall headstones. At first he thought he had imagined it. Maybe he *was* having a heart attack. But that didn't make you see things, did it?

Henry pulled into the cemetery's entrance and stopped the car. From this angle he couldn't see the headstone without getting out. He sat there, wondering again if he had imagined it. If someone was in the cemetery there wasn't anything wrong with that. People were free to come in and often did to place wreaths and flowers on the graves. So there was no reason to hide.

He backed out and pulled onto the road. Rosie would laugh at him, not about forgetting his blood pressure medicine, but about seeing ghosts. He glanced up in the rearview mirror as he started around another curve. Just as the cemetery started to disappear out of view he saw the man again. This time Henry pulled the car off to the side of the road, out of view of the cemetery.

He left the car and backtracked down through the ditch, keeping himself out of sight while he took the long way around. The cemetery backed onto a forest, and Henry could see a pickup parked deep between the trees where he knew there wasn't a road.

Henry climbed up a steep incline, hoping it would hide him until he got to the trees. The mud and rock kept crumbling beneath his boots and he thought for sure the guy would hear him. Finally a windbreak of spindly evergreens allowed him his first look.

The man had his back to Henry, but he could see the guy had a shovel and was digging. Okay, so he was a grave digger. But then why did he hide when a car came by? And did they use shovels anymore to dig graves? Hadn't he seen earth-digging equipment out here before? One of those miniature things with the claw? Yeah, he was sure that's how they did it. In fact, he thought Vargus and Hobbs had a contract with several of the funeral homes.

Henry moved closer to get a better look. That's when he realized the guy wasn't digging a new grave, he was digging one up. Just then the man turned enough that Henry recognized him. It was Wally Hobbs, and he was hurrying away to crouch down behind a tall headstone as another car drove by.

CHAPTER 59

Luc hadn't left the house all morning. Not even to get the newspaper. Ever since Agent O'Dell had left he had been pacing, trying to watch TV while he walked back and forth from one window to another with the baseball bat never leaving his hand. Scrapple had given up on him hours ago, finally settling down on his favorite rug. Except for a few ear perks now and then, the terrier was fast asleep.

Luc kept hearing vehicles up on Whippoorwill Drive. Maybe there was more commotion happening down at the rock quarry. He thought he had heard sirens earlier.

On the midday local news there was mention of a car being found in Hubbard Park, but that was in Meriden, not down the lane. He wasn't about to leave the house to go see. Ordinarily they wouldn't be able to keep him away. But today...today he couldn't seem to set foot on his porch without getting the shakes. Is this what he was turning into? An old man who couldn't leave his house and then couldn't even remember whether or not he had?

Agent O'Dell had asked him this morning if he would please consider calling Julia to let her know that he was okay. But if his daughter didn't know about this mess, she wouldn't need to know that he was okay. Or so went his reasoning. He knew he needed to call her. He wanted to call her. Ever since he had talked to her...jeez, what day was that? Was it a few days ago or had it been weeks?

He heard another car, only this one sounded like it was in his driveway. By the time he got to the door, Agent O'Dell was coming up the front porch. He opened the door for her and felt a flush of embarrassment when she saw the bat still in his hands.

"What's the excitement down the lane?"

"I'm not sure," she said, sounding a little out of breath. "I couldn't get hold of Sheriff Watermeier. You think you might be able to help with something, Luc?"

"Sure. I mean, I can try."

She had a map in her hands and started spreading it

out on his crowded coffee table. "You've lived around here for a long time, right?"

"Almost all my life. My wife, Elizabeth, was from Philadelphia, but she loved it here, too, so we stayed. Wish Julia would have loved it enough to stay, but…well, what can a father do, huh?"

"I wonder if you can tell me where Ralph Shelby's property is."

"Ralph the butcher? Ralph's been gone a long time. What's it been, maybe ten years. Jeez, I can't remember. Didn't I tell you this morning that Steve Earlman bought the butcher shop from Ralph? But now Steve's gone, too. I told you that, didn't I? Didn't we talk about that this morning?"

"Yes, you did tell me. But Mr. Shelby's property, the acreage where he lived, can you tell me where it is? It's close by, right?"

"Sure, it's up the road, past the Millers' old sawmill. Mrs. Shelby died just a few years ago, but I think her son still lives out there."

"Can you show me on the map?"

He stared at the lines and blue spots and nothing looked familiar.

"We're right here." She pointed to an area, but it didn't look like anything to him except some red intersecting lines. She was looking up at him with a frown. Or was it worry? He didn't know her well enough to know if she was upset with him or feeling sorry for him. He'd rather have her upset with him.

"Luc, can you show me?"

"I can show you, but I can't show you on the map." He went to the door and grabbed his black beret and a jacket.

"No, you can't come with me, Luc."

"That's the only way I know how to show you."

"Can't you just give me directions? How far up the road? Is it on Whippoorwill Drive?"

"I'm really not being stubborn," he said, and tried not to get embarrassed again. "But I can't tell you. I can't put it into words." His hands were already flying, trying to help him explain. "I have to show you by…well, by showing you."

She hesitated, standing with arms crossed, looking like she was trying to decide. "Okay, but you promise you'll stay in the car."

"Sure, I can do that. Why are you interested in the old Shelby place?"

"I need to check something out. Remember you told me that when the butcher shop closed someone bought all the equipment?"

"Oh, yeah. But I don't remember who it was. Seems like I should know."

"I found out. It was Ralph Shelby's son. He bought everything, every last piece."

"Really? Hmm…I wonder what he wanted with all that old stuff."

"That's what I want to find out."

CHAPTER 60

Henry knew he had the rock quarry killer. The entire trip back to the station Wally Hobbs kept complaining about his stomach hurting. In that tinny voice he begged Henry to stop the car so he could throw up. Well, at least the bastard waited until they got to the County Sheriff's Office. He thought about making Hobbs clean up the mess, but he knew he shouldn't push his good fortune.

Now he had Hobbs handcuffed to a metal folding chair in their interrogation room. Actually, it wasn't re-

ally an interrogation room but a break room with a cof-
feemaker and an empty plate of crumbs.

He had already read him his rights, or his version of
them. Sometimes he knew he left out a word or two.

"What do you think you were doing, Walter?" He
wondered if he could bully the little man into confess-
ing. Then he remembered that Hobbs's partner was the
biggest bully in town. He had probably built up some
kind of immunity. "You want me to call your sister?"

"No. Don't call Lillian."

"What's wrong? You don't want your sister knowing
you dig up bodies and slice them up?"

"What are you talking about?"

"I've seen your handiwork, Hobbs. What is it with
you? You kill some and when you get bored you dig
some up?"

"I haven't killed anyone."

"How could you dig up someone like Steve Earlman?
Don't you have any respect for the dead?"

"I didn't dig him up."

Wally Hobbs's eyes were the size of quarters and
sweat poured down his forehead. Henry could smell him.

"How many have you killed and how many have
you dug up?"

"Wait. You've got to listen to me. I didn't kill anyone."

"Right."

"Marley and Calvin and me, we just wanted to make
some extra money."

"Marley? Jake Marley?" Henry sat down on the edge of the table. "Marley's in this with you?"

"We didn't think it would hurt anybody. Life insurance policies usually pay for everything, so it's not like we were taking it out of the families' pockets."

"What the hell are you talking about?"

"I was just trying to fix it so that if anyone checked they wouldn't know."

"Check what?" Suddenly it was hot in the room and Henry needed to open a window.

"If anyone checked...you know, Steve Earlman's grave. Marley sells them the vault, but we don't actually use a vault. We divide the money three ways." Hobbs looked scared. "It was Marley's idea."

Henry rubbed a hand over his face and he couldn't help but feel disappointed. Wally Hobbs was a weasel and a thief, but he was no killer.

CHAPTER 61

Adam Bonzado didn't like what he was thinking. It couldn't be possible and yet it made sense.

He had driven back to West Haven, all the way to his lab at the university to retrieve the rest of the Polaroids Dr. Stolz had given him. It was bad enough that the victims' head wounds matched the exact angle of the pry bar he kept in the El Camino, but now he needed to check something else.

He grabbed the photos and rushed out of the lab, bumping into several of his students, barely mumbling a greeting. Now in the parking lot once again, he stood at the tailgate of his pickup. He stood there, hesitating with the Polaroid in his hand. It was a photo of the victim with the pronounced livor mortis on her back.

Adam knew that livor mortis was the result of gravity pulling and settling all the blood to the lowest area of the body. This victim had been laid on her back for several hours after her death. That's why the skin on her back was so red. Called the bruising of death, livor mortis also had the tendency of transforming the skin's texture. The skin often took up the pattern of the surface it was laid out on. So a body laid out on a brick sidewalk might have indentations resembling brick and mortar. A body found dead on a gravel road might have a pebbled texture. And in this case, a body laid out in a pickup with a waffle-pattern bed lining might have a waffle-pattern imprint.

Adam pulled down the tailgate and held up the Polaroid. The pattern matched the dead woman's back. And as much as he didn't want to believe it, he knew that Simon Shelby was the only person who had borrowed his pickup.

CHAPTER 62

Maggie knew she couldn't wait for Watermeier. Wherever he was he wasn't responding to any of her phone calls and her cell phone was on the verge of completely dying.

Jennifer Carpenter had to have been killed within the last twelve hours, which meant that the killer was becoming more and more paranoid. If he still had Joan Begley and was keeping her alive, Maggie knew it wouldn't be for much longer.

She drove slowly on Whippoorwill Drive, in the opposite direction of the rock quarry. Luc sat quietly beside her. She hoped he hadn't blanked out on her again. At least not until he showed her where Simon Shelby lived.

"Turn up here. In that direction," he said, pointing with an animated wave of his whole arm. "You can't see the buildings from the road. The mailbox is one of those big galvanized steel ones that sits on a barrel. You know, one of those big wooden barrels."

Maggie glanced at him. He had to be kidding. A barrel? But Luc didn't see the irony.

At the courthouse, the clerk who helped Maggie look up the estate sale records of Steve Earlman told Maggie that Simon Shelby was a very nice young man. "Poor fellow," she told Maggie without any prompting, "he lost his father when he was just a boy. Loved his daddy. I remember going to the butcher shop and seeing him there on Saturdays, helping Ralph. He had a cute nickname for Simon. I can't remember what it was, though.

"Simon really was crushed, just crushed when Ralph died. I don't think Sophie knew what to do with the boy. I think that's when he started getting sick a lot. We all felt so bad for Sophie. All that worry probably sent her to an early grave. But he's such a nice young man now." The woman rambled on and Maggie, who usually hated small talk, simply nodded and listened, noting all the coincidences.

But it was more than coincidence when the clerk said, "He's working his way through college now, the University of New Haven."

"Really?" Maggie had said, still more interested in the individual auction items.

"Something to do with bones, of all things," the clerk told her, and Maggie almost dropped the book of records. "I suppose that makes sense in some way, huh? I mean being the son of a butcher." The woman had laughed. "Frankly, I think it's a little morbid myself. But he must enjoy that sort of stuff. He works part-time at Marley and Marley Funeral Home, too. Such a hard worker."

"That nickname his father used?" Maggie asked the woman, although by this time she had felt certain she already knew the answer. "Was it Sonny?"

"Yes, that's it. How did you know? Ralph called him Sonny, Sonny Boy."

Now Maggie saw the mailbox on the wooden barrel before Luc's arm started waving at it, but she drove past the driveway.

"No, it's right there," he said. "You missed it."

"I'm going to park the car over here." And she pulled into what looked like a dirt path to a field. "I want you to stay here."

"Okay."

"I'm serious, Luc. You stay here." As an afterthought, she pulled out her cell phone and handed it to him. "If I don't come back in fifteen minutes, call 911."

He took the phone and stared at it, but seemed satisfied that she was letting him do something to help. Which made Maggie feel more confident that he would stay put, never mind that the cell phone's battery was dead.

CHAPTER 63

Simon stared at the tools on the wall, trying to decide which one to use on Joan. He had gotten used to her company. Despite hating to clean up her messes, he did like having her as his guest. He liked that she didn't even ask to be let go anymore. He had control over her and he liked that, too. But that reporter had ruined everything. And now he had to get rid of Joan.

He had called in sick, telling the receptionist at the funeral home that he might have the flu. It was something he had never done before. And he wasn't going to class this afternoon, either. Another first. Not since childhood had he missed a day of work or college classes. After all those missed school days growing up, he had always felt like he needed to catch up. Maybe he felt like he needed to prove something.

He hated missing. Hated ruining his regular routine. It didn't feel right. But this was important. Already he had cleaned out two of the chest freezers, one here in the toolshed and one back at the house. He had tossed all the parts he had saved, all those pieces he had saved and wrapped in butcher-block white paper. He had tossed it all in the woods, where the coyotes would take care of it once it thawed. He hated parting with the pieces, but none of them proved interesting enough to showcase. He really didn't need them. Besides, he needed some place to put Joan. At least until he found a new dumping ground.

He continued to stare at the tools. He had ruled out the chain saw, though it was tempting, especially since he still wasn't sure which gland caused her hormone deficiency. She tried to tell him she was fine. That she had only made it up to excuse her overeating. Poor girl. Like the rest of them, she didn't recognize what a valuable commodity she was in possession of. But it didn't matter. He'd just cut all of the glands out. Surely he would be able to tell which one looked diseased. And if he couldn't, he'd decided to keep all of them.

A knife would work. But which one? He had the entire collection now from his father's shop. Anything from the huge cleaver to the small, delicate filet knife. Maybe something in between. He really didn't want to do this. It was almost as if he had become attached to

Maggie couldn't see a vehicle, but there were enough outbuildings to store several. Had he gone to work already? Or if not work, perhaps he had a class. Maybe he was even back at the rock quarry, helping Watermeier and Bonzado. What a pathetic twist. The killer not only returning to the crime scene but helping to process it. Simon Shelby had stood by and watched, actually even helped at times, while they sorted through his mutilations, his butchery.

The acreage was well maintained. All the buildings were whitewashed, the grass and meadow cut short, no discarded old equipment. One of the buildings looked like it had huge solar panels on its sides, renovated for perhaps a workshop.

She made her way to the back door but hadn't peeked inside any of the windows yet. She decided to knock. Make sure he was gone, despite her certainty. And she slid her Smith & Wesson under her jacket, in case someone answered the door. When no one did, she tried to the knob, surprised to find the door unlocked.

She brought out her revolver again and swung the door open. She stopped to listen. Other than an electrical hum of an appliance, she couldn't hear anything. She entered slowly, watching, looking, searching as she eased down the hallway. She came to the kitchen first on the left. She glanced in. Nothing out of the ordinary. The electrical hum was coming from the old chest freezer in the corner. She continued down the hallway. An open stairwell was to her right and she looked up. Nothing.

She could see the living room beyond the stairwell, or perhaps a parlor, furnished like a showroom with what looked like antiques, lace doilies and curtains. She got to the entrance and was paying such close attention to what was in front of her that she didn't hear him come up from behind. She didn't hear him until it was too late.

Maggie turned just as something came crashing down on the side of her head.

CHAPTER 65

Luc didn't like waiting.

He wished Agent O'Dell had allowed him to bring Scrapple along. He didn't like being without the dog. They went everywhere together. And he really didn't like hearing Scrapple's howl of abandonment coming from the living room window as they drove away.

He tried to see beyond the trees. He tried to look down the path where Agent O'Dell had disappeared. He didn't understand why she hadn't driven up, or at least, walked up the driveway. She was being very secretive for someone who kept telling him not to worry. She reminded him of Julia. Before she moved to D.C. his daughter had always been going off checking stuff, stuff she probably shouldn't have been poking her nose into. Maybe that was just what law enforcement people did. Maybe it was in their blood. Although he and Julia did share some of the same blood.

He scratched his head, pushing back the beret and looking again to see if he could make out where in the world Agent O'Dell was now. He held up the cell phone. She said fifteen minutes. Well, it was close to that now, wasn't it? He glanced at his wrist, only to remember that he had stopped wearing watches long ago when he could no longer understand them. Numbers had become useless to him. He couldn't even write out a check anymore. They probably would have shut off his electricity months ago if he hadn't had the foresight to set up all the automatic withdrawals for his bills. Hopefully the money wouldn't run out before his time ran out.

He looked out the car window again and this time felt a slight panic as he tried to remember why he couldn't recognize anything. Oh, jeez! Where the hell was he? He twisted around in the car, trying to find something he recognized. Then he held up the black object in his hand. He was holding it so tight it had to be something important, but damn it, he couldn't remember what the hell it was.

CHAPTER 66

Maggie woke slowly. Her head throbbed. Her legs felt numb, tangled, somewhere underneath her. It was pitch-dark despite her attempt to open her eyes. No use. It was too dark. She couldn't move her arms. Couldn't begin to untangle her legs. She could barely move her hands and tried to feel around the small, smooth space above her. Whatever he had shoved her into, it was too tight to move.

Too tight and cold. So very cold.

That was when she heard the motor kick on. That was when she recognized the electrical hum. That same hum she had heard when she first entered the house.

Oh, God! He had put her in the freezer.

She couldn't panic. It wouldn't help to panic. She couldn't have been in here long or she wouldn't have woken up. She had to remain calm. She tried to twist her legs out from under her. It was useless. They were shoved in tight. Even her arms couldn't move more than a few inches to the side. It felt like she was squeezing herself down into the chest tighter and tighter. That couldn't be possible.

She needed to stay calm. She needed to breathe. It was already difficult to breathe. How much air could she possibly have inside here? And the cold. God, it was unbearable.

Her fingers hurt, but she balled them up into fists and pushed on the lid. There wasn't even enough room to pound. She remembered her weapon. Yes, she could shoot some holes in the lid. Of course, why hadn't she thought of that? She patted down her jacket. She tried to feel her pockets. And despair came quickly with the realization that, of course, he wouldn't have tossed her revolver in with her.

It was useless. She started to scream "help" as loud as she could. Over and over again until her throat felt raw. She shoved at the lid. She slammed her fists, now numb from the cold. She kept slamming them into the lid until she could feel what must have been blood dripping down into her face. And all she could think about was that the only person who might know where to look for her was back in her car with a cell phone that had a dead battery.

CHAPTER 67

Adam found Maggie's rental parked off the road but no one was inside. Did she know about Simon? How could she? He pulled his El Camino in behind the Ford Escort and jumped out, heading through the ditch until he thought of something. He ran back to the pickup and grabbed the pry bar from the back.

He barely got to the trees before he saw Luc Racine, wandering behind one of the buildings. The old man looked lost. Adam started to call out to him, then stopped, looking around for Simon. He had called the funeral home before he drove out here, hoping he'd catch Simon and be able to confront him in public. But they told him Simon had called in sick, and that alone sent a wave of panic through Adam. Simon never called in sick.

Now he wished he had tried to get ahold of Henry again, but each time he had tried, Beverly told him Sheriff Watermeier was in a very important meeting and could not be disturbed. That his deputy had been instructed to handle any emergencies.

Adam made his way to Luc, staying in the trees and watching for signs of Maggie or Simon. When he was close enough, he called to Luc in a low voice, "Mr. Racine. Hey, Luc."

The old man turned around so suddenly he almost tripped. His eyes darted everywhere and Adam worried he might be having one of his blank moments.

"Over here, Mr. Racine." He came out from the trees and walked to Luc, his eyes watching in all directions.

"Oh, Professor, it's you. You scared me."

"Sorry. Where's Maggie?"

"I don't know. But I think I heard someone in this cabin over here."

"Have you seen Simon?"

"No, no, not at all. We need to find Maggie. I just don't have a good feeling. I think she's been gone too long." He was shifting from one foot to the other, back and forth in almost a nervous dance.

"Okay, calm down. We'll find her. Let's check in here."

They couldn't see in through the windows and the door was locked with a chain and padlock. Adam used the pry bar, twisting and pounding at it until finally it broke open. The light in the room was dim. Adam thought it looked like a cozy cabin, except for the shelves that lined the walls. Shelves with rows and rows of jars and crocks that reminded him of his own lab back at the university. Then he noticed the bed in the far corner. Someone moved under the covers.

The woman curled up and strapped in the bed jerked awake. She cried out when she saw them, smiling and laughing. Then suddenly she winced and cried out with pain.

CHAPTER 68

Maggie felt the exhaustion. She needed to think. She needed to stay calm. No good would come from panic. Her hands throbbed with pain. That was good, good that she could still feel something even if it was pain. Yes, it was good that the cold bit into her skin, that it hadn't gone totally numb. Good that she could still hear her teeth chattering and feel her body shivering.

Shivering was the body's way of warming itself. Soon she'd be too tired to shiver, her blood too thick, her heart and lungs too slow to respond. Even her brain would become less efficient as she crossed the boundary into hypothermia.

She tried to remember what she could expect. She tried to remember what happens during hypothermia. If she could remember maybe she could look out for the signs and fight them.

She knew it was possible to survive several hours in extreme cold, but how many? Two? Three? She couldn't remember. What else was there? She needed to remember.

Soon the cold would shut down her metabolism. Her lungs would take in less oxygen and her breaths would become fewer so that it would look like she wasn't even breathing. That was good, because there couldn't be much air in this freezer. Oh, God! Would she suffocate before she froze to death?

She knew the same was true for her heart rate. It would slow down, too, which seemed impossible at the moment. It seemed so loud, hammering in her ears. But it would slow to a faint, almost inaudible rate, so that if someone were to feel her pulse, he might not feel one at all.

She kept telling herself that she had plenty of time until they found her. But who would come looking for her? Other than Simon the only person who knew she was here was Luc Racine. Would he come looking for her when she didn't come back to the car? Would he call for help? Oh, damn! How could he call for help? And again, she remembered that she had left him with a dead cell phone. What did it matter? He might not even remember where he was or who she was.

The panic clawed at her. She resisted the urge to beat her fists against the walls of the freezer again. She told herself that panic was also good. It was when the panic subsided that she'd need to start worrying. Although by that time she might not care.

She tried to concentrate again. She wanted to go through the list of things to expect. It would keep her mind working.

What other things were there? Oh, yes, the lack of oxygen would trigger hallucinations. They could be visual or auditory or both. She might see people when there was no one there at all. Or she might hear someone talking or calling to her, but it would only be her mind playing tricks on her.

There was also the sudden and extreme heat. Yes, heat after the cold. It was one of the cruel paradoxes of severe hypothermia. There was supposedly a burning sensation that made victims want to tear off their clothing and rip at their skin. No problem there. She couldn't move enough to do either. Ironically, the heat was one of the last things they remembered before losing consciousness. That's if they could remember.

Amnesia would eventually chip away at the brain. Maybe it was the body's last defense, a sort of odd blessing to replace the memory of pain and cold with a simple void.

She could feel her muscles already getting stiff. They throbbed and ached from the shivering. She tried to think of warm things. Maybe Gwen was right. Maybe she did need a vacation. And she tried to imagine a beach, hot sand between her toes, the sun beating down on her skin, warm, refreshing waves washing up against her. If not a beach then maybe her hands wrapped around a steaming mug of hot chocolate while her body cuddled into a thick down comforter while she sat in front of a roaring fire. So warm she could curl up, curl up and...sleep.

She was so exhausted. Sleep sounded good. She closed her eyes. She could feel her breaths coming slower, more and more shallow. The pain in her hands had gone away. Or maybe she simply couldn't feel the pain anymore. The panic had subsided. She felt it slipping away. She was so very tired, so sleepy. Yes, she'd close her eyes. Just for a moment or two. It was so dark, so quiet.

She'd allow herself to sleep. Just for a little while. She'd sleep under the warm sunshine. She could hear the waves splashing, a seagull up above. From somewhere in the back of her mind, someplace where her brain had slowed down but hadn't stopped working, from somewhere there came a faint whine, a soft, almost inaudible alarm insisting she open her eyes, pleading with her to not give in to the darkness.

At the same time came the realization that she had already stopped shivering. And she knew it was too late.

CHAPTER 69

Luc searched every room of the house and still hadn't found Maggie. Where in the world was she? Sheriff Watermeier seemed convinced Simon Shelby had taken her with him. His deputies searched the surrounding woods while the State Patrol were said to be setting up roadblocks.

Luc could still hear the ambulance's siren as it whined up Whippoorwill Drive. One of the paramedics said it looked like the woman named Joan had been poisoned. What if Simon had poisoned Maggie?

He fidgeted, wringing his hands, then raced back up the stairs to check closets and corners he knew he had already checked. The whole time he kept thinking that she had saved him once. He couldn't possibly let her down. He didn't even know how long it had been since she left him in the car. Simon could have taken her hours ago.

"Luc?" Adam was in the hall between the kitchen and the stairwell. "Any sign of her?"

"No. I've looked everywhere."

"Henry's put out an APB on Simon. If he has her with him, they'll find and stop him."

"I just don't have a good feeling about this."

"She's a tough woman. She can take care of herself."

But as he said it Luc could tell Adam hadn't convinced himself.

"What kind of madman does this?" Luc hated that the panic was still caught like a lump in his throat, making his voice crack. "Out back in the trees there's a bunch of white packages of frozen meat or something. He just threw it all out there to rot. What kind of a crazy man does something like that?"

"Wait a minute." Adam started searching again. "You say he threw out stuff from a freezer?"

"Yeah, piles of it. It was back—" But he saw it at the same time Adam did. They raced to the chest freezer in the kitchen corner, both of them hesitating and looking at each other almost as if they were as afraid to open it as they were hopeful.

CHAPTER 70

Out of the darkness Maggie thought she heard a hum, a faint whine that wouldn't go away. That kept getting louder, though was still in the distance. An annoying whine. Was it a voice? Was she only imagining it? Hallucinating?

She was too tired to care.

Her eyelids burned as a flash of light came at her, then was gone. Laser beams, another flash and then darkness.

"Gone."

Yes, they were gone as quickly as they came at her.

"She's gone."

No, wait. It was a voice. She could barely make it out.

Quiet and muffled, the words didn't make sense as they came through a wind tunnel.

"She's gone."

Her muscles were stiff. Her arms frozen at her sides. There was no willing them to move. Another flash of light and this time it came with a flash of color, blue and a blur of orange.

"No pulse."

She was too tired to ask what the voices meant. She couldn't ask if she wanted to. She had no control of her body. It seemed gone, stolen out from under her. She couldn't feel it or see it.

"She's gone" came the words again, and this time that alarm in the back of her brain said, "They mean you! They're talking about you."

But no. She wasn't gone. She needed to tell them.

"No pulse."

No, wait, she wanted to yell but couldn't because she was floating off in the distance and had no command of her body. They needed to listen to her chest. They wouldn't be able to get a pulse at her wrist. Her heartbeat had slowed down. It was a faint murmur, but it was beating. She could feel it.

"No dilation."

Please, wait. Why couldn't she see them? If they were looking into her eyes, why couldn't she see? The flashes of light. That had to be what it was. Her eyes wouldn't respond. But she was still here. How could she let them know she was still alive?

"She's gone."

No, no, no. Her brain seemed to be screaming it, but it was no use. They believed she was dead. She couldn't see beyond the black. She couldn't make her muscles respond.

No, wait. Maybe she was dead.

Wasn't this what dead felt like? A faint consciousness with no control over her body. No body to control.

Oh, God! Maybe they were right. Maybe she was gone. Gone forever. She felt herself slipping again. She'd close her eyes and sleep some more. Or were they already closed? She slept and woke again when she heard something. Nothing. More sleep. What felt like hours. A warm darkness slipped in tight around her. Liquid warmth ran through her veins. And she felt herself leaving again. Yes, maybe this was what it felt like. No second chances. No warnings. Gone.

Then suddenly she thought she saw…no, it couldn't be. Through a blur of gray haze she saw her father and then she knew it was true. She really was dead.

CHAPTER 71

"Maggie?"

It hurt to open her eyes. The light blinded her. The images swirled above her head. The humming of equipment filled her ears. And her mouth tasted like rubber and cotton. She tried to focus on the voice and where it was coming from. If it was real. Then she felt someone squeeze her hand.

"Maggie? You have to come back or I'll never forgive you."

"Gwen?" It hurt to talk, but at least she could. She tried again. "Where am I?"

"You scared us, O'Dell."

She turned her head to look up at Tully standing on the other side of the bed. Just the slight turn made her dizzy.

"What happened? Where am I?"

"You're at Yale-New Haven Medical Center," Gwen told her. "You suffered a severe case of hypothermia."

"They had to drain all your blood out of you, O'Dell, warm it up and pump it back in. So you can't complain about being cold-blooded, okay?"

"Very funny." Gwen shot him a look.

"What, we're not allowed to make jokes?"

"You really did have us scared, Maggie," Gwen said, caressing her forehead with the warm palm of her hand.

"What happened?"

"Look, Maggie, you're going to have amnesia and probably not remember everything that happened. We can go through it later when you're stronger, okay?"

"But how long have I been gone?"

"You've been out of it since Thursday."

"What day is it?"

"It's Saturday evening, sweetie." Gwen was still holding her hand and smoothing back her hair.

"What about Simon Shelby?"

"That she remembers. Always on duty, aren't you, O'Dell?" Tully smiled. "Maryland State Patrol caught him last night. We're not sure where he was headed. He actually had taken some of his specimens with him in the trunk."

"Specimens?" Maggie asked, trying to fight through the annoying haze.

"We were right," Tully said. "He was cutting out deformed livers, tumored brains, diseased hearts, crippled bones. Meriden's police lab thinks they may have already matched a pair of eyes to that reporter. They're running DNA tests on some of the other pieces. They'll probably be able to match some of them to the bodies in the rock quarry. You should have seen his work shed, O'Dell. Shelves and shelves of jars and containers. It's hard to tell how many victims or how long he's been doing this. And he's not talking. In fact, it looks like he might end up in a padded cell somewhere."

"My guess is it started five years ago," Gwen said, "when his mother died. I talked to a nurse at the local hospital. She remembered Simon Shelby and his mother, Sophie. This nurse told me she even felt sorry for him. The mother was constantly bringing him into the emergency room in the middle of the night. He always complained of terrible stomach cramps, but tests never showed anything out of the ordinary. His mother may have been poisoning him, just like he was poisoning Joan Begley."

"Is she okay?" Maggie asked. "Is she alive?"

"She's alive and she's going to be okay," Gwen said. "She's up at MidState Medical Center in Meriden. It looks like Shelby was giving her low doses of arsenic. She has a long recovery ahead of her, but they think she'll be okay."

"I thought I died," Maggie confessed. That much she could remember.

"So did the two men who found you," Gwen told her, moving in closer against the bed railing. "Luc Racine told me that he was sure you were dead. They couldn't get a pulse. Your eyes wouldn't respond to light. But he said Professor Bonzado wouldn't give up on you. You're really lucky he didn't, Maggie. Hypothermia can easily disguise itself."

"You're probably going to wish you died when Cunningham gets ahold of you," Tully said, but he was smiling.

"So I guess he knows."

"Let's just say he sent that white flower plant." Tully pointed to the potted plant on one side of the table. "The card says it's a false dragonhead, commonly known as an obedient plant."

"Are Luc and Adam here?" Maggie asked, hoping to change the subject.

"They'll be by later. In fact, Tully, why don't you go call them."

Maggie thought she saw Gwen and Tully exchange a look, some secret between them.

"I'll be right back," Tully said, and squeezed Maggie's shoulder. "Emma wanted you to know that she's taking good care of Harvey."

"Just don't let her think she gets to keep him, Tully."

"Yes, I know." And he left.

"Maggie, there's something I need to tell you."

She braced herself and suddenly tried to move her legs. Yes, legs worked. Arms worked.

"What are you doing?" Gwen laughed. "No, you're fine. Really. But I just thought I should warn you. Your mother is here. She's down in the cafeteria taking a break. She's been here since Thursday night."

"Oh. Okay. Wow! You really were worried about me, huh?"

"The procedure for bringing someone back from severe hypothermia can kill the patient," Gwen said, the pent-up emotion of two days revealing itself. "I'm sorry. But I was really worried. Your mother's not the only one I called. Now, you can be upset with me all you want, but there's someone else I called." Gwen squeezed her hand then went to the door. "You can come in now."

Patrick walked in, not hesitating, and came directly to the bed. But then he stood there, staring down at her.

"They've told you?" she asked.

"And it's a good thing. I wonder how many more trips and how many more Diet Pepsis it would have taken you." He smiled their father's smile.

"It was you," she said.

"What?"

"I thought I was dead. I thought I saw my dad…our dad. But it must have been you I saw."

"So you'll tell me about him sometime?"

"How much time do you have?" She smiled at him.

He sat down, taking Gwen's chair at the bedside. "My shift doesn't start for a couple more hours."

Three months later
Connecticut Mental Facility

Simon hated this room. It smelled of disinfectant, but it wasn't clean. He could see cobwebs on the ceiling in the far right corner. And the nurses or wardens or whatever they called them weren't very clean, either. The one with the tattoo had greasy long hair and bad breath. But at least they treated him okay. And Dr. Kramer had even given him something for his stomach that seemed to make it better...sometimes. It still hurt once in a while. Once in a while around midnight.

They had brought in two trays of food, which meant

he was getting a new roommate. Already he had drunk his juice and hidden the plastic cup under the bed, under a floorboard he had worked on and pulled up. That's where he kept his new specimens. He had to pace himself, but it was getting easier and easier to steal jars from the supply closet. The night clerk, better known as Broom Hilda, forgot to lock it sometimes.

He heard the door locks click open. They still made him jump.

"Simon." And here she was now. "Here's your new roommate. I want you to meet Daniel Bender."

He looked like a kid, skinny and pale with shaggy brown hair and empty brown eyes.

"Hi, Daniel," he said, standing up to shake his hand and disgusted to find it sweaty and cold. Simon wiped his hand off on Daniel's bedspread while Broom Hilda showed the kid where to put his few things.

After she left, Daniel sat on the edge of his bed, staring at the tray of food.

"The soup is usually good," Simon told him. "It's hard to screw up soup." He picked at his salad, poking the wilted leaves with his fork and pushing them off to the side of the tray.

"I can't eat just anything," Daniel said in a little bitty voice. "I have a bleeding ulcer."

Suddenly, Simon was interested, and he shoved his salad to the side.

Anyone who can simply not resist a great thriller
will not want to miss

ONE FALSE MOVE

A sensational new thriller from
Alex Kava

Available from MIRA Books in hardcover
August 2004

Turn the page for a sneak preview!

1:13 p.m.
Friday, August 27
Nebraska State Penitentiary—Lincoln, Nebraska

Max Kramer wore his lucky red tie with his power blue suit. While he waited for the guard to unlock and open the door, he admired his reflection in the glass security window behind him. That Grecian Formula for hair really worked. He could barely see any of the gray. His wife kept telling him the salt-and-pepper made him look more distinguished. Of course, she would say that. She always said stuff like that when she was suspicious, when she knew he was hunting for someone new. God, she knew him well.

"Big day," the hulk of a guard said to him, but he was scowling instead of smiling.

Max had heard the nicknames the guards had given him in the last several weeks. He knew he wasn't a popular guy here on death row. But that was the guards. To the inmates he had reached hero status. And they were the ones he cared about; they were the ones who counted. They needed him to right their wrongs, to tell their stories, or rather *their* versions of the story. Yes, they were the ones who mattered, and not because he was a bleeding heart liberal like the *Omaha World Herald* or the *Lincoln Journal Star* seemed pleased to label him. It was nothing quite as admirable as all that. Quite simply, all his hard work, all his efforts were for a day like today. A day when he could watch a client of his walk out of this concrete hellhole. A day when he could save his client from the electric chair and walk alongside him out the front doors and into the sunlight. The sunlight *and* the spotlight of about two dozen TV cameras from across the country. CNN's Larry King had already booked Max and Jared on his show for next week. And the red tie would show up wonderfully tonight when NBC aired his interview with Brian Williams.

Yes, this was what he had waited for his entire career. All the shitty pay and long hours and attacks from the local media would come to an end.

He stopped at the doorway, pretending to show some respect for his client's privacy. Pretending, because he didn't really want to spend any more time alone with Jared Barnett than necessary. So he watched from the doorway. Barnett was wearing the same faded jeans and red T-shirt he had surrendered that first day at the penitentiary five years ago. Now that he had traded in his orange jumpsuit for street clothes, Max couldn't help thinking how ordinary Barnett looked.

The guard at the door stepped aside.

"Paperwork's coming," he said. "You want, you can wait inside."

Max nodded as if grateful for the invitation—what the guard seemed to consider a courtesy—even though Max preferred for the asshole to let him wait in the hall. Too late. Jared saw him and waved him into the holding room. He stood up when Max entered, another courtesy. Jesus! Max hated this phony crap. What was this world coming to when convicted murderers stooped to being courteous?

"Relax. Take a load off," Max told Barnett as he shoved one of the metal folding chairs in his direction, scraping it against the floor, the noise grating his nerves. Only now did he realize he was nervous, nervous that Barnett could screw this up for him.

"Man, I never thought you'd actually be able to pull this off," Barnett said, taking the seat, seemingly unbothered that Max remained standing. It was a trick Max had learned long ago in his early years as a defense attorney. You get the client to sit down while you stand over him, instant authority. At five feet, seven inches, Max Kramer had to use every trick he could.

"So how does this work?" Barnett wanted to know even though Max had explained it several times during the appeal. He sounded as though he believed there was still a catch. "I'm really free to go?"

"Without Danny Ramerez as a witness the prosecution has no case. It was admirable of Mr. Ramerez to come forward and finally tell the truth—that he wasn't even there that night."

Barnett smiled up at him, but there was something about his smile that creeped Max out. Never once during the appeal process had he asked how Barnett managed to get Ramerez to recant his original testimony, but he suspected Barnett had, indeed, made it happen despite being locked up.

"You know I don't have a fucking dime to my name, man. I know you said I don't have to pay you anything, but I feel like I owe you."

Max knew Barnett was a man who wouldn't like feeling he owed anyone. He had heard rumors that after Barnett had been told that his sentence was to be death in the electric chair, he turned to his court-appointed attorney, poor James Pritchard, and told him that it looked like he didn't owe *him* anything more than a hole in the head. Max liked the idea that Barnett thought he might owe him something. In fact, he was counting on it, but instead he simply said, "I think we can work something out."

"Sure. Whatever you decide."

"But first I have to warn you. There's a media circus outside waiting for us."

"Cool," Barnett said, standing up. And that's exactly what he looked like—cool and collected, that same absence of emotion that had carried him through the trial and sentencing and every aspect of the appeal process. "I don't mind talking to them for a few minutes, but then I have a few things I need to take care of."

Max scratched his head, a nervous habit he immediately caught and turned into a smoothing of his hair. He couldn't believe Barnett was going to fuck up this opportunity for him. Shit! So much for this lowlife showing his appreciation and wanting to pay off his debt. But Max had to watch his temper. He couldn't make it sound like this media shower would benefit *him* or that he even cared whether or not they did them. He certainly didn't want Barnett thinking he could pay him off by simply agreeing to an interview or two. No, Max already had something else in mind. He needed to think quickly. He needed to appeal to Barnett's core values, those few essentials that made him tick.

"You're going to be a celebrity overnight, my friend," Max told him, smiling and shaking his head like he could hardly believe it. "I've got messages from *NBC News*, *60 Minutes*, *Larry King Live* and even Bill O'Reilly's *The Factor*. You can talk to whoever you want, whenever you want. Just remember, the media has a short attention span. Tomorrow they could already be hounding someone else."

Barnett got up out of his chair, hands in his pockets. "Bill O'Reilly actually wants me on his show?"

"Yep, tomorrow night. It's up to you, though. I can tell him… Hell, I can tell them all you don't want to put up with the whole lot of them. Whatever you want to do."

"That O'Reilly guy always thinks he's so tough." And now Barnett was smiling again. Max tried not to, but he was thinking he had just hit the nail on the head.

"I think I'd like to tell a few of these assholes what I think."

For the first time since he met Jared Barnett, Max allowed himself to look deep into those dark, vacant eyes, and this time he allowed himself the truth. He knew that Jared Barnett had, indeed, killed that poor girl seven years ago. And not only did Max know for sure, he was counting on it.

From the *USA TODAY* bestselling author of
The Parting Glass comes the story of
three generations of women who discover
the healing gift of family, memories and love.

EMILIE
RICHARDS
WEDDING RING

Tessa McRae has never been close to either her mother or her
grandmother, but she reluctantly agrees to help them repair the old
family home in Virginia's Shenandoah Valley, hoping that the time away
will help her to reflect on her failing marriage.

With the passing weeks, Tessa restores a tattered wedding-ring quilt
pieced by her grandmother and quilted by her mother years ago. Through
days of hard work and simple living, the three women will discover that
what was lost can be found again—if they look deeply into their hearts.

"[A] heartfelt paean to love and loyalty…"
—*Publishers Weekly* on *The Parting Glass*

Available in July 2004 wherever books are sold.

MIRA®

"M. J. Rose is great."
—*New York Times* bestselling author
Janet Evanovich

M. J. ROSE

THE
HALO
EFFECT

Cleo Thane is a high-priced prostitute and a special patient
whom sex therapist Dr. Morgan Snow connects with immediately.
And when Cleo asks Morgan to read her unpublished tell-all
book about her exclusive clientele, Morgan realizes that what
she has in her hands could be explosive.

Then Cleo disappears.

Certain that the answers to the disappearance lie in Cleo's
manuscript, Morgan delves into the private confessions of
a woman paid to act out the sexual fantasies of some of
the city's most powerful men. And too late she realizes
she's ventured into dangerous—deadly—territory.

"Dr. Morgan Snow, sex therapist turned murder detective, will
keep you spellbound and guessing from the first page to the last."
—Stan Pottinger, author of *The Fourth Procedure*
and *The Last Nazi*

Available in July 2004 wherever books are sold.

MIRABooks.com

We've got the lowdown on your favorite author!

☆ Read an excerpt of your favorite author's newest book

☆ Check out her bio

☆ Talk to her in our Discussion Forums

☆ Read interviews, diaries, and more

☆ Find her current bestseller, and even her backlist titles

All this and more available at

www.MiraBooks.com

ALEX KAVA

66915	SPLIT SECOND	___ $6.99 U.S.	___ $8.50 CAN.
66824	A PERFECT EVIL	___ $6.99 U.S.	___ $8.50 CAN.
66701	THE SOUL CATCHER	___ $6.99 U.S.	___ $8.50 CAN.

(limited quantities available)

TOTAL AMOUNT	$_____
POSTAGE & HANDLING	$_____
($1.00 for one book; 50¢ for each additional)	
APPLICABLE TAXES*	$_____
TOTAL PAYABLE	$_____

(check or money order—please do not send cash)

To order, complete this form and send it, along with a check or money order for the total above, payable to MIRA Books, to: **In the U.S.:** 3010 Walden Avenue, P.O. Box 9077, Buffalo, NY 14269-9077; **In Canada:** P.O. Box 636, Fort Erie, Ontario L2A 5X3.

Name:_____
Address:_____ City:_____
State/Prov.:_____ Zip/Postal Code:_____
Account Number (if applicable):_____
075 CSAS

*New York residents remit applicable sales taxes.
 Canadian residents remit applicable GST and provincial taxes.

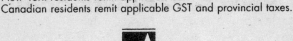

MIRA®

www.MIRABooks.com

MAK0704BL